GHOST NATION

A LACY MERRICK THRILLER
BOOK 4

ROBIN MAHLE

HARP HOUSE PUBLISHING, LLC.

Published by HARP House Publishing

October 2018 (1st edition)

CHAPTER
ONE

WINDOWS DOTTED the Battery Park high rise and the lights that shone through them resembled stars against the night sky. Inside the high rise, in his penthouse apartment, Sergei Koslov overlooked the Hudson River, its surface shimmering with the lights of lower Manhattan. He placed the shot glass brimming with vodka against his lips and threw it back, savoring its icy smooth finish.

He eyed the empty glass, spinning it between his thumb and forefinger before placing it on the bar top. "I expected a permanent replacement to have been announced by now. It has been two months since the appointment of the acting director." Koslov turned away from the captivating view and regarded his partner. "And with Janz no longer in play, I am beyond arm's length to those who matter, which leaves us all in a position of weakness."

"Casper Janz was a disease that the US government has eradicated for us." With a thick Russian accent, Maxim Abramov, the heavy-set man with a bulbous nose and blonde crew cut, hair sat at attention. "His recklessness brought you dangerously close to exposure. Brought us *all* dangerously close."

Koslov approached. "Had he accomplished what had been envisioned, our homeland would have benefited tenfold."

"But he didn't and now here we are. What we need to do," Abramov continued, "is to bide our time. Wait until the Americans have forgotten what their country tried to do and with whose money they tried to do it with."

"Wait. Wait." Koslov threw up his arms. "That is exactly what we have been doing now for too long. Meanwhile, the relationship between our countries continues to deteriorate." He sat down on the chair next to Abramov. "Do you know what will happen if the US companies, under demands from their government, cease to do business with Moscow as they did with Beijing?"

"That will not come to pass," Abramov replied. "The man who is now the acting CIA director will not want what happened as a result of sanctions placed against China to happen again. This country is not yet over the turmoil. And that is where this government's attention lies. Not with us or our organization. We have been flying, as they say, 'under the radar,' and will continue to do so."

Koslov laughed. "And you know this for a fact? Surely your connections reach far higher than mine to make that assertion."

Abramov stood with a degree of ire. "Our objectives have not changed, Sergei. Janz is gone, yes. But there will be others. Those who will sell their services just as he did to the highest bidder without fear of reprisal from their government. Our goal remains the same and Acting Director Axell has no bearing on how we will continue to conduct business stateside. It matters not who runs the CIA but who inside the CIA and the rest of the intelligence community is willing to sell their patriotism."

"Perhaps," Koslov replied. "But Janz's connections to the corporate world were invaluable. That is where I am most concerned. We need those connections."

As Abramov started toward the door to leave, he stopped and turned his attention again to Koslov. "Those connections you shall have. In the meantime, your focus should be on the organization and continuing on that front with business as usual." He closed the door behind him.

"Mʊ'dak." *Asshole.* Now alone in his apartment, Koslov retrieved his cell phone and waited for the line to answer, and in his native tongue, he began speaking. "He just left." Koslov poured another shot of vodka. "He has promised to garner further connections and suggested we not worry about Director Trevor Axell." He turned to his reflection in the exterior glass door, approving of his slender physique, clothed in a Brioni suit. "I will do as you ask; however, we are losing ground with our most trusted partners and that must be stopped."

———

Upon hearing the knock on his door, Acting CIA Director Trevor Axell, former inter-agency liaison and covert operative of the presidentially appointed task force, closed the file on his desk. He pushed his hand through his short salty hair and squinted at the door for a better view of who waited on the other side, a dead giveaway of his aging eyes. "Yes."

Lacy Merrick opened the door. "Trevor. Thanks for taking the time to see me."

"As if I could ever say no to you." He gestured to the chair opposite his desk. "Please, sit down. I'm glad you're here. I was just reviewing Koslov's file."

With brunette locks that now hung past her shoulders and donning her usual blouse and slacks, Lacy took her seat. "Good, because he's the reason I'm here. Aaron intercepted intel that Koslov had recently been in touch with the Russian Ambassador.

And from what I understand, the ambassador has just welcomed an attaché who arrived from Moscow a few days ago."

Axell raised a brow. "Hunter must be working overtime. I assume you two believe the diplomat's arrival and Koslov's meeting with the ambassador means something?"

"I don't think it's a coincidence. It's time we understand Moscow's position on Koslov and if they intend to protect him."

"You're suggesting a sit down with this new diplomat? You know as well as I do that we'll never get the Kremlin to admit any knowledge of Koslov's activities here in the States, especially as they relate to Casper Janz or anything to do with funding terrorist activities. They barely acknowledge his existence. So any attempt to extract information from this new arrival would be pointless."

"Then what do you suggest? We've been monitoring Koslov since you discovered his alias, Malcolm Ford, and how he helped fund Shen Yang's efforts to unleash the attack on Beijing."

"Oh, and don't forget the former administration's involvement," he added.

"How could I? It's the reason you're sitting where you are right now. So again, it's been two months and still no evidence Sergei Koslov, aka Malcolm Ford, has any other ties to Russia or has attempted to fund other terror plots in the US or abroad."

"Where does Caison stand on this?" Axell leaned back in his chair and folded his arms across his chest.

"You know Will. He wants to jump in with both feet. Go after Koslov and eliminate him as a sponsor of terrorism. It's why he came on board with the task force on a permanent basis and left the Bureau," Lacy replied.

"And your position is?"

"It's time. Koslov won't sit idle for long and in fact, may already be engaged with another like Casper Janz. Our goal was to unearth Janz's other connections, and with that, dismantle the entire network Koslov belongs to. That starts with meeting with the diplomat and reminding him that the US is not afraid of harsher sanctions against Russia to get what we want."

"That is well beyond my scope of authority. You know that, Lacy. I won't have you threatening a diplomat with sanctions I have no control over. Besides, the point I believe you're getting at is to get information from him, not to scare the pants off him. And if you're hell-bent on that, and you really think he'll open up about Koslov, then the best way to achieve your goal is to get him talking."

"Wine and dine him," Lacy replied.

"Yes. And forgive me for sounding sexist, but I'm looking at the best person for the job."

Lacy smiled. "And why is that? You don't think Aaron could do it?"

Axell laughed. "Not a chance. His personality is more suited to wooing a laptop. No. If you want to open a dialog with the Kremlin and you think the diplomat is the conduit, then this is a job for you."

"Then we're in agreement." Lacy stood from the chair. "If you can get me a contact, I'll get a meeting set up."

"There's one more thing, Lacy," Axell began. "I need you to remember who we're dealing with. Koslov is no neophyte. He's been operating under the cover of Malcolm Ford for a long time, probably since he met Janz. We know who he is, yes. But we don't know who supports him, the Russians or some other entity. It's best not to go in with the idea this attaché is going to cooperate. He might know something about Koslov, but he might be working for him too."

———

The task force, which awaited a formal designation, was still headquartered in the same facility. However, the building had been substantially upgraded and now housed more than the four people who brought down a corrupt government and foiled a potential civil war in China. There was another member of the support staff under Aaron Hunter's guidance who assisted him in matters of cyber-intel. Jill Goddard was hand-picked by Hunter, and she was among the best of the best in her field.

Lacy Merrick's long-time friend Aaron Hunter was one of the last people to see Jay Merrick alive, and was Lacy's confidant; the friend she turned to when she needed to find the truth about Jay's death. They had worked side by side for almost a year now, moving beyond their casual friendship that began in college, evolving into something deeper. Both were enraged by the injustice of a corrupt administration. Both were angry about Jay's death. And now both were like family, even if he had wanted more.

"Aaron, I found something I think you might be interested in." Jill Goddard wasn't an Ivy League college graduate. In fact, she wasn't a college graduate at all. Hunter brought her on board because she was simply one of the best hackers he'd ever seen. In her mid-twenties, she knew almost as much as he did, perhaps more, if he was being honest.

"Yeah? What do you have?" Aaron approached her desk in the open area workspace, akin to a bullpen.

"I found a way to access Koslov's GPS in his car. We can track his whereabouts at any given time and find out who he's meeting with on a regular basis."

"Hang on." Aaron held up his hands. "This is great, Jill, but we can't do that. We might operate with relative autonomy, but we're still a government agency. What you've done is illegal. We can't use it."

"What? Are you serious? Koslov doesn't play by the rules, so why should we?"

"Because that's what separates us from the criminals. This is excellent work, but we can't do it this way. I'm sorry. You'll have to find another way to keep tabs on him."

"Like how?"

"Through our contacts at the FBI and CIA. In case you forgot, our boss is the Director of the Agency. We get intel from Axell and use that to further the investigation," Aaron replied.

"He hasn't given us anything of value in weeks. We're going to lose this guy, Aaron."

At that moment, Lacy entered the room. "Morning. Sorry I'm late. I stopped by to see Trevor." She approached Aaron. "How's it going?"

"Speak of the devil." Goddard appeared irritated.

"What's that?" Lacy asked her.

"Ask Aaron."

"Okay." Lacy turned to Aaron. "What's going on?"

"Jill figured a way to gain access to Koslov's GPS in his car, only I told her we can't use it. That we have to play by the rules."

"I see," Lacy replied.

"You don't agree?" Aaron asked.

At this, Goddard seemed to have a spark of hope in her eyes.

"I do agree that it isn't the 'by the book' way."

"By the book? Lacy, it's completely illegal. You know that. Look, I get that we've all bent the rules in the past, but this is different."

"Is it?" Lacy asked.

"Yes. It is. And I can't believe you'd think any differently. In fact, I figured you would be behind me on this one."

Lacy sighed. "I am behind you. I'm just frustrated by our lack of progress. I stopped by Trevor's office this morning. I told him you intercepted that communication from the Russian ambassador."

"Wait," Goddard began. "It's okay to do that, but not use his GPS to find out where he goes every day?"

Lacy turned to Aaron. "She's got you there. Anyway, I'll be initiating contact with the new diplomat from Moscow and get him to talk about Koslov."

"You? He wants you to do that?" Aaron asked.

"Yes."

"He is aware that almost everyone in the intelligence community knows who you are and what you did. What we've all done."

"He is well aware. This has dragged on for too long, Aaron. Which is exactly why I think what Jill has done could be useful. And it is also the reason I have to be the one to meet with the diplomat. And whatever you have to say about it doesn't really matter."

"Doesn't matter?"

"What's going on?" Caison approached them. "Why are you two arguing?"

"We're not arguing," Aaron replied.

"Well, you sure as hell aren't sharing a joke." He turned to Lacy. "What's the issue here?"

"No issue. I ran the concept you and I discussed about meeting with the new Russian attaché to find out what he knows about Koslov. Aaron doesn't like the idea. And Jill here has figured a way to get inside Koslov's GPS in his car."

"Fantastic. That's exactly what we need," Caison replied.

"What? Come on. Are you serious?" Aaron shook his head. "What the hell is going on here? Have you all forgotten where the line is? We aren't supposed to be like them. We're supposed to be the good guys here."

"Hunter, I get it," Caison started. "But it's only a matter of time before Axell's replaced. This is exactly the time to do these things because who knows who the new director will be and if we'll be able to skirt around the system. This is exactly the reason Goddard is here. Now if you don't agree, take it up with Axell."

"I can see I'm on my own here." Aaron turned to Jill. "Do what you gotta do. Guess it doesn't matter." He walked toward the hall.

"I'd better go talk to him." Lacy followed.

He walked into the breakroom and stood at the sink, arms braced against the counter and his back to the door.

"Aaron, come on." Lacy approached him and placed her hand on his shoulder. "I know you're trying to do what's right. I get it. But we've ventured into the gray more times than I can count. Why is this time different?"

Aaron turned to face her. No longer the man scraping by with odd computer jobs, he had changed. They all had. Even his appearance had changed. The graphic tees, shorts, and flip-flops computer geek was long gone. What remained was a mature, even cynical man who might have grown tired of the fight. "Because, Lace, you know how easy it is for that gray area to disappear altogether? We keep going down this path and we'll forget whose side we're supposed to be on. I'm trying to keep us all from getting into trouble. We serve at the pleasure of the president. Do you really think he wouldn't turn on us if he had to? Do you think it matters to him that you helped put him in that office?"

She moved in closer and held his gaze. "I've asked you to do things well outside your comfort zone. I know that. And it's changed you. I'm not blind. But, Aaron, I don't think we're in any danger of forgetting who and what we're doing this for. Casper Janz was in bed with a lot of people who were working against our country's interests. Sergei Koslov was one of those people. And Trevor believes he will lead us to many others."

Aaron eyed her hand and placed his over it. "I just don't want you to be a casualty of these people. I don't want you to lose who you are. You're one of the good ones, Lacy."

"I know who I am. But I also know what they've done to my family. You should know better than all of them what I would do to make sure what happened last year doesn't ever happen again. And if that means I have to use what I have to get what I want, no one is going to stop me. Not even you."

"Okay. I get it. But with you and Caison siding with Jill, what do I tell her?"

"She's an incredible talent and we're lucky to have her here. I say we let her do what she does best. The more intel we have on Koslov, the better for all of us, even if we have to swim in the gray to get it."

Aaron peered at her. "I'd follow you to the ends of the earth, you know that, Lacy. And if this is what you want, then we'll do it."

"Good. Let's get back out there. I need to make a call and get that meeting set up." She led the way back to the bullpen, where Caison stood by Goddard's desk as the two continued discussions. "Okay. Here's the deal." She looked to Caison. "I'm going to meet with the new diplomat. Jill is going to monitor Koslov's whereabouts through the GPS in his car and hope we get something useful."

"And you're good with this, Hunter?" Caison asked.

"As good as I'm going to be."

"And Axell is aware of what's going on?" he asked Lacy.

"On my end, yes. He isn't aware of what Jill's been able to do. But he'll be here in a couple of hours. So, Jill, why don't you line it out so you can explain it to Axell? He'll have to make the final call and give you the thumbs-up to proceed."

"Got it." With a smile, Goddard returned to her computer to

work, but not before casting a glance at Aaron. "I could use some input on this."

"Sure." Aaron eyed Lacy and pulled up a chair next to Jill.

"Hey, you mind?" Caison nodded to Lacy as he started toward his office.

She followed.

"Close the door for a second." Caison sat down.

"Okay. What now? Are you still unconvinced?"

"Not about that. We'll have to see how that plays out. Right now, I want to know how you plan on getting in front of this diplomat, Usenko."

"Anton Usenko," Lacy replied.

"We haven't vetted him yet. That's something we should do before we go down this road."

"How long will that take?" she asked.

"I don't know. A day, maybe two."

"As soon as it's done, then. Too much time has passed already. Who knows how many people Janz was in contact with who've already gone back underground, figuring we'd come after them. It's now or never." Lacy began to leave.

"Hey, Lacy?"

She turned on her heel. "Yeah?"

"Is Hunter going to be okay with this? I mean, you know how he gets."

"He's fine. We all have a job to do and he won't get in the way of what he knows needs to be done."

"Maybe not when it comes to the rest of us. I'm not so sure about that when it comes to you."

CHAPTER
TWO

WHILE THE UNREST had subsided in the aftermath of the former president's resignation, the country had a long way to go toward healing. The wound of the mall attack was still fresh and relations with China were still tense. But it was Trevor Axell who had worked to bring more transparency to the CIA, as had FBI Director Mobley within his ranks. Neither, however, had the full support of their respective agencies. Some were resistant to change. Some felt China had been let off too easy. Perhaps they had. But the time had come for Axell to move the agency beyond the attack and focus on what he believed could be an emerging enemy, one that never really went away and just waited in the wings for the US to be distracted. That distraction was now gone and Axell had his work cut out for him. With Mobley's help, the two would bring down Casper Janz's network and the man known as Malcolm Ford, a Russian.

A knock on Axell's door pulled him back into the moment. "Yes." He sat tall in his chair and waited for the man he knew would arrive.

"Axell." FBI Director Mobley appeared in the doorway.

"Good morning. Please come in." Axell rose to greet the director with a friendly handshake. "I appreciate you carving out some time from your schedule for me."

"Not at all." Mobley took a seat across from Axell. "You were somewhat vague in your email. What is it that I can do for you?"

"Pardon the ambiguity of my request. I guess you could say I'm still leery of leaving electronic trails."

"Really? I can't imagine why." Mobley smiled. "So what do you need, Trevor? I'm all ears."

"What do you know about a Russian diplomat by the name of Anton Usenko? He arrived a few days ago and I haven't yet been able to get a read on why he's here. I'm hoping you might know."

"I am aware of his arrival. And I suspect the reason you're asking is because you believe he might have ties to Sergei Koslov."

"Possibly. Or he's here to relay a message from the Kremlin regarding Koslov. Am I off-base?" Axell asked.

"I can't say with certainty, but I'll get the ball rolling. Consider it done."

"He'll have diplomatic immunity, so your people will have to tread lightly," Axell continued.

"Absolutely. I already have someone in mind who will be more than up for the task." Mobley stood. "If there's nothing else, I still need to have a sit-down with your counter-intelligence on another matter."

"That's all I need for right now. Once we know who Usenko is here to see and why, I'll plan on sending in Merrick to take it from there."

"You sure she's right for the job?" Mobley appeared concerned. "She tends to draw attention even now."

"I've done some recon on the new arrival, and from what I know as of now, her fame is what I'm banking on." Axell stood again and offered his hand. "Thank you, Director Mobley."

"Anytime." Mobley started toward the door. "Oh, and I assume you'd like to keep this out of our weekly briefing with the president?"

"For now."

Mobley nodded and left the room, closing the door behind him.

Axell returned to his seat and picked up his phone. "Caison, where are you?"

"At the shop," he replied.

"I asked Mobley to put someone on Usenko. Once I get the name, I want you to meet the agent."

"Copy that."

———

Lacy walked into the kitchen and slipped off her shoes before grabbing a Diet Coke from the fridge. She started up the steps and headed to her bedroom but not before a quick stop to check in on the kids. They were both sound asleep.

She slipped into a long T-shirt and crawled into bed. Her eyes fell shut and she saw Jay standing in their bedroom doorway. His tie loosened, the cuff of his pants brushing the carpet as he stood in socked feet. He looked at her with tired but playful eyes. Alone in her bed with the memories of him swimming in her mind, Lacy smiled before drifting off to sleep.

"Mommy. Mommy?" Jackson shook Lacy's arm. "I heard something. Mommy, wake up!"

Lacy opened her eyes, forgetting for a moment where she was. Then his words sounded clearer. "Jack, what is it? What's wrong?"

"Mommy, I heard something downstairs."

"It's probably just Celeste, baby."

"No, it isn't. Mommy, you have to get up and go look. Please!"

"Okay, okay. I'll get up." Lacy tossed the covers from her legs and sat on the edge of the bed. "I don't hear anything." And as she strained to listen, the sound came.

"Did you hear that? I told you!" Jack said.

Lacy stood, wide awake now. "Stay here, you understand? Don't move!" She opened her nightstand and retrieved the gun. Before all this, before terror attacks and assassins, Jay's gun was kept in the closet, locked away in a safe. Now she kept it in a locked case next to her bed.

She started toward the door but turned back and whispered, "Stay here!" She made sure he understood as he nodded before she continued through the door, closing it behind her.

Lacy tiptoed through the hall and to the staircase. There were no lights on and she hadn't heard the sound again, but continued nonetheless. Her pulse raced as she aimed the weapon at the darkness.

Now on the bottom step, Lacy searched for the source of the noise. A glance to the front door. It was closed—and locked. The kitchen was just ahead and to her right was a hall that led to Celeste's room, Jay's study, and the utility room. As she started down the hall, a light caught her attention. It was coming from Jay's study, a room she hadn't touched since he passed and rarely entered. And as she walked inside, the light shone from a printer and that printer was printing something. That was the noise.

"For God's sake." She lowered her weapon and continued inside, walking toward the printer. "I almost shot you, you know. That would've been hard to explain to the cops." The printer stopped and Lacy picked up the page that it spat out. "What the hell is this?"

It was at that moment she recalled Jackson sitting in her room, probably terrified. Lacy ran back up the stairs and opened her bedroom door. "Jack, honey. I'm so sorry. Everything's fine."

He was in her bed, the covers pulled up over his face.

"Baby, it's okay. It was only Daddy's printer. It was on. That's all it was. Come on now." She returned the gun to its case and secured it before picking up the boy who had grown quite a lot this past year and carried him back to his bed.

"You're sure that's all it was?"

"Yes, baby. I'm sure. I'm so sorry it woke you up. I'll go back downstairs and turn it off."

"Okay."

She tucked him back into bed and started to leave.

"Mommy?"

"Yes, sweetheart?"

"Why do you have a gun? Are those bad men coming to take us again?"

"Oh, no, honey. No. That's never going to happen again. I promise. I—I don't know why I have it. I guess I just feel better. I'm supposed to be the mom and dad now, right? Well, this was Daddy's gun."

"Oh. Can you teach me how to use it so I can protect the family like Daddy did?"

"Maybe someday, when you're much older. Goodnight, sweetheart." She pulled the door until it rested on the jamb. He didn't like it shut all the way.

Lacy returned downstairs and back to Jay's office, where the paper lay on his desk. She flipped on the switch to the desk lamp and sat down in his chair. The room had been virtually untouched since the attack. In fact, nothing of Jay's was gone except for his car and that was because it had been damaged at the mall. His clothes still hung in her closet. His shoes still rested on the floor. And his office, minus his laptop that, too, had been damaged in the attack.

Lacy held up the paper once again and began to read it.

Someone was offering information about Sergei Koslov. And that someone went by the moniker, Graybear. But who was Graybear, and how could this person have accessed her printer? She supposed it did still have a wired internet connection and the only person she could think of who could possibly hack into it was her dear friend, Aaron Hunter. And what would be the reason for that? No. This was someone else. Someone who knew the task force's plan to find Koslov and the rest of Janz's connections.

But the real problem was that this Graybear knew how to get to her. Friend or foe, it was impossible to decipher in this instance. Was the information going to be valuable or was it a trap? Lacy eyed the time. It was almost 2 am. She had to tell someone about this and the only person who wouldn't completely lose his mind was Trevor. Will would want to come over. Aaron would want her to leave her house. Neither was going to happen. Trevor it was.

She walked back upstairs and grabbed her cell phone by her bed. The line rang. "Come on, answer." She leaned back against her headboard.

He picked up. "Lacy, what's wrong?"

"Someone gained access to the printer in Jay's office."

"What? What the hell are you talking about?"

"It's okay, Trevor, we're safe. Someone accessed the printer and printed a sheet of paper. The paper says they know we're looking for something on Koslov and they know how to get to him."

"Wait. Hang on a minute. Are you telling me someone hacked into your computer?"

"Well." She tried to assuage his nerves, but it was a little frightening even for her to think about. "Not my computer. It was a printer, which is connected to my Wi-Fi, so yeah, I guess someone hacked into my router and my IP provider."

"Christ's sake," he replied.

"Trevor, I'm fine. Look, they're trying to tell us something."

"Okay. But how the hell did they know we were looking for Koslov?"

"It has to be someone on the inside. Someone who thinks they're better off concealing their identity. I don't know, but what I need to understand is, does this person have real intel or is it a ploy?"

"Ah shit, Lacy. It's two in the damn morning."

"Yeah, I know that. This woke up my kid and I pulled out a gun, which I'm sure scared the crap out of him."

"Great." He released a heavy sigh. "Okay, look. I'm coming over."

"What? No. You don't need to do that." This wasn't the answer she expected. What she expected was for him to say bring it to the shop in the morning and talk about it. "There's no need. I just wanted you to know so we could discuss it later. Like when the sun comes up."

"I don't know. I don't feel good about this. Did you call Caison?"

"No, I called you. I figured you would be the most reasonable in this situation."

"You're probably right. Okay. Fine. Listen, just keep your gun handy. Not that I think you'll need it, but it'll make me feel better. Bring the paper with you in the morning. I'll head in there first thing before I go to Langley. In fact, why don't you get everyone in there by 7 am? We'll meet and figure this out."

"Got it. Okay. Thanks, Trevor. I'm sorry to wake you," Lacy replied.

"Don't be. Just try to get back to sleep. I know you, so I'm sure that won't be easy."

"Doubt it will be easy for you either."

"Probably not," Trevor replied. "I'll see you at seven." He ended the call.

Lacy started back toward the hall and the stairs, but not before double-checking the front door. "It's locked, Lacy." She continued up the steps after stopping a few more times to check over her shoulder. How many times had she done that this past year?

"More times than I care to remember."

CHAPTER
THREE

IT WAS 7 am on the dot, but after Lacy revealed in the night that she had received mysterious intel via a personal printer, they'd come in early and were ready to swoop in on her. "Glad you all got my message," she said. "I hope I haven't kept you waiting."

"You have the paper?" Caison approached her without so much as a morning greeting.

"I do." Lacy retrieved the evidence from her laptop bag. "I'll go make some copies so we can all take a look." Without further delay, Lacy walked to the copier. She was just as anxious as the rest of them to find out not only the meaning of the information sent but also the true identity of the sender.

"Okay." She stepped away from the copier and handed out the sheets. "This came in on my family printer in Jay's office. It's on Wi-Fi, but it wasn't connected to the internet at the time."

Hunter jumped in. "So we're dealing with someone who figured out how to get access to your IP address. That's not a good thing."

"No," Axell began. "But more important is that the information I'm seeing here is intended to give us a leg up on Koslov's actions and communication efforts."

"Someone's trying to help," Caison replied. "This Graybear person."

"Or at least making it appear as such."

"Are we not going to address the fact that someone got to her?" Hunter asked. "This is no amateur we're talking about."

"That'll be your job to figure out, you and Goddard," Axell replied. "And it will be priority number one."

"Does that mean you want me to pull off the GPS tracking?" Goddard asked.

"Yes," Hunter replied. "Your resources will be needed on this."

"Hang on," Lacy began. "That will still give us more information about who Koslov is meeting with, including if he's meeting with the diplomat, Anton Usenko."

Axell seemed to consider the idea. "Here's what I think. Whoever sent this to Lacy is, I believe, someone inside Koslov's circle. And for whatever reason, they're looking to get him out of the picture. So I say, Goddard, continue monitoring Koslov's locations." He raised a preemptive hand. "With the understanding that we will only use that intel if we deem it absolutely necessary. I recognize the ramifications of illegally monitoring a US resident, which he is. That said, finding out the true identity of this person is, in my opinion, critically important and could change the course of our investigation."

"I have to agree with Hunter on one point and that is like he said, they got to her," Caison began, "meaning she's exposed."

"Will, I understand where you're coming from, you and Aaron both," Lacy began. "But you have to remember, I've been in the public eye for almost a year. If someone wanted to find me—to harm me—they could've done it by now. I don't think this person wants to put me out of commission, or else I would be."

"She's right." Axell walked toward the whiteboard and started writing. "Number one, Hunter will find out who Graybear is. Then," he scribbled faster, "we determine if this individual is a friend."

"Do I get a say in this?" Lacy leaned against her desk. "We have a way to possibly reach out to the person who sent this. Viewing the logs on my IP server is the best way to do that. Aaron and I can find the passive digital footprint left by whoever accessed my printer. Not to mention, the intel provided appears too generic. Look here." Lacy pointed to a sentence on the page. "Malcolm Ford, aka Sergei Koslov, has ties to more than just the Kremlin. You need to look inside the EU." She peered at her team. "Okay. The EU as a whole or are we talking about one or two countries? It's vague and I think it's vague on purpose."

"You mean it's a setup?" Hunter asked.

"I mean if they want to string us along for the purpose of diversion, possibly. Or worse, to send us on a wild goose chase. We've been down that road before and I don't want to go down it again."

"So what are you saying?" Axell asked.

"I'm saying Aaron and I need to analyze the intel and trace the hack back to its origins. I want to know who Graybear is before we take what's on this paper as truth."

Axell began to walk toward his office. "Then I suggest you two get on it. Caison, I need to see you."

Will eyed Lacy for a moment before hustling in line with Axell.

"Sit down." Axell sat at his desk. "What do you know about Mobley's agent? Can he be trusted?"

"From what I discovered, *she's* an expert on the Russian mafia. Her name is Anya Balfour. She works out of the WFO. I ran the name by SSA Adam Fraser, and although they work in different departments, he knows a little bit about her."

"We're going to entrust her with assessing Usenko before Merrick meets with him?"

"By all accounts, she's the one to turn to. Her parents were Russian-born. She was born in the Bronx in 1986. Worked her way through college, studied International Relations at NYU. Recruited by the Bureau during her senior year."

"They recruited her." Axell leaned back in his chair. "What did her parents do in Russia?"

"After working in the Russian ministry, both defected in 1985 and were protected by the US government. The docs were sealed, but I have to assume they supplied intel in exchange."

"Explains why the daughter was recruited."

"Partly," Caison added. "But from what I understand, they saw something different in her—special. And with her parents' history, well, the Bureau decided it was better to have Balfour on our side."

"I would agree. Okay. I'd like you to work with her on Usenko's background clearance. Mobley won't object. But it needs to be sooner rather than later. I need to get Merrick inside, especially now."

"That could be exactly what they want us to do, the person who sent the intel," Caison replied.

"We'll see."

Caison returned to the bullpen where Lacy and Aaron huddled around Goddard's desk and had already started tracking down this so-called Graybear who so willingly offered up intel on Sergei Koslov. "Listen, I have to run out. Axell's sending me to meet with an agent at the WFO."

Lacy turned to him. "Oh yeah? Anyone we know?"

"Fraser knows and I'm about to. I'll catch up with you later. Let me know if you track down the hacker."

"We're on it," Aaron replied.

"You need any backup?" Lacy asked him.

"Nope. I got it." He grabbed his cell from his desk and headed out the door. He didn't turn back, knowing Lacy would want more details. She always did. But this time, Axell wanted her out of the equation until the time came for her to meet with the diplomat, Usenko. The fewer people who knew of Lacy's intentions, the better. She was still a trending figure, as they say, and while that might appeal to Usenko, it wouldn't so much to anyone else who might be associated with Koslov.

————

Caison headed to the WFO, where he would stop and say hello to his friend and reliable ally, SSA Adam Fraser, the same man who he had worked with on the murder of Undersecretary Drew Kendrick and Deputy Secretary Wendell Turner. If it hadn't been for Fraser, it was likely Caison might have seen Trevor Axell spend the rest of his life in prison after CIA Director Handley attempted to frame him for Turner's murder.

He entered the building and presented his credentials before clearing security. He recalled being in this very spot not so long ago when he ran into his former classmate at Quantico, Kate Reid. Caison smiled at the memory of her that flashed before him. She had worked here until very recently, he remembered. Now she was a big shot with the BAU at Quantico. How times had changed. He wondered what had become of her and if she was happy. Their all-too-brief romantic relationship seemed a lifetime ago. Now there was someone else who consumed his thoughts.

Caison figured he must have a thing for unattainable women. Seemed he always fell for them. He knew there would never be anything between Lacy and him, and he'd come to accept that. It was probably best anyway. They worked together. Besides, there was another who had fallen for her.

"Caison! Good to see you, my man." SSA Fraser approached with an outstretched hand.

"How you doing, brother? Good to see you too." He returned the gesture. "Thanks for meeting with me."

"Hey, no problemo. Come on, let's talk in my office." Fraser led the way to his office and closed the door behind him. "So you want to know about Balfour, huh?"

"Whatever you think might be useful," Caison replied.

"Well," Fraser made his way to his desk and took a seat, "I already told you her background. I can only add that she speaks four languages, Russian being one, of course. She's highly regarded here. The Bureau has recognized her work. I don't know, man. What else do you want to know about her?"

He turned serious. "Her ties. Specifically, her Russian ties. Does she know Sergei Koslov or any of his associates?"

Fraser eyed him. "She's been in on a lot of deals with the Russians. Mostly as it relates to the mafia, which as you know..."

"Goes right back to the Kremlin," he replied.

"Exactly. But it's her job to get chummy with those guys. And she's pretty damn effective."

"Okay. So when Mobley puts her on the new Russian Diplomat Anton Usenko, she'll be effective there too?"

"I'd stand behind her if that's what you're asking. I don't know her personally, but I'd trust her."

"With your life?"

Fraser shrugged. "Got no reason not to. What's this about, really?"

Caison pulled forward and placed his elbows on his knees. "We're planning an op and she's going to be a big part of it."

"Anything else you can share?"

"Not yet."

"Copy that. Listen, I believe she's one of the good ones. And I know after all the bullshit we went through what that means."

"So you think I can trust her?" he pressed on.

"I think you can trust her."

Caison slapped the arms of his chair and stood. "That's good enough for me. Better go meet this Balfour and get a read on her myself."

"Okay, man." Fraser stood. "Hey, you need anything more, you know where to find me."

"Appreciate that. Let's go grab a beer soon." He started to leave.

"Anytime, anyplace, my friend."

He left and started toward the floor where Balfour worked. The elevator doors parted and he rode to the sixth floor of the WFO, remembering for a moment that Agent Reid had worked very near here. He wondered if anyone there would know how she was doing, but cautioned himself about making the inquiry. Word would likely get back to her and he didn't want her thinking he wanted back into her life or anything stupid like that.

The doors parted and Will stepped through the opening in search of the admin desk. On approach, he spotted a woman behind it on the phone. He waited patiently for her to finish her call.

"Sorry about that. May I help you?" she asked.

"I'm here to see Agent Anya Balfour. I'm Will Caison." He still carried FBI creds because, officially, he was part of the FBI. The task force, while it wasn't as covert as it once was, still maintained a high-level security clearance and only those at the top knew of its existence.

"I'll see if she's available." The young woman called into Balfour's office.

Inside the FBI's Criminal Division was a department dedicated to working transnational organized crime. This was where Balfour's skills were put to use.

"She'll be right down. You can have a seat if you'd like." The woman gestured to the chairs alongside the wall.

"Thank you for your help." Caison walked to the chairs and sat down, thumbing through one of the magazines for a few minutes when she arrived. Her high heels clicked on the tile floor and Caison's eyes drew up, noticing her legs first, then her pencil skirt, and finally, her deep-set brown eyes and black hair that brushed her shoulders in a thick, blunt line.

"Will Caison, I'm Anya Balfour. What can I do for you?" She offered her hand.

"Pleased to meet you, Balfour. I'd like to speak with you about a mutual friend. Do you have five minutes?"

"Of course. Follow me." She started back into the corridor.

Caison followed, trying hard not to stare at her backside. She was a beautiful woman. Not at all what he expected.

"Right through here, Caison." She held the door for him as he entered.

"Please, call me Will."

"Okay, Will. Have a seat. You mentioned a mutual friend?"

"I did." He sat down after her. "Director Mobley."

"Yes, of course." She seemed hesitant to elaborate.

Caison picked up on her hesitation and figured he would have to be more forthcoming, which was something he wasn't generally very good at. He preferred to wait for others to reveal their intentions. Still, the silence had become awkward. "Right. I understand he has asked you to look into the Russian diplomat, Anton Usenko."

She regarded him with caution. "And this is of interest to you, why?"

"Please, forgive my vagueness. I understood you had been informed as to why Usenko needed vetting."

"You're going to have to cut to the chase, Caison," she replied.

"All right, then. I'm here to work with you on that endeavor."

"I don't need a partner."

"Of course not. However, other operations will rely heavily on what you discover about Usenko. That's why I'm here."

"Should I call the director about this?" she asked.

"Feel free." He sat back, more than a little perturbed by this woman. However, he had to respect that she was doing her job and he would react in precisely the same manner were he in her shoes. But that was too logical at this moment in time when he'd begun to feel heat under his collar.

Balfour peered at her desk before returning her sights to him. "Caison, if we are to work together, then you shouldn't be angry that I double-check your request. It's what any good field agent would do."

"You're right. My apologies. Please, call Director Mobley. I don't have a lot of time to waste."

"Nor do I." She picked up the phone and smiled as she held the receiver to her ear. "Director Mobley, please. It's Anya Balfour. Thank you."

Caison tapped his shoe on the carpet while he waited. This was not going as he would've expected. Nothing about this woman was as he would've expected.

"Thank you, Director. I'll ensure complete transparency." She ended the call. "Okay, then. Where do you want to start?"

"How about you start by telling me what you know about Sergei Koslov?"

CHAPTER
FOUR

INSIDE THE TASK FORCE HEADQUARTERS, Hunter studied his monitor before turning his attention to Lacy. "Whoever did this knew you had an unsecured port. He wrote an automated script that searches for open printer ports. I think we're going to have to go to your house and look at the printer. I need to see if it has IPP or LPD ports that are open to external connections."

"Internet printing ports or line printer daemon ports," Goddard replied.

"That's what I said." Hunter creased his brow. "Lacy knows what I'm talking about, right, Lace?"

"Sure. Yeah." She looked at Jill. "Thanks for the clarification, though. And if we find that my printer has one of those connections, what then?"

"We close it. Disconnect your printer. Then we can try and track him down," he replied.

"What makes you so sure a man did this?" Goddard asked.

Hunter glanced between the two women who flanked him.

"Um, well, I just figured," he stammered. "I've seen this before. Some guy did this a couple of years ago, only he hit hundreds of thousands of printers."

"So you think this person is taking cues from another hacker?" Lacy let him off the hook.

"I think he—or she—got the idea from someone else. But it would've taken specific knowledge to hit just your computer and that's what we still need to figure out."

"Then let's head back to my place and take a look," Lacy said. "Jill, will you continue working to track down the mysterious Graybear while we're out?"

"You got it. If I get a hit, I'll text you," she replied.

"Great. Let's head out." Aaron started toward the door but not before scanning the office. "Where's Axell?"

"He headed back to Langley for a meeting," Lacy replied. "Said he'd be back by the end of the day."

The two walked into the parking garage when Aaron added, "How long is he going to keep pulling double-duty? He's running the CIA, for Pete's sake."

"I know. He does have an assistant director, though. But yeah, as much as I think he appreciates what the president did, I think he wants to be back here with us. And especially now that we're starting to get somewhere with Koslov."

"Not to mention the politics involved." Aaron opened his car door. "I was only at Langley a few weeks and I saw it. Can't imagine what it must be like at the top. And Axell isn't exactly a political guy."

"No, he's not." Lacy stepped inside while Aaron started the engine. "Look, I'm not so sure I want to close off this line of communication."

"What are you talking about?" He pulled out of the garage.

"I mean the printer. What if this person is for real? Are we cutting off a potential source?"

"It's too risky, Lacy. If he got into your printer, he can get into a lot of other things, like your security system. No. I can't take that chance. We need to close the loop. If he is truly looking to help, he'll reach out another way."

"I hope you're right."

Within minutes, they arrived at Lacy's home and Aaron cut the engine after parking alongside the front. "Kids out of school yet?"

"Next month. Can't believe it," Lacy said. "Olivia will be going into third grade and Jack into second. Doesn't seem possible," she reflected. "I wish Jay could see how much they've grown."

"He can, Lace. I'm positive." Aaron stepped out of the car and waited for Lacy to join him.

She pulled out the keys from her purse and unlocked the front door. "I always tell Celeste to keep the door locked when she's home."

"I bet you got no argument on that," Aaron replied.

"No, sir. No argument at all." She pushed it open and called out, "Celeste, it's me. Aaron's with me too."

Celeste was getting just a little slower as time caught up to her. And this past year had aged her a lot. It had aged Lacy too. "Well, I wasn't expecting to see you two here at this time of day. Can I make you some lunch? I doubt either one of you has eaten."

"I could eat," Aaron said.

"Just some sandwiches, Celeste. That would be great. We're going to be in Jay's study for a few minutes."

"Oh. Okay. I'll bring in the food shortly." Celeste walked into the kitchen.

Aaron followed Lacy down the hall. "She looked a little surprised."

"I don't usually go into the study. No reason to." Lacy pushed open the double doors to reveal Jay's desk.

Aaron seemed to pick up on the fact that nothing had changed and appeared slightly alarmed. "Okay, so this is the printer in question. Let me see what kind of connection we have here." He stopped to look at her. "Can you do me a favor and grab your laptop? I want to see how you're connected to this."

"Sure." Lacy started back into the hall and ran into Celeste.

"I've got lunch."

"Oh, thank you so much. Just go ahead and set it down in there. I need to run upstairs and grab my laptop."

"Everything okay in there?" Celeste asked.

"Absolutely. Just double-checking the connections to the printer. Nothing to worry about."

Celeste continued on her path while Lacy ran upstairs. She recognized the look on Celeste's face. It was worry and it wouldn't matter how many times Lacy would tell her not to worry, it never did any good. And she had every right to feel that way, especially after all that had happened. But Lacy couldn't think about that now. In her heart, she felt Graybear was trying to help and an itch in the back of her mind told her that cutting off the connection was a mistake.

She grabbed her laptop and returned to the study where Aaron crouched over the printer with a sandwich in his hand and a bite in his mouth. "Any luck?"

He turned, and with a full mouth, replied, "Can't tell much until I get a look at your printer protocol, but this brand is one of the vulnerable makes. Let's see what you have."

Lacy placed her laptop on Jay's desk and opened it. "I'll just log in for you." She stood over him and entered her credentials while he sat down at the desk.

"You haven't changed this room at all. Figured you would've made it your office instead of the small room upstairs," Aaron said.

"Guess I haven't had time to do that. What with all the running for our lives and taking down corrupt government officials." Lacy tried to laugh, but the sound she produced was forced and awkward. "Anyway, here you go. Have at it." She turned the screen toward him.

Aaron keyed in a few strokes until the printer setup appeared on the screen.

"Are you sure this is the right way to go?" Lacy asked.

Aaron looked up. "Yes, it is. I already explained that." He pushed back in the chair. "You clearly don't think so."

"I'm still trying to wrap my head around the fact that someone reached out to me. Not you or Will. Me. And he's telling us that Koslov's connections aren't all that they seem. That they can be found in places we haven't even considered looking. Why is that, Aaron? What could this individual possibly gain by handing over information like that?"

"I can't answer your question because I don't know. Maybe it's someone Koslov or Ford or whatever his name is burned and he's looking for payback. He or she."

"It is possible it's a vendetta. But even so, what harm does that do us?"

"What harm? Well, that depends on who Koslov is tied to and what those people are capable of doing. Look, my main concern is your safety. You and the kids and Celeste. I'm closing the port. I'm sorry, Lacy, it has to be this way." Aaron returned to the laptop and began typing once again. "Yep. I see it here." And with an exaggerated thump of a few more keys, he added. "Done. I've just installed a firewall. No more rogue print jobs."

———

The halls of Langley were studded with officers and staff as Caison made his way through the international emissaries toward the office of the acting director. After having to confirm his identity on multiple occasions along the way, he made it to Axell's office. His assistant, or rather, guard waited nearby.

"Hi. Can I help you?" the woman said.

"I'm here to see Acting Director Axell. Will Caison. He's expecting me."

"Thank you. I'll let him know you're here."

The austere woman buzzed into Axell's office before returning her attention. "Door's open."

"Thanks." Caison made his way inside. "Axell, I know you're a busy man. Thanks for taking some time."

"Sorry it couldn't be at the shop. I've been slammed with meetings and congressional hearings. You know, fun stuff."

"Sure." He sat down. "So I had an interesting meeting of my own."

"Agent Balfour," Axell replied. "I hope you didn't get any pushback. I did confirm with Mobley."

"Pushback. I guess that would be the polite way to put it. Anya Balfour is, um, I'm not quite sure how to put this in politically correct terms. Suffice it to say, she was none too pleased to have, what did she call me, a shadow."

"I see. You are muscling in on her territory, but I wouldn't take it personally. And I have a feeling if the shoe was on the other foot..."

"Maybe. Nonetheless, she confirmed with Mobley. I'm now allowed to work with her on looking into the diplomat."

"Good. Mission accomplished, then. What have you two planned out? I assume you'll get started asap."

"Yes. I'm meeting up with her again in a few hours. We'll be heading to a place where she says Usenko will be. We'll get a feel for how he operates. Who he sees. And if Koslov might be on his agenda."

"That's a good start, but I want you to figure out everything you can about this man. I want to know when he wakes, when he sleeps, who's in that bed with him, and when he takes a shit. You understand me?"

"Roger." Caison stood up to leave. "By the way, Lacy means as much to me as she does to you. I won't see her in any danger. Frankly, letting her get close to this man could be dangerous enough."

"I have my reasons for assigning her that task. Unless you want to question my judgment."

"No, sir."

Axell appeared resigned. "Look, Caison. You may not agree with the plan, but getting Lacy out there with Usenko, knowing what I know about him already, is a good idea. He wants people to notice him, which means he wants to be around people who are noticed. There's no one better suited for that than Merrick."

"You're right. I appreciate that you know what you're doing. Doesn't make me feel any better about it, though."

"I wouldn't expect it to, all things considered." Axell returned to his duties.

Caison eyed him with the distinct feeling there was a thinly veiled message in his words. Without taking further notice, he left Axell's office, and upon leaving the building, he made the call to Lacy.

"It's me. Where are you?"

"Just leaving my house. Aaron fixed the issue and we're heading back to the shop. Why? You have something going on?"

"Not yet, but soon. I'm just leaving Axell's office now. Going to head back to the shop for a little while."

"See you back there soon." Lacy ended the call.

"What's he got going on?" Aaron asked as they stepped back into his car.

"Not sure exactly. Says he'll see us at the office, but then he's off again."

"Interesting." Aaron keyed the ignition. "Axell must have him working on something to do with Usenko."

"That'd be my guess. Vetting him before he'll let me set up the meeting. I think that could backfire, though, especially if Usenko catches wind he's being shadowed." She shook her head. "I need to get to this guy's inner circle, and the longer we wait, the more chance Koslov has of erasing his footsteps."

"I know how you get, Lacy, but Axell and Caison are doing this for your safety."

"Everyone seems to do everything for my safety. I guess none of you remember what I've done to change things around here."

"We all remember. And you know that's not what this is about. Your life has changed, Lacy, and not just with what you and the kids have been through. You're in the public eye now."

"Hardly."

"Think what you want, but people know who you are. People who aren't all good. Some might say there are people out there who want to harm you. Hence our printer hacker."

"You don't know that."

"I don't. But given our history, all signs seem to point in that general direction."

———

Caison was on the highway headed back to the shop when his phone buzzed in the center console of his car. He pressed the answer button on his steering wheel. "Caison here."

"It's Balfour. Where are you?"

"Headed back to my office. Why?"

"I'm going to text you an address. I need you to meet me there in thirty minutes."

"Okay. Where am I..." Before he could finish the sentence, she hung up. "What the hell?"

The text came through and he eyed the address. No need to plug it into his nav; he knew where he was going. He veered right off the highway and started back in the opposite direction. "This should be fun."

It wasn't going to take him thirty minutes to get there. In fact, it should only take fifteen, which would give him time to scope out the area. He had to assume since Balfour was so kind to elaborate, that she got a lead on where Usenko was going sooner than she expected. Which was fine by him; the sooner the better.

Caison arrived at the hotel. It was the Watergate Hotel. And why not? If this guy wanted to be seen, why not there? The five-star hotel still had a great deal of prestige in and around Washington. It was no surprise a junior Russian Diplomat would want to stay there, for its infamy alone.

He cut the engine and stepped out, approaching the grand entrance of the well-appointed and modern hotel. He eyed his surroundings. Caison had seen a picture of Usenko, but so far hadn't caught sight of the man near the hotel's entrance, and once inside, he surveyed the lobby.

Caison continued to the bar area and found it near-empty. Then again, it was only four in the afternoon, not yet happy hour. He checked the time on his phone. She would be there soon. Just enough time for him to have a walk around and check out the place. The exits, the elevators. Anywhere he would find people coming and going, even the staff elevators. Caison had been trained by the best in Louisville. In fact, he was still in contact with ASAC Mendez. Counterterrorism had been his specialty, and while he was still technically a member of that division, this type of work wasn't exactly what he had had in mind. But Caison was glad he made the choice. It was important work. And then there was Lacy. She'd changed his point of view on a lot of things. Cyber-related and otherwise.

"Caison."

He spun around. It was her. And now he was pissed someone got the drop on him. That never happened. Maybe he was slipping. Or maybe she was that good.

"Balfour. You're early."

"I could say the same thing about you." She turned on her heel. "Follow me."

"Great. I'll follow you, then," he muttered.

"Excuse me?" She spun her head around.

"I'm right behind you." He plastered a smile on his face until she turned back around. His smile quickly fell flat.

"Usenko is due here in twenty minutes," Balfour began. "We need to get a table and a drink and look like we've been here for a while." She continued into the bar. "This looks good."

"Perfect." Caison waited for her to slide into the booth and he sat across from her.

"No. On this side. That way we can both see him."

He pulled back up and walked to her side. "Okay."

"We'll order drinks. You'll put your arm around me so it looks like we're a couple."

"Can't wait." Caison raised a hand to get the attention of the cocktail waitress.

"Hi. What can I get for you two love birds?"

His expression hardened. "I'll take a beer. Bud Light's fine."

"He'll have a Stella, in a glass, please," Balfour said. "I'll have a house chardonnay. Thanks."

"Be right back with your drinks."

He turned to her. "Why can't I have a Bud?"

"Because if Usenko happens to see you, I need you to appear slightly more sophisticated like you're from D.C. It's hard to do that with a Budweiser."

"I beg to differ, but whatever you want. This is your op."

"That's right. It is. And you're an observer."

Caison eyed the time on his phone and did whatever else he had to do to keep from having to speak to this uncooperative, self-righteous, aggravating field agent. Finally, the drinks arrived. "None too soon. Thank you."

"Uh, if you don't mind, there'll be no need to check up on us. We need to have a conversation and it's best if we aren't interrupted," Balfour said.

The waitress furrowed her brow. "Whatever you say, ma'am." She eyed him and noticed his slight shrug, a reaction that brought a hint of a smile to her lips.

As she walked away, he began, "I don't think there was any need..."

"There he is."

He peered straight ahead and recognized the man immediately.

"Quick. Put your arm around my shoulders," Balfour said. "We need to look like a couple. Not a couple of government spies."

Caison reluctantly conceded, knowing she was probably right and refusing to admit it to her. "We got ears on him?"

"No. There was no time. I just want to know who he's meeting with."

"Copy." It was only a few moments that he had to pretend to be in a relationship with this woman, when Usenko's companion arrived. Caison didn't recognize the man. "Do you know who that is?"

Balfour was silent, only staring at the two until she turned to him. "That's Maxim Abramov."

"Name doesn't ring a bell."

She looked at him with almost pure disgust. "Maxim Abramov is the head of the Russian mafia in New York."

"Oh. That seems like it could present a problem for us."

"You think?"

CHAPTER
FIVE

THE CONVERSATION that had transpired between the two Russians sitting at a bar, the idea of which had begun to sound like a bad joke, was indecipherable for the "couple" sitting in the nearby booth. With no audio and a bar now full of patrons, Caison and Balfour could only imagine what was said. However, the important detail was that the two had met. But now Maxim Abramov, the head of the New York Russian mafia, and Anton Usenko were parting ways.

Caison cast a casual glance to Balfour as one of the men headed toward them, on his way to the exit. "We should follow them out."

"Yeah." She started to nudge her way out, but he was in her path. "Um, you might want to move."

"Sorry." He slid out of the booth and both started toward the hotel's entrance. "I see them standing near the valet." Caison retrieved his cell and began snapping pictures.

"What the hell are you doing?" she asked.

"Documenting something we might need to reference in the future."

"You're drawing too much attention." She launched in front of him.

He peered around her. "Great. They're leaving—separately. You happy now?"

"Look, you're here out of the kindness of my heart. We have the intel we need. We know Usenko is in bed with the Russian mafia."

"And that means what exactly?" Caison asked as he placed his phone back into his pocket. "We're looking for ties to Koslov. And right now, I'm not seeing any."

"I can see you're new to the whole Russian thing. I don't know exactly what your background entails, but I've been watching men like Maxim Abramov and Anton Usenko my entire career. They're all tied together, and it all points right back to the Kremlin. You want your friend to get inside Koslov's inner circle and you think putting her in front of Usenko will do that. What I'm telling you is if Usenko is talking to the Russian mafia, so is Koslov."

"And how do we go about proving that?"

She flung her arm back toward the cars that had now pulled away. "By seeing these two together. Geez! Are you not paying attention?"

Caison took a few steps back. "Look, I don't know what your operation is, but I know what mine is. I don't give a shit about the Russian mafia. I care about Sergei Koslov, a man I know helped fund or sourced the money to fund an attempted terror attack in Beijing. One I helped to prevent. So you go on and look for money laundering or drug dealing or whatever the hell it is you do, and I'll stick to the important stuff. The work that protects Americans' lives." He started back toward his car, not giving her a second glance. He was pissed. He'd just wasted three hours watching two Russians get drunk together and he was no closer to knowing how

Koslov fit into any of it. And to top it off, he had to deal with her. "Screw this." He unlocked his car and stepped inside, and as he turned the ignition, a knock sounded on his driver's side window.

Balfour stood, hunched over, pursed lips and a hand on her hip. "Hang on."

He rolled down the window. Her face was partially obscured in shadow as the sun had lowered in the sky and dusky light filtered around her. "What? Did I forget to pay you for the drinks or something?"

"I want to show you something. You mind letting me in?"

He paused to consider what fresh hell this was going to bring. More insults? More backhanded compliments? But in holding her gaze, she appeared sincere for the first time since they'd met. "Fine. Get in."

Balfour walked around the car and stepped into the passenger seat. "I'm sorry I was an asshole back there. It's just that I've been around enough men to understand that in order to hold on to the lead, you have to be just like them—an asshole—or else they'll walk all over you."

"Yeah, well, I'm not like most men. And you'd know that if you cared to let me get a word in edgewise at all earlier. What is it that you want to show me?"

"Head north and I'll tell you when to stop," she replied.

———

Lacy helped Celeste with the dishes and finished wiping the table. "Thank you for dinner, Celeste. It was delicious."

"You're very welcome. Is there anything else you need tonight? Should I help get the children ready for bed?"

"No, thank you. Why don't you go and settle in for the night? I'll get them cleaned up for tomorrow. Only another month of school and they'll be in your hair every day. Might as well take advantage of the solitude now."

"I suppose you're right." She untied her apron, folding it neatly before setting it on the counter. "Good night, sweetheart."

"Good night, Celeste." Lacy made her way into the living room. "Hey, guys. Why don't you go and get ready for bed?"

Olivia groaned first, and right on cue, Jackson followed. "Do we have to?"

"Yes, ma'am, you do. No complaints. You only have a few weeks left of school. Now go on upstairs. After that, you can watch two cartoons, then it's off to bed for both of you."

"Fine." Olivia rolled her eyes. "You know, I am older than Jack. I should get to go to bed later than him. It's not fair."

"Life's not fair, Liv. Now go."

Once she was alone and Celeste returned to her room, Lacy opened her laptop, which lay on the side table next to the sofa. It was a relatively easy fix, remove the firewall and see what happened. There were a few things to be concerned about, however. The first is not knowing if this hacker had malicious intent. Secondly, she would have to lie to her team. And that was something she wasn't accustomed to doing. She trusted them with her life and they'd saved her a time or two in the not-so-distant past. Could she really deceive them?

"We need answers," she said to no one but herself. "Who do you know?" Her desire to get something on Koslov was winning in the battle over her need to comply with orders. Axell's orders, something she rarely rebuked without just cause. But was this just?

Her only task was to uninstall the firewall and leave her connection open on the internet. If she did that, the hacker known as Graybear could access her once again. Only this time, she would make this a one-man show, or rather, one woman. She could run him like an asset. Perhaps she'd spent too much time around Axell and Delgado, and of course, Keith Colburn. But maybe they'd taught her something too.

With a few keystrokes, it was done. "Now all I have to do is wait."

———

Balfour peered through the windshield. "Pull up here and park along the curb."

"What is this place?" Caison rolled to a stop in front of the building. It had been almost forty-five minutes and Balfour had hardly said two words. He had reached an even higher level of irritation with this woman.

"My apartment. Come on."

She was already halfway out the door before he cut the engine. He joined her on the sidewalk as she started toward the building and watched her punch in a key code. The door clicked open.

Caison decided he wouldn't waste any more words on her, realizing it wasn't likely she'd answer his questions anyway. That seemed to be the way she preferred to operate. "You're not exactly a Chatty Cathy, are you?"

She shot him a stern glance before starting up the stairs. "This will be worth your time. Trust me."

Trust me, he thought. Not likely. Balfour might have been handpicked by Mobley for this assignment, but trust wouldn't enter into the equation for Caison any time soon. Trust wasn't something he casually doled out to just anyone. It had to be earned. And right now, she hadn't earned it.

Then they entered her apartment. He was agape at the surveillance equipment inside. "What the...?" He turned to her. "Does Mobley know about this?"

"Of course he does."

"I find that hard to believe." He approached the monitors. "You do remember the Fourth Amendment, don't you? You have a warrant for any of this?"

"Okay, look." She turned on her heel. "Do you want to know what it is I'm doing and who I'm watching, or are you going to start spouting off surveillance laws to me? Cause I got better things to do than to let you in on my op."

"You're right." He raised his hands. "Not my problem. I just want to know about Usenko and his supposed ties to Sergei Koslov."

"Good. Then I'll show you." She sat down and keyed in something on the laptop in front of the monitors. "I don't know how much Mobley told you about me, but I've been on these Russian mafia guys my entire career at the Bureau."

"He said something about that. Well, my boss said it anyway."

"Acting Director Axell. He seems legit."

"How old are you again?" he asked, noting her vernacular and vaguely recalling his research into her background.

"Old enough, why? How old are you?"

"It doesn't matter. I was also told your family has Russian ties."

"My parents are Russian. Defected in the early eighties. I remember growing up and they were always getting invited to government things. Dinners and such. They're both academics now, teaching Russian studies."

"Is that why you joined the Bureau? Because of your parents' history?"

"Partially, but mainly because I speak fluent Russian. Turns out, the Bureau likes that in a candidate."

Caison noticed she glossed over the fact that she'd been recruited and not the other way around. Meaning, she had more to tell about her story. But right now, Koslov needed to be the subject. "So what do you know about this diplomat?"

"I know he has a penchant for pretty American girls. Barely eighteen, from what I can tell. And, he likes to spend money."

"For a low-level attaché, sounds like someone must be fronting him cash to satisfy his needs."

"You get first prize, Caison." She smiled.

"You mean I get a participation ribbon?" He chuckled, but she didn't seem to find the humor in that. He cleared his throat before adding, "You believe the mafia leader, Maxim Abramov, is the one keeping him flush?"

"That's one consideration, and if that is the case, it's most probably under the direction of the Kremlin. Because, of course, nothing could be funneled through to Usenko directly from the Russian government. Not for those purposes, anyway."

"Got it. So what's your strategy, then? You're trying to pin something on Abramov? Tax evasion, money laundering, something like that?"

"Something like that, yes. Most importantly, and the reason I brought you here, is this." She pulled up a camera inside the diplomat's office.

"What am I looking at?"

"Usenko's office, leased by the Russian government."

"How did you...? Never mind. Again, not my business. Is that how you knew Usenko was going to be at the hotel earlier?"

"Yep. I had his office wired when I knew where it would be and when he would arrive. That little bit of intel, I got from my CIA friends."

"And this is what you'll use to find out who Usenko is palling around with? Including our elusive Sergei Koslov?"

"That's the plan. Your side of the plan. I have other dealings I'm working on, but for you, for Director Mobley, this is what I'm going to get for you. So, you see, I can offer assistance and you can trust me."

"You'll share your findings with me?"

"Yes, I will."

"Then what are your thoughts about me sending in a member of my team? She may not be as young as Usenko likes them, but she has prominence. That might appeal to him."

"Right, Lacy Merrick," she said. "Everyone knows about her and what she did for this country. She took down an entire administration. I'm sure in no small part thanks to your help too."

"I played my part, but it was her show."

Balfour seemed to consider Caison's inquiry. "I don't know if I could protect her."

"That won't be your responsibility," he replied.

"And you're hoping she'll be able to draw out information about Koslov, am I correct?"

"That's the goal."

"I can get the word out to some of my contacts and get them to keep me abreast of his objectives." She paused a moment. "If you're willing to hang her out as bait, then who am I to object?"

CHAPTER
SIX

IT TOOK the better part of the night before Lacy could rest. Her mind churned with thoughts of what Graybear might yet expose via the portal she reopened. Now that morning had arrived, it was time to see if her hunch was right, that he would again make contact.

She pushed up from her bed and wrapped herself in a robe before walking downstairs to check for herself. And as she entered Jay's office, disappointment masked her face. "Damn." Perhaps Graybear wasn't as eager as she assumed. Lacy turned and headed into the kitchen.

"Good morning." Celeste was already there with a fresh pot of coffee. "Can I pour you a cup? I'm getting another myself."

"Yes, please." Lacy sat down at the breakfast table and gazed through the window at the rising sun. "How'd you sleep?"

"Oh, same as ever," Celeste replied. "And you?"

"Well enough."

Celeste walked toward her and placed the mug on the table. "Here you go, hon."

"Thank you." She sipped on the steaming brew.

"You look like you're far off in the distance. Everything all right?" Celeste continued.

"Yeah, of course. Just work stuff."

"If you say so. I'll go and get the kids up."

A familiar sound arose from the back of the house and a flicker of anticipation grew in Lacy's eyes. She stood from the table and walked quickly to Jay's office. And that was when she saw it. The printer began to spit out a piece of paper. She retrieved it.

"I thought I'd wait until a more reasonable hour this time. I see you changed your mind?"

So Graybear knew she'd installed protections and then removed them, meaning she was being watched, at least, from this standpoint. And as she continued to read, Lacy got the feeling that perhaps this anonymous individual knew far more than he or she initially led on. The meeting between Anton Usenko and Maxim Abramov was mentioned, although it appeared that Will's presence had gone unnoticed. But what this meant was that Graybear was most certainly in the know on a variety of subjects.

There was something she had picked up on about this message. There was no new information, only a rehash of what had already come to pass. First and foremost, the time had come for Lacy to initiate a direct contact with Graybear. And she would have to find a way to make that happen without further exposing herself, or her family.

———

Koslov switched off the financial news and opened his door at the sound of a knock on the other side. "Good morning. Please, come in."

"I have news."

"I gathered that was the reason for your early arrival, Maxim. May I get you a coffee?" Koslov started toward the kitchen.

"Yes, thank you." Maxim Abramov pulled off his suit jacket, exposing the oversized belly beneath his button-down, and carefully draped it over the side chair before sitting. "I had a very productive meeting yesterday. And, as promised, have news of developments from home."

Koslov soon returned with two mugs in his hands. "Good developments, I hope."

"Someone has arrived who will assist with expediting your reemergence from the shadows. And I met with this someone yesterday afternoon. I think you will be pleased."

"And why wasn't this relayed directly to me?" Koslov, who modeled himself after the movie-style gangsters, hiked up his pants and sat on the sofa.

"It is unwise to risk your association with the diplomat."

"If this diplomat is supposed to offer assistance in my return, it seems difficult to understand why I cannot meet with him directly. Am I to go through you for this guidance?"

"For now. Until such time as the consortium and Moscow believe it safe."

"We have lost time and influence that will be difficult to reestablish," Koslov said. "However, at this point, I am willing to agree to the terms you have set forth. So who is this individual?"

"Anton Usenko."

Koslov laughed. "You cannot be serious. That *child*?" He stood. "A boy more interested in celebrity and wealth?"

"Wealth is not a bad thing, Sergei," Abramov said. "He is our best hope at reestablishing ties within the US government, regaining access to those at the top. We had that once with Casper Janz. And, as I stated before, we will have that once again. You will need to allow the process to develop, Sergei."

Koslov paced the room. "I can see I have no choice in the matter. Maybe the boy has matured since I last knew of him."

Abramov thrust out his arm. "There, you see! You have found the bright spot. I knew you were capable." He started toward the door. "I will act as the go-between until the directive comes that you will be able to meet with him. Good day, Sergei. I will be in touch."

Koslov held open the door for his companion. As he stood in the opening, he considered the consortium's directive and how important it was to regain the ties he once shared with the former CIA operative. It appeared Anton Usenko was their solution.

————

Inside the offices of the task force, Lacy waited for the others to arrive. Axell had an update as to the status of Sergei Koslov and how they might infiltrate his inner circle and had called a briefing. Armed with the new message from Graybear, Lacy believed this could further advance their goals, although it was something she was prepared to take on her own for now.

Trevor Axell made his way to the bullpen. "Sorry I'm a little late. Let's head into the conference room so we can get started." He started into the hall. "We have a lot of ground to cover and not a lot of time to do it in."

Aaron Hunter and Jill Goddard started into the conference room when Hunter looked back over his shoulder. "Lace, you coming?"

"Be right there." She slipped the latest message from Graybear inside her desk drawer and made her way toward the others. "Anyone seen Will yet?"

"Right behind you." He appeared from the kitchen with a coffee in hand.

"I didn't realize you were already here. How did yesterday go? I figured I would've heard from you."

"I'll tell you all about it in the meeting." He patted her on the shoulder. "We're making progress."

Axell flipped on the lights. "Okay. Everyone have a seat." He stood at the head of the table. "First things first. I had a productive meeting with Director Mobley late yesterday afternoon. The cooperation between our task force and his agency has been very effective, as has the level of cooperation within the CIA. That said, I have a meeting scheduled with the president's chief of staff later today, so I'll let you know how that goes."

"Do you think the president has selected a permanent director?" Lacy asked.

"Your guess is as good as mine."

"It would be nice to have you with us on a more permanent basis right now," Hunter replied. "We need someone here to keep the rest of us above board."

"What's that supposed to mean?" Caison asked.

"Just what it means. Look, I know everyone in this room has the best of intentions, but there is protocol. Rules. And we can't disregard the rules just to get what we want. Otherwise, how does that make us any different from the people we're searching for?"

"Point taken, Hunter," Axell replied. "That's a discussion for a later date. Right now, I want to throw the ball over to Caison, who has an update on his meeting with the Bureau's Russian expert."

Caison made his way to the front of the room, where images flashed on the wall-mounted screens. "These were taken yesterday afternoon." He pointed to the man on the right. "This man here, waiting for his car, that's Anton Usenko, the Russian diplomat who arrived in Washington last week. He's staying here at the Watergate. Agent Balfour and I sat in the lobby bar, where he met with a man by the name of Maxim Abramov, the head of the

Russian mafia in New York." He pointed to another image. "This is Abramov."

"Do you know what they were talking about? Did it involve Koslov?" Hunter asked.

"Balfour didn't have time to get audio on the conversation, however, given what she knows about Usenko, she believes he is here to act as a liaison between Koslov and the mafia leader, Abramov, in order to keep him on the QT. Which leads me to believe they assume we're going after Koslov after what happened in Beijing. And that brings me to my next point. Axell and I think the time has come for Merrick to make contact with Usenko and find out how involved he is with Koslov's plans."

"I'm on board with that. When and where?" Lacy said.

"Hang on. Are we going to put surveillance on Usenko first?" Hunter asked.

"We have help with that from Balfour. That said, you and Goddard will need to do your jobs and figure out how to keep tabs on Usenko as well. It's important our team is in on this and not just Balfour," Caison continued.

"Regarding Koslov's GPS," Goddard interrupted. "I have some raw data that suggests he's doing a lot of traveling back and forth from New York to D.C."

"I'm wondering if that has anything to do with Usenko's arrival?" Lacy replied. "How do we do the introduction between Usenko and me?"

"I'm glad you asked," Axell began. "There's a state dinner in three days. Usenko will be there and so will you."

———

A knock sounded on Lacy's door. "I'll get it." Celeste emerged from the hall. "Well, Mr. Axell, don't you clean up nicely."

"Thank you, Celeste. Is the lady of the house ready to go?" He walked inside.

"I am." Lacy descended the steps dressed in a stunning blush-colored evening gown.

"Now this one here." Axell pointed to her. "She cleans up good. You look beautiful, Lacy. I am a lucky man to have you on my arm tonight."

"Yes, you are." She stepped off the final stair and reached for Trevor's arm.

"Are you ready for this?" he asked.

"Yes, sir."

The two stepped outside into the tepid evening air and Axell opened the door to his Audi SUV. "After you, ma'am."

Lacy slipped onto the supple leather seat while Axell closed the door. She was nervous. Probably more nervous than she had been even when faced with Shen Yang's men. Perhaps that was because her children's lives were at stake. And a mother could muster incredible strength and courage in such instances. But this was different. She was going to have to be someone she wasn't. She was going to have to feign interest in a man she didn't know nor believed was a man of integrity.

Trevor pressed the ignition. "Let's get this show on the road."

Lacy was quiet for most of the drive, contemplating her words carefully as she figured out how best to approach a young Russian diplomat who valued celebrity above all else.

"You're awfully quiet," Axell said. "You sure you're okay? It isn't too late to pull the plug."

"Yes, it is. I'm okay. Just thinking about what I should say and do. How I should react, things like that."

"Once you make the connection and break the ice, it'll get easier. You'll see how he operates and how best to play on his weaknesses. Just remember, you're going in as yourself, the woman who brought down a president. That alone will get you in with this kid. I guarantee you that. Your only job then will be to get closer to him. He thinks you're still FBI, so remember that. No one outside our team, Mobley, and the president knows about the task force. And don't forget that I'll be there with you and so will Caison."

"He's going to be there?"

"Yes. He and the FBI's Russian expert, Agent Balfour, will be surveilling. So if you see him, just walk on by. Here we are." Axell pulled into the valet parking. "Put on your happy face, Merrick. It's show time."

The attendant opened Lacy's door first and she stepped out in her high heels and gown. Axell caught up to her and tugged to straighten the coat of his tuxedo. He pressed on a tiny earpiece in his right ear. "We're onsite."

Lacy walked inside and was dazzled by the glow of the chandeliers and the gilded walls that abutted the cathedral ceilings. "Taxpayers paid for this?" she whispered to Axell.

"'Fraid so." He placed his hand against the middle of her back and guided her inside the ballroom, where the dinner was taking place. "Entering the building now," he said in a hushed tone, all the while smiling as he passed people on their way in.

"You're the director of the CIA now. All eyes are on you." Lacy stood inside the ballroom and surveyed the room. "That should get Usenko's attention pretty quickly."

"That's the plan. Once we set eyes on the target, I'll make the introduction."

The two strolled into the room, greeting a few people, and stopping at the bar for a drink. That was when she spotted him. With a wine glass to her lips, she muttered, "That's him over there, right?"

"Good eye, Merrick," Axell replied. "Let's go have a chat with

Mr. Usenko." He led Lacy toward the younger man also dressed in black tie.

His light brown hair was cut short on the sides and left long on the top, swooping over in a sort of pomade bouffant. Not unattractive, but not Lacy's cup of tea. Usenko seemed to recognize them both right away as indicated by his smile on their approach.

"Mr. Anton Usenko." Axell offered his hand. "Acting CIA Director Trevor Axell. I heard you were new here in D.C., so I thought I'd come on over and get you familiar with some of us around here."

"I'm well aware of you, Director Axell. And this, I believe, is Mrs. Lacy Merrick with the FBI."

"You've done your homework." She held out her hand. "Pleasure to meet you. I didn't realize I was that recognizable."

"Mrs. Merrick, everyone knows who you are." He returned the greeting. "You brought down a president."

CHAPTER
SEVEN

WITH HIS HANDS clasped at his front and an eagle-eyed expression, Caison looked more like Secret Service and appeared conspicuous in the room full of smiling statesmen and donors. And his partner, Anya Balfour, seemed to take note.

"You know, you can relax a little. This is a social gathering."

"I'll relax when I know my team makes it safely back home. Until then, my eyes won't leave them."

"If you're not careful, someone's bound to call you out. You need to chill. I get that you guys have been through a lot together. And what your team has done for this country is admirable, but you gotta relax or you'll blow it for them."

"What's he doing?"

"Who?" Balfour peered in the direction in which Caison had his sights trained.

"Axell. He's leaving her."

"That's kind of the whole point. Am I right? Her job is to get to know Usenko. That's a little hard when there's a third wheel."

"It's too soon."

"We're at a state dinner, Caison. What do you think is going to happen?"

"I don't know. I just don't like it, okay?" His eyes were glued on Lacy and the Russian diplomat.

"Oh." Balfour smiled. "I get it. You're into her. Now it makes sense."

"What? No. I'm concerned about a colleague. You have no idea what we've been up against over this past year. I don't take any situation for granted. And frankly, neither should Axell."

"You mean CIA Director Axell? He is one of the most powerful figures in the intelligence community. You speak of him as if he's just an annoying uncle."

"I don't have time to explain to you the dynamics of my team. Right now, I believe it's too soon to throw Lacy into the fire with Usenko."

"Okay, but that's not what you said a few days ago. But I see now that it's actually happening, you're up in arms about it."

Caison noticed Axell's approach as he tossed him a sideways glance. "Excuse me for a moment."

"Sure thing. I'll keep an eye out for your *colleague*."

Her use of air quotes on that last word irritated him, but he continued to follow Axell as they stepped out into the hall.

"Looks like we've got the ball rolling," Axell said, looking pleased with himself.

"I'm not feeling quite as confident as you are right now," Caison added.

"Of course you're not. But that comes as no surprise to me. Point is, she's ready and she can do this."

"What happens after this? After tonight?"

"I don't expect her to go home with Usenko if that's what you're asking." Axell held up his hand before Caison could reply. "I expect she'll spend the next several minutes talking to him, laughing at his jokes. Eventually, she'll casually mention that it would be nice to talk again, maybe at lunch sometime in the near future."

"Is that what you two agreed on? Because it might have been nice to let the rest of us in on the deal."

"What's going on with you, Caison? You don't think Merrick can handle this? You were the one who signed off on this after working with Balfour, who by the way, seems to be doing a good job keeping her eyes on the prize."

He glanced at Balfour, then at Lacy, who did appear to have things under control.

"I realize you want to protect her. Okay, we all want to. On this issue, she is more than capable of running this kid. Let her do the job. Your only job is to help keep the way clear for her."

"Right. I got it." Caison knew Axell was on point, but that didn't change the fact that Lacy wasn't a spy. She wasn't any sort of covert operative, she was a cyber analyst. And this would be a stretch for anyone with that background. "I'd better get back to Balfour."

"Good. I'm going to press the flesh with a few more folks, then I'm calling it a night. Stay close to her, but not too close. Comprende?"

"Copy." Caison started back toward Balfour as Axell continued making the rounds.

"All okay with Papa?" she asked.

He glared at her. "Are you always such a condescending asshole?"

"I told you, sometimes it's part of the job." Balfour seemed genuinely contrite. "She's your partner. I respect the fact that you give a shit about her, just as I imagine you do for the rest of your team." She turned her sights back to Lacy. "Looks like she's making a move."

He appeared at attention once again. "Stay close."

"I know." Balfour followed him.

"He's walking her out." Caison pressed on his earpiece. "Are you seeing this?"

"I'm on it. In the hall now and I'll keep eyes on her. You two go out front. I think that's where he's headed. He might be leaving," Axell replied.

Caison continued navigating through the people in fancy clothes as the two made their way outside, near the valet parking. "Axell's got her."

Balfour creased her brow at him, appearing to wonder who he was speaking to. "Are you talking to yourself?"

"Huh? No. Never mind. We'll just sit tight here and see if they leave together."

"I doubt that would happen, but sure."

Lacy emerged through the grand building's entrance with Anton Usenko closely behind. They appeared to be engaged in light-hearted conversation. She smiled and even tossed her head back a time or two, appearing to laugh at something he said.

"Be smart, Lacy," Caison said.

"Give her some credit," Balfour replied.

Usenko moved in front and handed a ticket to the attendant. He was getting his car. He was going to leave.

A newer-model Mercedes sedan rolled to a stop in front of Usenko.

"That must be his car. Axell, are you seeing this?"

"I am. Just relax, Caison. She's got it under control. If she leaves with him, we'll follow. I've already got someone ready to go if that happens."

Caison felt his heart pump hard against his chest. The last thing he wanted was for her to get in that man's car. He was still an enigma. No one knew whose side he was really on. Perhaps only his own.

Usenko turned to Lacy and reached for her hand. With a subtle nod, he bent down to kiss the top of it.

Caison couldn't make out what was said, but Lacy appeared flattered.

A moment later, Anton Usenko stepped into his Mercedes and drove off. Lacy stood outside alone.

"Don't approach her. Not yet," Axell said through the earpiece. "Give her a chance to give us the all-clear."

"Roger," Caison replied, keeping his eyes on her, waiting.

Lacy's smile faded as the car disappeared with Usenko inside of it. She inhaled a deep breath and stepped away from the curb. She appeared to be searching for something.

"She's looking for us. Axell, are we good?" He continued watching her when Lacy turned and started back inside.

"We're good. You go, but keep contact under wraps. If Usenko has anyone else there, I don't want them to see you two together. Get word to her and get her out of there."

———

It looked like a sort of dismal high school prom. Lacy leaned against her desk, still dressed in her blush gown. Caison sat on the edge of his, still wearing his monkey suit. And Axell was the principal who appeared ready to punish his students for spiking the punch. Only Hunter was dressed in ordinary clothes and that was because he wasn't at the dinner.

"So Balfour left?" Hunter asked.

"As soon as we got Lacy out, she said she didn't see much point in staying but asked that we relay any intel on Usenko we think might be relevant to her." Caison shifted on his desk, pulling open his coat.

"You did great, Merrick." Axell moved toward her. "Exactly as we discussed. I think you might make a good spy after all." He placed his hand on her shoulder.

"I don't know about that. I felt like I was sweating bullets the entire time, but I got a date."

"For when?" Caison asked.

"Day after tomorrow. He asked to have lunch tomorrow, but I didn't want to appear too eager. I had to play a little hard to get. I agreed to drinks on Thursday. That'll buy me some time to get to know him a little more and then we'll see what happens after that."

"Good call. Drinks will get him loosened up. Get him talking," Axell said. "Okay then. I think we've all had a busy night. We should hit the sack and start fresh tomorrow. Unless there's anything else?" He looked directly at Caison.

He shook his head. "I'm good. Thanks for running audio, Hunter." He pushed off the edge of his desk.

"No problem. Glad I could help. I have to say, man, you got your hands full with that Agent Balfour."

"That is a fact," Caison replied. "Hopefully, I won't have to shadow her for too long. Sounds like Lacy's got a handle on this situation." He eyed Hunter, knowing he must've overheard Balfour mention that Will had a thing for Lacy. It was a subject the two had avoided at all costs, neither wanting to truly know how the other felt. Both tried to pretend it didn't exist.

"I got it handled. So long as you all have ears on us on Thursday too."

"That won't be an easy task," Axell replied. "I'm concerned if Usenko has people around him, those same people might've seen Caison or Balfour tonight and I don't think we can risk that happening."

"What are we supposed to do while she meets with him?" Caison asked.

"You'll be nearby, and Hunter will have to set up an emergency signal through her cell phone that will reach us. All of us. Even if I'm not there. I need to stay abreast of what's happening."

"I can get something set up. I can track her signal, and if she turns off her phone, then back on, that'll be our sign something's gone amiss."

"Excuse me, but what happens then?" Lacy asked.

"Like I said, Caison will be nearby. Look, I wouldn't put too much thought into any problems. Not when you're out in public. Now if he wanted to meet you at his place or something, then I'd take issue. But it'll be fine. Get to know him, Lacy. Find out if he's in contact with Koslov. Because if he is, then I can guaran-damn-tee you that the Kremlin's running Koslov too." He continued toward the door. "Don't forget to lock up. We have a lot of expensive shit in here. That's all, folks."

———

Lacy entered her home, immediately shedding the high heels and evening bag. She was proud of her work tonight and had a hard time not patting herself on the back for it. She did what she'd set out to do. Maybe she would make a good spy.

Lacy started up the stairs but was stopped short by a sound coming from Jay's office. Her heart jumped. It must have been Graybear. She'd almost forgotten about her asset.

She quickly stepped back down and padded into the study. A page had just been printed. She snatched it from the tray and began reading it.

"Hope you had a nice time this evening. You looked beautiful,

by the way. And what do you think of Anton? There is much to tell you about him. Get some rest. I'm sure you must need it."

Lacy turned deadpan. Graybear had seen her. No one else knew she would be at that dinner tonight except for the team.

So far, Graybear was holding all the cards and Lacy was feeling more vulnerable by the moment. She picked up her cell phone and made the call. "Hey, I didn't wake you, did I?"

"No. I just got home," Aaron began. "Is everything okay?"

"No. Look, we need to figure out a way to track back to this hacker."

"What are you talking about? The printer thing? We took care of that already."

"I know you did. But I sort of undid it."

"You what?"

Lacy had to pull the phone from her ear. "Calm down, Aaron. Please. I felt it was the only way to get intel on Usenko and Koslov and I was right."

"Did he contact you again?"

"Yes. Twice."

"That's it. I'm coming over," Aaron replied.

"No. Wait. Not here. I'll bring my laptop. We need to be on a secure connection. We'll have to go back to the office. Or, I can go alone and try to work through it."

"I'll meet you there in twenty." The line went dead.

———

Lacy pushed through the doors at headquarters, appearing sheepish. This was her fault and now she had to own up to it. She thought she could handle it, but this development frightened her. Not only because Graybear had seen her, but because he knew when she arrived home, which was precisely the reason for

Aaron's initial concern. "Thanks for coming down. I'll put on a pot of coffee."

"Don't bother. I brought some. Come and sit down." Aaron was at his desk, the glow of his computer screen leaving a hint of sickly blue on his face. "The sooner we can take down Graybear, the better off we'll be. And this time, we cut him off for good."

"I understand." She pulled up a chair next to him and retrieved her laptop. "We have to assume it's a botnet. Possibly P2P with a C&C."

"I'm impressed. I thought maybe you'd forgotten what you used to do for a living," Aaron replied. "So the first thing we need to do is determine if you have a zombie computer. Everyone's moving away from Internet Relay Chat because they're too easy to take down. P2P, however, makes that much more difficult."

"Right," Lacy began. "However, if I recall, P2Ps search random IP addresses. This wasn't random. Maybe we should look elsewhere."

"First things first. Let's open this up and take a look. I'm installing BotHunter to check for bots first."

"How did you get hold of that? That's military-grade software. I don't even think the Cyber Division has access to that."

"I bet they do. You just might not know about it. And besides, I have people. They have access to things. We'll leave it at that." Aaron ran the program and after several minutes, it became clear.

Aaron pushed away from the screen. "Did you open a suspicious email attachment recently?"

"No. Of course not. I would never do that."

"Okay. Then the only other way, apart from the printer, which I see now is just another bot, which I attempted to eliminate..."

"Yeah, I screwed up. I get that. Get to your point, Aaron."

"Someone had to have access to your computer."

"No way. Not a chance. No one has access to this laptop except me. I promise you that."

"Lacy, someone installed spyware that allowed the botnet in. If you didn't open an attachment or click onto a link or get into a weird website, then the only other way it could happen was if someone had physical access to your device."

"Meaning someone got into my house and did this," Lacy replied.

"That's one possibility."

"No, Aaron. That's the only possibility."

CHAPTER
EIGHT

OUTSIDE THE OVAL OFFICE, where the president's personal secretaries received visitors, was where Trevor Axell waited. The last-minute meeting had been scheduled in the night and Axell was only informed of it at five o'clock this morning. It could have been called regarding a few issues, though the primary issue running through Axell's mind was the decision to announce a permanent CIA director. He had known this time would come and had expected it much sooner. It had been a good run, he thought. But the time had come to hand over the reins to another. This wasn't his kind of gig anyway. Axell had never been the political type and this job required a political puppet master.

"Director Axell, the president will see you now." One of the secretaries opened the door to the Oval Office.

"Thank you, Chris." Axell entered the room, where the president sat at his desk. "Good morning, Mr. President," he tendered a greeting.

"Good morning, Trevor. How are you?"

"Doing well, sir, thank you."

"Good. Let's sit over here." The president walked to the

seating area where two sofas sat opposite each other with a small coffee table in between. "I wanted to talk to you about something. Something I'm sure you've been expecting."

"Yes, sir." Axell took a seat, and it appeared his initial assumption had been correct.

"For the past, what, two months now, you've been the CIA's acting director?"

"I have, sir, yes. It's been an honor to serve."

"Well, as you know, the term 'acting' implies temporary and that I would eventually have to name a permanent director. And I believe that time has come."

"Of course, sir. I have been expecting this."

"The work you've done, and I don't just mean with the CIA. I mean with the task force. It's been invaluable. And it appears you have become quite indispensable to me."

"That's very good of you to say, sir." Axell shifted in his seat, never one to readily accept praise.

"That said, I'm sure it must be difficult juggling the two, especially considering what a hands-on leader I know you to be. However, I also know that you have excelled at your current position, on both fronts. Frankly, I'm not sure how, but as I choose to surround myself with people smarter than me, you were a good choice."

Axell wondered when he would get to the point. The flattery was confusing and he didn't know which way this would break.

"So, my point is. I'd like to make you the permanent director of the CIA. Will you accept the position?"

"And my current role in the task force?"

"I'll leave that up to you, if you elect to appoint another in your footsteps, or if you prefer to stay."

"I am absolutely honored that you would ask this of me, sir, however..."

"However?"

Axell took in a breath to ensure the words in his head came out as he intended. "However, I do feel it would take away from what I believe the task force can accomplish. I feel the work my team is doing is beyond compare. Not quite CIA, not FBI, but acting in its own space. Doing work that both agencies have the capacity to conduct, but are somewhat hamstrung in their ability to act due to congressional constraints."

"Ah, you prefer the relative hands-off approach and freedom the task force offers. Well, I certainly don't blame you. While my predecessor created the task force, to his own detriment, the nature of its work and its clandestine operation is unique in the intelligence community."

"And necessary, as we've seen," Axell added.

"And necessary, indeed," the president replied. "But that leaves me with a difficult course of action. Who, then, should I appoint to take your place in the Agency, as it sounds as though you are declining my request."

"Respectfully, sir, yes, I am afraid I will have to decline your extraordinary offer. But I do have another in mind who I believe would do better than just fill my shoes. She would blaze a trail within the Agency that would take it beyond its already world-class status. It would become something you and I could have only dreamed of. It would be unparalleled on the world stage."

"Well, tell me then, who is this trailblazer?"

"Washington Chief of Station, Elizabeth Ward."

"Of course. She was instrumental in seeing your name cleared, among her many other talents." The president stood and offered his hand. "I will think about your suggestion. And it is a good one at that. Thank you, Director Axell. It has been my absolute pleasure to have worked with you."

"That won't end, sir. Not as long as you allow the task force to continue. Good day, sir."

A secret service agent opened the door and Axell made his way back into the secretaries' office.

"Goodbye, Director Axell."

"Bye, Chris." Axell started through the halls, feeling lighter than when he'd entered. It wasn't really a difficult decision. He never wanted to be director. Well, maybe for a minute. He wanted to get back to the work his team was carrying out. That was where he felt most at home. Perhaps it was Lacy who made him feel that way. She had begun to fill a hole left wide open by the distancing of his own daughter. Regardless, his heart was lighter and he would return to the task force offices this morning and relay the news to the team.

―――――

Upon Axell's arrival, he spotted Lacy and Aaron at Aaron's desk. "You two are here early." And on further inspection, he noted it appeared neither had slept. "What's going on? Have either of you been to bed yet?"

The look on Lacy's face revealed all he needed to know. "What happened? What did you find?"

She glanced at Aaron and returned her attention to Axell. "I was hacked."

"Yeah. I thought we knew that and Hunter shut it down. The printer thing, right?" Axell leaned on the corner of Lacy's desk.

At this, Aaron shifted his gaze and replied, "It looks like it was worse than we thought. The person who sent the rogue print jobs, probably via a botnet..."

"This isn't the time to get technical on me, Hunter. Speak English," Axell said.

"Sorry. So, this person, it now seems, had gained access to Lacy's laptop. And probably more than that."

"Graybear knew I was at the dinner last night," Lacy began. "I don't know how, but when I got home, I got another message on my printer. He or she knew I was there, saw what I was wearing, and knew exactly who I was speaking to."

"For God's sake." He stood in frustration. "Wait. So Hunter fixed the hack or whatever on the printer. But somehow, this hacker—Graybear?"

She nodded.

"Stupid name. Graybear also had access to your laptop. Okay. But that doesn't explain how he/she knew you were at the dinner."

"It does if the laptop was open," Aaron said. "Audio, turning on the webcam. Lots of ways people can listen in. And if Lacy mentioned that was where she was going at home, there you go."

"There you go." Axell started to pace the bullpen and his tone grew abrasive. "There you go. With all the damn tech we have here, all you can say is 'there you go.'"

"Trevor, this was my fault. It's my computer. I let my guard down. And," she paused a moment, "I reopened the connection Aaron fixed so I could maintain contact with Graybear. This is on me."

"You did what?" He marched toward her. "After everything you've been through, you did this? Do you recall nothing of what happened in Beijing? Of what happened here, to your husband?"

"I screwed up. I get that." Lacy became heated and the discussion was going down a path she hadn't wished it to travel. "I wanted intel on Koslov and I thought, I still think, Graybear can get it."

"Oh, I'm sure that's the case," Axell started. "And what happens when Graybear gets to you? Your kids?"

"That's enough," Aaron jumped in. "Arguing isn't going to

solve this problem. We're all concerned by this, but it isn't too late. We can fix this. That's why we're still here. Neither one of us has had any sleep. We're trying to find Graybear."

Hunter was not usually the voice of reason, but this time, that seemed to be the case. Lacy backed down and so did Axell. "Okay. Are we all calm now? I'd like to get back to work."

Caison arrived at the silence in the bullpen and immediately questioned it. "Did I miss something?"

Lacy peered at him. "Just another day in paradise." She retreated to the kitchen to calm herself. Bringing up the safety of her children wasn't something Lacy expected from Axell. He knew how much she blamed herself for what they had already been through. It was a low blow and it would take time to get over this one.

She was reaching for a bottled water when Will entered.

"You mind telling me what the hell is going on? After last night, I thought we'd be all smiles in here. I come in and instead, you all looked pissed off. And you'll forgive me for saying this, but you also look like hell. Like you haven't slept."

"I haven't. I've been here with Aaron all night." She set the bottle on the counter. "I messed up. Big time. I let my guard down and I got called out for it."

"You're going to have to start from the beginning."

After she relayed the troubling news, Caison began, "I can see why Axell's in a tizzy. This is bad, Lacy."

"I know it is. But I'm telling you, I can use this Graybear for intel."

"That's a dangerous game and you know it." He poured two cups of coffee and handed Lacy one of them. "Here, you look like you could use the caffeine."

"Thanks."

Axell appeared in the doorway and leaned against it, thrusting his hand into his pants pocket. "Listen, Lacy, I'm sorry for jumping down your throat. That's the last thing you need right now. And, I'm sorry about, you know."

"It's okay, Trevor. It's a problem and I'll deal with it."

"Not alone, you won't," Caison added. "If Graybear can find you, then we can find him."

"There was something else I needed to talk to you all about," Axell said. "Why don't we all huddle for a few minutes."

They returned to the bullpen, where Hunter remained at his desk.

"Where's Goddard? She should hear this too," Axell asked.

"She mentioned something about an early morning appointment. She'll be here around ten," Hunter replied.

"Okay, then. I guess it's just the four of us. As usual." He smiled. "I was called to the president's office this morning. I'm sure you can all guess as to why I was there."

Lacy held her breath, unsure if this news would be good or bad. Though she supposed, either way, it would be good for Trevor. But she missed him and wanted him back where he belonged, with the team.

"The president asked me to take on the director role on a permanent basis." He paused, seemingly for dramatic effect. "I declined the offer. I told him I wanted to be back here, with you all."

Lacy finally released the air in her lungs. "Are you sure this is what you want, Trevor? Being director could've been a huge stepping stone for you. I mean, who knows, you could've eventually become president."

"I've never wanted that. Hell, I didn't want to be acting director, but someone had to step in and I did feel some responsibility after Handley. Besides, we're doing work here that the other agencies can't. We have little oversight..."

"For now," Caison added.

"For now, and for the foreseeable future. Our funding isn't approved by Congress, so we aren't beholden to them either. We're an agency that is free to operate as it sees fit."

"Which might be concerning to the general public," Hunter said.

"Were it in the wrong hands, yes, but it's in our hands. We've all risked our lives for this country, more than once. This task force is beyond reproach and I fully believe that."

"So you're back with us—for good," Lacy said. "What did the president say when you rejected the offer?"

"I think he half-expected it. I did make a recommendation and we'll see if he takes me up on it."

"Who?" Caison asked.

"Elizabeth Ward. Who else? The best thing that could happen to our task force is to have her on board at the Agency. I just hope the president makes the right call." Axell clapped his hands. "Okay. That's all I've got. So we'd better get started, or rather, continue searching for the elusive Graybear. Stupid name." Axell shook his head.

"You heard the man, let's get back to work," Hunter said. "Lacy, come take a look at this." He moved back to his monitor.

She raised her index finger. "Give me one second, would you?" Lacy caught up with Axell as he walked into his office. "Can I talk to you for a second?"

"Sure."

She closed the door and took a seat. "Have you told Elizabeth you recommended her for the job?"

"Not yet. I honestly didn't know if I planned on declining the offer or not. I guess I needed to hear it from the president directly. Then it became clear to me. So I'll be giving her a call here shortly.

I don't know how she'll feel about it. My gut tells me she'd accept if the position is offered."

"Well, the president wouldn't be the president if it weren't for you, so I think you have the man's ear."

"If it weren't for all of us. But we'll see. Is that what you wanted to ask? Because somehow, I think you're still ticked off about what I said earlier, and rightly so."

"It's not that. I understand you were angry."

"Worried, more like," he replied.

"Okay. Worried. But I don't think I'm as worried as the rest of you. I still maintain that Graybear wants what we want. I don't know why this person would go to the lengths they did to surveil me at the dinner. But there must have been a reason."

"What do you propose we do about this, Lacy?" Axell leaned over his desk and rested his arms atop it.

"After getting over the initial shock of the fact that I let a hacker into my own computer, I started thinking. Maybe I should try to get closer to him. Or her. Or whatever."

"Isn't that what's already happened? And I'm sorry to say, it doesn't make me happy."

"Trevor, if this person wanted harm to come to me or my family, it would be done by now. Believe me, I have enough enemies and I've started to recognize a pattern of behavior among them. This person is not an enemy."

"Then why not come forward? Why the cloak and dagger routine?" Axell asked.

"Maybe this individual wanted to be sure they could trust us. That we were on the right side of this."

"The right side of what? They've made no demands; only offered intel on Koslov, but have delivered virtually nothing useful."

"In the past year, we've taken down how many government

figures? What's to say we aren't among the corrupt, according to this person? We were directly responsible for inserting a new President of the United States. Us. Our team."

"Okay, so Graybear is feeling us out. Fine. I'll accept your premise. But how do you plan on getting closer? You plan on leaving your webcam on and letting this individual into your home every night?"

"No. Of course not. And I've already put a piece of tape over the camera on my laptop. Problem solved. And I'll be shutting it down every night too. No internet, no audio access."

"Good. Then your solution is?"

Lacy considered her proposal for a moment. "I have no idea if Graybear is a man or a woman, a citizen of this country or a foreigner. So I'm going in blind. But what I do know is that Graybear seems to want to expose Koslov. So I ask myself, why? What is Graybear's motivation for wanting Koslov or whoever Koslov works for caught? And I think Anton Usenko could be the answer to that."

"What are you trying to say, here, Lacy? What is your plan?"

"I'm saying this. Graybear got into the state dinner, meaning he or she was invited. This person might be an excellent hacker, but forging an invite to a state dinner is no easy task. Not with the background checks done these days."

"I'm with you."

"And we only heard from Graybear after Usenko arrived. So what I propose is this, we stick to the plan of moving inside Usenko's circle. When Graybear reaches out, I'll give them the download. See what reactions I get."

"What about money?" Axell added.

"No. I think Graybear wants infamy. And just like Usenko, I think he or she will place fame above money."

"How are you going to offer up Usenko? The kid is an attaché. Nothing more, from what I've seen."

"An attaché Will's new friend, Agent Balfour, seems well acquainted with. And in fact, Graybear mentioned only in vague terms something about Usenko. So I don't know what he knows, if anything about him. But if I work with her to get intel on Usenko and offer that to our friend Graybear, maybe he'll be more inclined to open up. More inclined to trust us."

"I don't know, Lacy. That would mean understanding the Kremlin's infrastructure here in the States. A dark and dangerous web I don't think we want to get tangled up in."

"Balfour has a handle on that, from what Will has said. Trevor, it's the only way I'm going to find out who Graybear is and if he can get us to Koslov..."

"Then don't let me stop you."

CHAPTER
NINE

LANGLEY HAD BEEN HOME to Trevor Axell for a good part of his career with the agency. He'd worked within the confines of this facility for the past ten years. Prior to that, he was a case officer in the field, working in parts of the world most people preferred to forget, including himself. One such location was Egypt, the very place he first crossed paths with the now-deceased Casper Janz. He knew then the type of man Janz was and was still cleaning up his mess. The worst kind of American, Janz sold his services and his secrets to forces that wished to see the United States suffer.

But once the team obtained solid intel on Sergei Koslov, aka Malcolm Ford, the man who helped fund Janz's and former Director Handley's plans to start a Chinese civil war, the mess would finally be cleaned. He knew, however, that there would be another Koslov, another Janz, which was precisely the reason he wanted to return to the task force and leave these hallowed halls once and for all.

"Good afternoon, Director Axell." Elizabeth Ward leaned in

his doorway, arms folded and smiling as though she carried a secret only the two of them shared.

"Elizabeth." He pushed back from his chair and stood to greet her. "Please come in. It's so good to see you."

"And you." She accepted his hand and sat down. "I just had a very interesting meeting with the president."

"Is that so?"

She regarded him with suspicion. "Like you didn't know."

"I didn't, but I'm glad to hear it."

"Trevor, I don't know what to say. I expected you to accept the permanent position when it was offered. Instead, you recommended it for me."

"Why wouldn't I, Elizabeth? You're more than capable of handling the assignment. And I couldn't think of anyone better," Axell replied. "So you accepted?"

"I did. The official announcement is slated for 3 pm today. Then I'll have to play nice with the Senate for confirmation."

"That won't be a problem, I assure you. No one, not Republican or Democrat, would find fault with the job you've done. I imagine I'll be getting a call soon then to inform me as to when I'll need to vacate, assuming you'll be taking command immediately following confirmation."

"That is my understanding. And of course, filling my shoes at the Washington station won't be too difficult a task. I've had plenty of officers nipping at my heels for years for the opportunity, least of all, the deputy chief."

"I'm excited for you, Elizabeth. It's everything I could've wanted for you."

"You know, Meg asked about you the other day."

"Oh yeah?"

"Since you were appointed acting director, she's been talking about you more than she used to. Maybe it's time you offered an olive branch. She's your daughter, Trevor. And as her father, it's up to you to try to make amends."

"And as her mother, I would expect you to explain to her that the things she's angry with me for are the very things that I had to do to help this country."

"I think she knows that now. I told her it was you who recommended me for director. She said it was commendable on your part."

"Maybe once I'm out of here and can focus on the task force, maybe I'll reach out to her."

Elizabeth stood. "Don't wait too long, Trevor. She's just as stubborn as you and now that she's married, well, it won't be long before you'll be a grandpa. I don't think that's something you'll want to miss out on." She began to walk away. "I'll see you at the press conference."

————

Sergei Koslov turned on the seventy-inch wall-mounted television in his New York apartment. The news conference was about to begin and the president had just arrived at the podium. He poured himself a shot of vodka and listened as the president spoke. He eyed the crowd, looking for those he knew were also on his trail. The woman and the two men who destroyed Janz's plan and Janz himself. But he saw no one matching their descriptions in the rows of seats displayed in front of the podium in the Rose Garden.

That could only mean one thing. Acting Director Axell told his people not to attend. Sergei nodded. "Makes sense." He knew their operation had top-secret security clearance and only a handful of high-ranking officials were aware of its existence. And the only reason he was aware was thanks to Janz. It was also the only reason he remained underground, unable to draw in the partners and the money to the organization. He feared his capture.

It didn't take long before Koslov spotted the current acting director move closer to the president and the woman next to him. He wondered, was she to be the new director? "And who are you?"

He picked up his cell phone and called Abramov. "Are you watching the conference?"

"I am," Abramov replied on the line.

"Good. Do you know who stands next to the acting director? I do not recognize this woman."

"She is not someone I am familiar with and this is concerning. I believed the next director would of course have to be the current assistant director, were Trevor Axell to refuse. Seems the president has bypassed etiquette in this instance."

"Could this present a problem for us?" Sergei continued.

"It is too early to say. I had already worked to establish a relationship with the assistant director through Usenko. Apparently, I have targeted the wrong individual. That will have to be rectified and soon."

Sergei turned up the volume. "The president is about to introduce her." And as he listened, the name, one he had heard of before but only in passing, was finally spoken.

"The Washington station chief," Abramov said. "Elizabeth Ward. Well, at least we know who we will be dealing with."

"I don't think the consortium will be affected, not in the immediate aftermath of this announcement. It's too soon to know how she will affect policy. Not much, I have to assume. As with most government agencies, and particularly, government intelligence agencies, the United States follows rules no one else does." Sergei began to snicker. "To their disadvantage."

———

Lacy switched off the monitor on the wall. "I guess that's it. We have him back."

"Good," Hunter began. "I mean, he would've been a great CIA director. Has been a great CIA director, but we've been stymied without him here. That's going to change and now we can put all our efforts into tracking down Koslov."

"Speaking of that," Caison chimed in, "what's the deal with Anton Usenko? You're supposed to be meeting him for lunch, wasn't it?"

"Drinks, actually." Lacy walked back to her desk. "I'll head out by four. I'm meeting him at five. I'm sure the announcement will come up. After all, it was Trevor who introduced me to him. So at least we'll have an ice-breaker."

"And you and Balfour will be keeping watch?" Aaron asked.

"I'll be there, Balfour will not." Caison eyed Lacy for a moment. "Usenko left the timing to the last minute."

"He did. I only just got the call from him about an hour ago," Lacy began. "Too late to set up surveillance."

"Sounds like he knows how to avoid Big Brother." Hunter turned to Lacy. "Just be cool."

"Be cool? That's your advice? I'll be fine. This is just drinks. Will is going to be there. I'll be fine. My goal is to get to know him and not ask too many questions that might raise suspicions."

"That's my girl." Caison patted her shoulder.

Hunter seemed annoyed by Caison's lackadaisical behavior. "You do understand this man has ties to the Russian mafia. You're not concerned about that? Or about the fact that we still don't know who Graybear is?"

"Calm down, Aaron. It's a meeting in a public place in daylight. Please don't worry so much, okay?" Lacy asked.

"Fine. I'll just sit here and keep working with Jill to find the person who hacked into your personal computer."

"That's what you should be doing." Lacy returned to her desk. "I need to wrap up a few things, then I'll head out."

———

They had arrived and Lacy sat in the car with Will as he pulled curbside about a block from the bar.

"I'll come in about ten minutes behind you," Caison said. "That should give you enough time to get your drink and strike up a decent conversation to keep him distracted when I get inside. Oh, and remember to make sure his back is to the entrance."

"What if he won't sit that way?"

"Make your move first. This guy won't ask you to get up. He's going to try to impress the pants off of you and asking a woman to move seats isn't a good way to do that."

"Right. Okay. So you'll come in and I'll be talking. I thought I should keep my phone's mic on."

"I wouldn't risk it. Not at this stage in the game. He's not going to give you what you want today. This is just to feel each other out. Then we'll talk about wires."

"Okay. I'd better get in there. Don't want to arrive after he does and miss my chance to pick my seat." She opened the passenger door.

"One more thing. I know you'll be fine, but if you feel at all uncomfortable with the conversation or where it's headed, just make an excuse to use the restroom. I have a guy who will be there to get you out if need be."

"You have a guy in the ladies' restroom?"

"No. Just outside. There's a window. Use it if you have to. And —be careful, Lacy. I know you've been through this route before, but this time's different."

"I'll be fine. I have on my big-girl pants today." She smiled and stepped out of the car. "See you soon."

Dressed in a long summery skirt and short-sleeved top, Lacy wanted to make a good impression without being overstated. And this man valued appearances.

She entered the bar, which was growing busier with happy hour having approached, and it appeared she was the first to arrive. Lucky her. Lacy scoped out a good location that would place her facing the front door and would also face a couple of tables, where she assumed Will would sit.

From what she knew about Anton Usenko, he was a man who believed himself smarter than those who might surveil him, like the US Government. He thought he had a keen eye. Perhaps he had, but that behavior hadn't been exhibited the other day when Will and Agent Balfour observed him from afar.

She placed her bag on a bar top table and sat on the stool.

A waiter approached and flashed a youthful and not at all hard to look at smile. "Evening. What can I get you to drink?"

"I'll have a white wine. House is fine. Thanks."

"I'll have that out to you in just a moment. Anything else? Appetizer?"

"No, thank you. Just the drink." Lacy turned her sights to the door, where she expected Usenko to arrive at any moment. She thought she would be more nervous but then figured after her life had been in danger countless times already, this should be a piece of cake.

The waiter returned with her drink. "Would you like me to start a tab for you?"

"That won't be necessary." She pulled out a twenty and handed it to him.

"I'll bring you your change."

In the moment she was distracted by the waiter, Usenko had

entered and begun his approach. In fact, when he stood only feet away, she was startled by his arrival.

"Mrs. Lacy Merrick. What a pleasure it is to see you again." Usenko sat down, seemingly not bothered by the fact his back was to the door.

"Anton, good to see you too. I'm so glad you could set aside some time tonight."

"The pleasure is mine to accompany such a beautiful and remarkable woman."

The waiter approached again and regurgitated the same line he asked Lacy.

"I'll have a vodka tonic," Usenko replied.

After the waiter took his leave, Lacy began, "You know, I always thought it was a movie cliché when Russians were always on screen drinking vodka."

"Oh, we take our vodka very seriously in Russia. I assure you, it is no cliché. Much like beer here in America."

"You have me there." She sipped on her wine. "Did you happen to watch the news conference today?"

"As a point of fact, I did. It was—unexpected. But I see that it is likely a good thing. A woman director. Hurray for feminism, yes?"

Lacy smiled even as his words came off as condescending and not at all how he truly felt. She brushed it off and continued to make small talk. That was when she spotted him. Will had arrived and slipped virtually unnoticed, except by her, into a booth nowhere near where she had expected him to go. But he was there and she suddenly felt a surge of strength and determination. "So, Anton, your recent arrival here—what role are you fulfilling?"

"My job is to help reestablish relations with the new administration, as you know. Well, of course you know; you brought down the last president. As you know, we need to continue on a positive path forward with America and perhaps relook at existing sanc-tions imposed by the last president."

"I see. You do have your work cut out for you."

"Yes." He sipped on his vodka tonic. "And you have returned to your job at the FBI? Is that correct? What exactly does an analyst do?"

"I'm a regional data analyst. I look for hackers."

His eyes sharpened. "Oh, then I suppose Russia must be high on your list of targets."

"Among other countries," Lacy replied. "It's hard to keep up on the ever-changing dynamics of cyber security and information control."

"You are quite an intelligent woman, Lacy Merrick. Not that I would have expected anything else. Do you suppose you are being watched right now as you are speaking with a Russian?"

Her heart jumped into her throat, but she maintained her pleasant veneer. "I'm sure they're not that interested in me. There are far more interesting people who work for the Bureau with far greater access to intelligence than me."

"That is good to know. What a pity it would be were your own agency keeping tabs on you and without your knowledge."

"It would be a pity—yes." She inhaled a breath, and with a pleasant smile playing on her lips, Lacy tried to calm her nerves. She couldn't shift her gaze to Will because Usenko was watching her closely, much too closely.

Usenko blotted the corner of his mouth with a cocktail napkin and began to rise. "Would you excuse me for just a moment? I must find the little boys' room. Please, order another if you'd like. I'd enjoy further conversation if you have the time."

"Of course." She watched as he walked right past Will and then veered right toward the restrooms. Once he was out of sight, she looked at Will with renewed panic.

He subtly nodded in a reassuring manner and held his beer to his lips. She figured he wasn't overly concerned by what had just happened. Perhaps Usenko was used to being followed and just assumed she had eyes on him.

"Much better." He returned. "Oh, did you not place your order yet?" He snapped his fingers at the waiter. "Let me. I could use another as well." When the waiter approached, he asked for another round of drinks. "Oh, do you have chips and salsa too?"

"Of course, sir."

"Ah. We'll have some of those too. It is rare I get to eat such ethnic-type foods. Do you enjoy chips and salsa as well, Lacy?"

"One of my favorites."

"Excellent."

Maybe she had overreacted. It didn't seem as though Usenko suspected anything was going on. And maybe now was the time to get into the meat of the situation. "Anton, I understand you enjoy social gatherings."

"Well, of course I do. Doesn't everyone?"

"I suppose so. There is one thing I would absolutely love to attend and, if I'm not being too forward, maybe you and I could attend together..."

"What is it? Anything." He sounded more confident now. "I can take you just about any place you would like to go, Lacy Merrick."

"There is a gallery opening next week. A Russian artist I have recently come to admire."

"I know of this artist. I too am a champion of his work. In fact, I know of several important Russian figures who will be in attendance. And I would be honored to have you on my arm."

"Wonderful." She raised her fresh glass of wine. "To the arts."

He joined her. "To the arts."

She nursed the second glass of wine for nearly another hour

and the conversation was winding down. Perhaps now was the time to leave him wanting more. "It is getting late. I should get home to my kids."

"You have children?"

Her expression fell for a split second. She had revealed too much. "Yes. Two. A boy and a girl."

"I adore children. Perhaps one day I might meet them."

"I would like that very much." Lacy began to rise. "Thank you for a very enjoyable few hours. And I can't wait to see you next week."

"Nor can I. Shall I walk you to your car?"

"I took a cab, but thank you. Goodbye, Anton."

"Goodbye, Lacy Merrick."

Lacy started toward the door and tossed a sideways glance to Will. She continued outside, and in the event Anton had his eye on her, hailed a cab. But she was out, and as far as she knew, Will hadn't been identified.

She stepped into a cab and dropped her shoulders. A brief but overwhelming feeling to break into tears washed over her, but it soon faded. It was just nerves. And it wasn't until her cell phone rang and she saw it was Will that she began to feel better. "Are you out of there?"

"I am. I'll meet you back at the shop. Are you okay?"

"Yeah. I'm okay."

"You did good tonight, Lacy."

She closed her eyes. "I hope it was good enough."

CHAPTER
TEN

ALTHOUGH ONLY A FEW hours had passed, upon Lacy's return to the task force headquarters, she felt like it had been much longer. Adrenaline still surged in her veins. That rush that came when something had gone right took time to diminish. She'd done as was required of her and believed it would make a difference.

As she approached her desk, Aaron stood nearby, arms folded, like a father whose daughter had broken curfew. "Well, you're here," he began. "Must mean things went well. Where's Caison?"

"On his way back. And yes, I think it went well. I'm meeting him next week at an art exhibit opening. He's going to introduce me to some Russian VIPs. Maybe Koslov will be among them." She turned at the sound of footsteps behind her. "Speak of the devil."

"What? Koslov's here?" Caison smiled and turned his head as if searching for the man. "Just kidding. I'm back. Go on, keep talking about me."

"Aaron was just wondering where you were," Lacy replied.

"Right behind you, as always."

"I know it's getting a little late in the evening, but can you set up a meeting between us and Agent Balfour? I'd like to discuss with her what happened today and find out how much she knows about this exhibit next week, assuming she knows," Lacy said. "Maybe she can get us a guest list."

"That's probably a good idea." Caison started back toward his desk. "I'll call her right now, see what her schedule is like."

"Thanks. Hey, has anyone heard from Trevor?" Lacy picked up her cell phone to check for messages. "I haven't received any calls."

"To my knowledge, he's at Langley," Aaron said. "Briefing Station Chief Ward or something."

"Right. Well, maybe I'll give him a call and let him know how things went." She started dialing his direct line. "Damn. No answer."

Caison turned his sights to Lacy once again. "Balfour can meet in twenty if you want to do this tonight."

"Absolutely. The sooner, the better. While everything's still fresh in my mind."

"Do you need me for anything?" Aaron asked.

"Not right now." Lacy shut down her computer. "Any luck tracking down Graybear?"

"If I had, you'd know about it."

"You might as well head home, then. Nothing more for you to do tonight. Will and I can meet with Balfour and we'll go from there. Good night, Aaron."

Hunter watched as the two left the office. "Good night."

Jill Goddard, who had been quietly working away at her desk, peered at him. "She doesn't know?"

Aaron was pulled back into the moment. "Huh? Know what?"

"That you installed a keylogger to monitor her laptop?"

"I did that to find out who has access to it. And for no other reason."

"Then why not tell her?"

"Because I can't trust that she won't disable it. No one knows who Graybear is. These types of people are dangerous. And now she's trying to worm her way into Koslov's circle via this Anton Usenko. God knows what kind of mess that'll bring."

"I don't get it," Goddard continued. "I thought you wanted Koslov's head on a platter. Now you don't want any part of him?"

"It's not that. I do want Koslov. Just in the right way and not with Lacy being used as bait. Look, we haven't worked together long and I understand the questions. But I need to know that you and I can work together and I won't have to worry about you running off and spilling the beans to Axell or anyone else on the team about our plans. I know what I'm doing. And I know you're more than capable of handling what I toss your way. Are we a team, or what?"

"We're a team. I won't say anything more." She turned back to her screen but stopped again and peered over her shoulder. "Maybe the real problem here isn't that you don't want Lacy to know you're tracking her every move on her computer. Maybe it's the fact that you're afraid she'll be put in danger."

"We're all at risk of getting into danger unless you haven't figured that out yet."

"Yeah, we are," she added. "But your feelings about Lacy are getting in the way of her doing her job."

Aaron was about to respond, but doing so would only add fuel to his anger. Because at the end of the day, she was right. They were usually in some sort of peril at any given time. All of them. And yet it was only Lacy who had his concern. Now he was spying on her for the purpose of catching Graybear in the act. And the worst part was, he didn't want to tell her. After what she'd done with the printer, he almost felt he couldn't trust her not to put herself in more potential danger. "Maybe you're right. I do care about what happens to her. She lost her husband, a man who was my friend too. If I lost her, I don't know what I would do."

———

Agent Anya Balfour opened the door to her apartment, where Will and Lacy waited in the corridor. "Evening. Come in." She closed the door behind them.

"Thanks for agreeing to see us." Lacy offered her hand. "I'm Lacy Merrick."

"I've heard a lot about you, Merrick, and your performance the other night was exceptional. I'm Anya Balfour. Pleasure." She returned the greeting. "Come, I'll show you what I know so far."

Balfour's surveillance setup was impressive and potentially illegal, but Lacy wasn't one to split hairs. She wanted Koslov just as badly as the rest of them and long gone were the days she worried about doing what was right. Now she only worried about doing what was best to get to what was right. After all the under-handed deeds she'd seen in just the span of a year, her innocence in the ways of those in power had been shattered into oblivion.

"I was aware of this artist's gallery opening, and I had a chance to look into him again after Caison called." Balfour sat down in front of the monitors that rested on a folding table between her living room and kitchen. "He seems pretty legit."

Lacy eyed Will for a moment. Will shrugged his response and Lacy returned her attention to Balfour. "So Usenko just wants to rub elbows with these people?"

"Possibly. But from what I know of Anton Usenko and his connections, I'd say he garnered an invite probably from Maxim Abramov's people as a gesture of good faith. And, it seems he might want to impress you. That's a good thing." Balfour smiled.

"Is there a way we can find out, maybe from the gallery owner," Caison began, "who will be in attendance at the event?"

"It's possible if I ask the right questions, which I'm pretty sure I can handle."

Lacy noticed Balfour's tone dripped with sarcasm. "That would be really helpful. Then we can run background on them and go in armed with knowledge about who we're dealing with."

"She's got her head on straight, this one," Balfour said to Caison.

"No doubt about it. Anything else we need to know about today?"

"Like what? I mean, it's not like I sit here all day watching Usenko. I do have a job. This is mainly for you guys."

"We appreciate it. I just wanted to know if Usenko made any calls afterward to anyone of significance. Or if he met with anyone after Lacy left."

Balfour turned again to her monitors. "I'll look into it and let you know."

"Thanks." Will appeared frustrated. "We should be going. Appreciate your time once again, Balfour. Please let us know if you get anything else you think might be important to us."

"Will do." Balfour stood. "It was really nice to meet you, Merrick. You really are an inspiration."

"Thanks, but I don't see myself as inspirational. I just don't like to be taken advantage of."

"That makes two of us." She eyed Caison. "Good night."

Lacy started out the door and Will followed. When she was

sure they were clear of her apartment, Lacy began. "You mind telling me what the hell that was?"

"Oh, her?" He thumbed back in the direction of Balfour's apartment. "Yeah. Nice girl, right?"

"Um. She seems a little angry." Lacy continued until they reached the stairs and started down to the first floor.

"Oh yeah. She's always like that. Got a little bite to her." He snapped shut his jaws. "She's an acquired taste and I haven't acquired it yet."

"I can see why. I hope she'll help us and not try to screw us over." Lacy recalled the conversation she'd had with Axell regarding getting to know Balfour better to get a feel for finding Graybear. But after today, she wondered if the woman would want to help at all.

"She'll do as she's told. Axell has already made that clear, thanks to Mobley. I have no idea why she always seems on the offensive."

"You clearly did something to piss her off. You know how you can get." Lacy pushed through the door into the parking lot.

"What do you mean? I didn't do anything." He raised his hands in defense. "I don't know what her deal is. Maybe she doesn't like working with people."

"Maybe. Or maybe she just doesn't like working with you." She laughed.

"Go ahead and laugh, Chuckles. You'll be dealing with her now too." He opened the passenger door for her. "You'll see what I'm talking about." Will continued to the driver's side and stepped in, turning the ignition. "I'll have to drop you back at the shop so you can get your car."

"Yeah. I've got a few more things to take care of, so I'll stay there for a while."

"You sure? Anything I can help with?" Will asked.

"No, you go home. I don't plan on staying long anyway."

"Suit yourself." Will turned away from the curb and headed south.

————

Inside, the office was already dark, except for the security lights that flashed as Lacy entered. The alarm had been set too and she keyed in the passcode. Upon arrival at her desk, Lacy switched on her computer and checked her emails a final time. Nothing of any importance. But as she sat there alone, in the dark, the sound of something falling, a book maybe, reached her ears. She spun around at the noise. It was probably nothing, but Lacy couldn't be sure.

Pushing up from her chair, she began toward the hall where she thought the sound came from. Axell's office was down this hall, as was the conference room. His office was quiet. "Must be the conference room." She started down the hall again and turned on the lights, peeking inside. Everything appeared as it should have.

Lacy furrowed her brow and headed back to her desk. She began to recall that she'd missed a couple of the firearms training Will had set up for her and now regretted it. "I really need to get that done."

She arrived at her desk and sat back down. An image appeared on her computer. This wasn't her own personal laptop. This was her office computer—highly secured.

A Russian flag waved with background music that could've been Russian too. Lacy couldn't be sure. But she stared at the image, unclear of what to do, and suddenly feeling as though she wasn't alone. "Is someone here?" she said to the empty room. As expected, there was no reply.

The screen changed. It was now a DOS prompt like something out of the movie *War Games*. Someone was messing with her and that someone had to be Graybear.

She began to type at the prompt. "Is this you, Graybear?"

The cursor flashed, ready to receive a reply. None came.

Lacy placed her fingers on the keyboard again, this time feeling more anxious than before. "I think we're on the same side. We should be working together." She pressed the enter key and again the cursor flashed, awaiting a response.

Finally, one came. "The man you are looking for won't be there."

"Be where?" she typed.

"At the art gallery." The cursor flashed again.

Lacy pulled back. Only two other people, besides Usenko, knew she would be in attendance. Those were Caison and Agent Balfour. "I don't know what you're talking about." Lacy bit her bottom lip, feeling slightly lightheaded with a combination of fear and a desire to figure out how this person knew. The cursor kept blinking. "Come on. Answer me," she said.

"Is that how we're going to help each other, Lacy? You're going to lie to me? I know you were with Anton Usenko today. Please try to remember, I know all there is to know about who you're after."

Lacy turned white-lipped and typed, "Then why not tell me how to get him? Why play games?" She stared at the monitor, tapping lightly on her keyboard, waiting for an answer.

"It has to be this way. I can't make it easy because I will be found out. You will have to work harder, Lacy Merrick. But, to answer your question, yes, we are on the same side."

"Fine." Lacy typed again. "Are you saying I shouldn't go to the art gallery because Koslov won't be there? Don't you think I should stay on Usenko's good side?"

A few laughing emojis floated on the screen. Lacy figured

Graybear was very good at his job to make that happen. This was no ordinary hacker. Graybear was beyond anything she'd ever seen, either at the FBI or here, at the task force.

"Usenko has only one side—his." The screen went black. Graybear was gone.

Lacy's computer rebooted and the Windows screen kicked on again. "Damn it."

————

Inside the large office building, men and women, most appearing to be in their twenties, sat at desks inside the open industrial-style room, each one with eyes fixed on computer screens and typing feverishly.

Johanna Wolff, a thirty-something German national in an expensive pantsuit, walked through the passageway next to a man who appeared to be equally as powerful. She spoke in English to her Bulgarian cohort, a man who went by the name Lukas Barkov. "He is ready to move the operation forward."

Lukas Barkov, a member of the board, began, "The time is right, I believe, for him to continue. We have lost ground and much needs to be done to regain our position."

"I agree. Too much time has passed," Wolff replied.

"I will meet with the rest of the board and get their blessing. At that time, Sergei should make arrangements to be here. The board is anxious and he must assure them that work will continue as it had prior to the loss of our most valued asset, Mr. Janz."

"I will inform him of our discussion. Good day, Lukas." Wolff walked into the lobby and through the glass doors of the building and now stood outside. Her car had arrived and the valet opened the driver's side door. "Thank you."

"Of course, madam. Good evening."

She pulled away from the curb and made the call. "Sergei, I have been informed that upon notification to the board members, you are to return here to discuss operating again at full capacity."

"Excellent news. I can again begin to reach out to my contacts and work to establish new ones?"

"Yes."

"Then I know exactly where to begin," Koslov replied.

CHAPTER
ELEVEN

WHAT STARTED as innocuous hacker stunts had turned menacing. And as Lacy stared up at the ceiling while the morning light saturated her bedroom, she contemplated Graybear's endgame. The idea of revealing to the team what had happened last night still weighed heavily on her mind too. Their concern for her safety would result in her being cut off from Graybear by any means necessary. And she just wasn't sure that was the right way to go. There was something about Graybear she couldn't quite pin down, but she still maintained the hacker wanted what they wanted: Koslov in a six-by-eight cell.

Lacy tossed her legs over the edge of the bed and quietly walked down the stairs. The coffee was freshly brewed, thanks to the one woman Lacy could always lean on, Celeste. And as she poured a cup, as if by osmosis, Celeste appeared.

"Good morning, honey. How did you sleep?"

Lacy grabbed another mug from the cabinet and poured a cup for Celeste. "Okay, and you?"

"I heard you come in late. Are you sure everything is all right?"

"Yes. I had some things to wrap up at the office." Lacy turned away and checked her phone. "I'd better get ready for work. I'll give you a call if I'm going to be late again tonight." She started toward the stairs.

"Lacy?" Celeste asked. "I know the job you have is very important and that what you're doing is for the protection of our country, just like you always have done. But please remember that you selected this life; your children did not."

"I know it was my choice. I chose to avenge my husband's death. I chose to make those responsible pay for what they'd done to my family. I don't regret that."

"And you shouldn't, but we all believed the worst was over and that things would return to as normal as they could be. Lacy, that hasn't happened. At some point, you must let go of the past because if you don't, Olivia and Jackson won't either."

———

With Celeste's ominous words replaying in her mind, Lacy arrived at work and vacillated about whether to inform her team of Graybear's intrusion. If she didn't, her decision could expose all of them to dangers she couldn't quantify.

Upon entering the office, she spotted Axell carrying a box. "Morning. What's that you have there?"

"My personal effects from the Agency. I'll be booted out of there soon and figured I should clean out the place." He set down the box on his desk and returned to the hall, where Lacy waited. "I heard yesterday's meeting with Usenko went off without a hitch."

"It went well enough."

"That's what Caison relayed to me. Do you feel it could've gone better?"

"No. I think it went as well as could be expected. He's taking me to a gallery exhibit opening on Friday night. Will and I talked to Balfour about that, who, by the way, doesn't seem too eager to talk to us."

"She's young and has a chip on her shoulder. That's all it is," Axell replied. "She knows the deal on the Russian scene, that I can guarantee."

"I agree with you on that point. She also said a lot of key figures are likely to be at this opening. Apparently, this artist is heavily funded by his government."

"I'm sure that's what they're saying."

"She's going to see if she can provide a list for us so we can do some recon before Friday," Lacy replied.

"Sounds like a plan. Any word yet on your friend Graybear?"

She hesitated for a split second. "No. Aaron's still trying to trace back the digital footprint, but Graybear appears to be very good. It's been tough to crack that nut."

He peered at her as if he could tell she was holding something back. "Okay. I'm going to be back and forth for the next few days, but I'll plan on being here all day on Friday in the event we need all hands on deck for the upcoming date."

"Good. I'd better check in with Aaron and see if he's come up with anything new." Lacy started inside the bullpen and arrived at her desk.

"You were here late last night." Aaron peered at his computer as he spoke. "Anything you want to share?" At this, he turned his sights to her.

He knew. Somehow, he knew and now she was going to have to confess because she couldn't lie, not to him. Their friendship spanned decades and she wasn't a good liar in any case, not to the people she cared about.

She approached his desk and leaned on the corner. "You obviously know what happened."

"I saw that your computer flagged a virus. I thought I'd wait until you got in to check it. I didn't want you to think I was invading your privacy."

"Graybear got into the network. We exchanged several messages through an old DOS prompt screen."

"He's good," Aaron replied.

"Tell me about it. He warned me that Koslov wouldn't be at the art exhibit on Friday, like we hoped. And that Usenko had his own agenda."

"It doesn't take a rocket scientist to see that," Aaron said. "How do you want to handle this? We can't have someone rummaging through our network. I think you know that."

"I do. I made it clear to Graybear to only contact me through my personal server, and if he hacked into our servers again here, we would hunt him down and throw him in jail for the rest of his life."

"I bet he thought that was hilarious." Aaron shook his head. "I doubt this punk is even a US citizen. Probably Russian by the looks of it."

"Graybear wants something and I need to find out what it is. He won't cut off ties with us. I think he needs us as much as we need him."

"You'd better be right."

"I am. But look, can we keep this between us for the moment? Just until I can establish Graybear's motives. Then we can re-evaluate."

"I don't agree, but I'll go with it. If that's what you want."

————

Under the white light of the LEDs in the ceiling, the young woman examined her monitor, keying in parameters until she hit one that worked. A smile arose on her lips. Data scrolled down her screen in a beautiful array of numbers and signs. She was in.

In quick fashion, she worked to capture the data. She accessed the servers to store the valuable information and quickly retreated —undetected. Now her job was to decipher the data and determine its worth. It would take at least the day, but if she was right, as she suspected she was, this would please her bosses very much, likely fetching upwards of $1.5 million US dollars.

The young woman, one of many talented cyber experts in this building in a remote town outside of Kyiv, began to sift through the information. She'd just hacked a US aeronautics company that had recently developed software for non-commercial airlines. This software would detect a problem and initiate a backup protocol before a pilot could. It would be extremely valuable on the black market.

Recruited by the consortium, Daria Liski, a native of Ukraine, had been caught hacking into the government's Ministry of Information. The ministry had been recently established as a means of combating Russian propaganda as well as ensuring free speech. Daria attempted to prove they were failing miserably on the latter, except that she was caught.

After spending several weeks in prison, Daria was set free. Well, free wasn't quite the right word. She was free to go to work for the consortium or continue in prison for the remainder of her sentence. She chose the consortium. That was last year. And she'd already stolen other intellectual property from US companies whose cyber-security measures were a joke. Her place here was solidified. And with this new intel, she just might get a raise.

By the end of the day, Daria had the reports ready to present.

She stood from her desk and approached her supervisor. "Sir, I have a new report for your review," she spoke in her native tongue.

"English, please, Daria." The supervisor was Bulgarian and didn't speak the language of the country in which he was employed.

Daria hadn't learned to speak English until she was hired on and it was still pretty rough. "Excuse me, sir. Yes. I have a report for you on M1 Communications. They have new software for airplanes. Small ones."

"Thank you, Daria. I'll take a look and pass it on if it meets our criteria. Excellent work."

"Thank you." She left his office.

The supervisor reviewed the report and appeared pleased. He headed straight for his superior to relay the news. "Madam? I have something I think might be of interest." He handed the report to Johanna Wolff.

"Who gave this to you?"

"Daria Liski. She has provided excellent intelligence for us to date. And again, she has not let us down."

"Please, sit down. Walk me through it," Wolff said.

After Daria's manager informed her of the proprietary information contained inside the report, Wolff nodded. "Yes, this is exactly what we need. I will add it to the bid for tonight's auction. Please, relay my congratulations to Daria. And you should also be commended. Thank you."

"Shall I remain in attendance for this evening so that I may answer any questions that arise during the bidding?"

"As this was derived by a member of your staff, yes, that would be wise. That will be all."

"Thank you, madam." On his return, he stopped at Daria's desk. "They are pleased, Daria. I would like to ask that you remain on board this evening, with me. They will be sending out your report for bid. And, as this is your success, perhaps it is best to have you nearby to answer questions."

"Of course, sir. I will be honored," Daria replied. Before her supervisor started leaving, she called out again. "On that note, what time, exactly, will the bidding begin?"

He eyed her. "2100 hours, GMT."

"Thank you, sir." After he was out of sight, Daria sighed. She would have to stay until midnight tonight and it was only 7 pm now. Still, this was an opportunity she would not discard.

———

Daria gazed through the window nearest her desk at the black sky. The building was tucked away off the main road with only one other building nearby and that appeared abandoned. And while it was approaching midnight, the work never stopped. Shifts changed, but people were doing the work she did on a twenty-four-hour basis. The sheer amount of data collected was beyond enormous and required a full staff at all times. Her usual schedule saw her working from 7 am to 7 pm. Not tonight. Tonight, Daria would be a part of the auctions, something in which many of her colleagues would never get the chance to participate. It was a golden opportunity.

"Daria, it's time." Her supervisor tapped her on the shoulder. "Huh? Oh, yes, sir." She grabbed her report and followed him inside the room few were allowed to enter. She marveled at the scene. Rows of tables with laptops open. A person sitting in front of each one. There must have been fifteen people inside this room, most of which she recognized to be supervisors or senior management. These were the people who made the real money. She was just a grunt.

"Take a seat here, next to me. The bidding will start soon," her supervisor said.

"What should I do?"

"If someone asks a question, I'll look to you to answer. And you'll need to be quick about it, so I hope you know exactly what is in your report."

"I do, sir." She pulled out a chair and sat down next to him.

"Good." He placed a headset over his ears and handed her one as well. "This is so you can listen in."

She put it on.

A man stood at the front of the room. She didn't know who he was, but he began to speak.

"The bidding will commence in two minutes. The rules are the same as always. Highest bidder, verified funds. And tonight, we have a few new participants in the bidding." A final nod and the gentleman walked away.

"Who bids on these?" she asked her boss.

"Companies, foreign governments, document-dumping sites."

"I see."

"Shh. It's about to begin."

Daria listened in on her manager as he announced the information being sold. The program she stole was now about to be put up for auction for whoever or whatever ended up as the highest bidder. Once he finished the announcement, all she could hear was typing. But what she saw were bids on screen. Her manager kept upping the amount as each bidder placed a bid. So far, no one asked anything. Dollar amounts were on the rise. It was like they almost didn't care what it was, but they had to own it. Whoever "they" were.

Her manager peered over at her briefly and smiled. He nodded to the screen where she noted the bidding had now reached $1 million US dollars.

Daria tried to identify the bidders, but they all had screen names. Maybe whoever won the auction would have to reveal who they were. Right now, it looked like it could go to someone with the screen name Sky Raider. Not very original, she thought.

As the dollar amount reached closer to $1.5 million, Daria was sure the bidding war would end, but it didn't. And to her surprise, it didn't slow down until it was nearer $2 million. The screen names were dropping. Only a few people were left standing. One was Sky Raider.

Finally, it ended. Sky Raider won the information for $2.2 million dollars. Her manager removed his headset and peered at her. "Well done, Daria. How do you feel after your first auction?"

She smiled at him. "Do I get to come here again?"

————

The entire process took about an hour and the consortium sold over $6 million dollars' worth of stolen intellectual property. Building plans, software, even US defense plans. She could only imagine how one was able to garner that sort of material. Of course, everyone had a price, even government officials in the US.

She returned to her desk to prepare to leave, but not before opening a small notebook she kept in her handbag. Surveying the room, everyone paid attention to their own tasks, so she took a moment before she could forget, to jot down the names of the bidders. Screen names only, but it would give her something to go with.

"How did you enjoy this evening, Daria?" Her supervisor appeared as if from thin air.

She quickly returned the notebook to her purse and reached for her keys, also inside her purse. "It was an amazing sight, sir. Thank you for allowing me to participate."

"You are most welcome. I certainly hope it won't be the last time. You should go home now. Get some rest. It's late. I'll see you tomorrow morning." He walked away.

Daria shut off her computer and started toward the door. The parking lot was just ahead. She slipped into her car, retrieved the notebook once again, and peered at the names she could remember.

Daria typed a quick text message. "I have names." She pressed send.

CHAPTER
TWELVE

THE BLACK-HAIRED WOMAN with an athletic build entered the task force headquarters. It was 9 am and Agent Balfour had come to deliver the list of names in person. Her arrival came as a surprise, considering she didn't have the clearance.

"Agent Balfour, good morning." Caison offered his hand. "Can I get you a coffee?"

"Do you have any Chai tea?" She waited while he appeared perplexed. "Never mind. I wanted to get to you that list of names for those who are currently slated to attend the exhibit on Friday night."

Lacy approached. "Thank you so much for this, Agent Balfour. It will be very useful."

"I'm here to help. And you're welcome." She surveyed the room. Hunter was at his desk and hardly took notice. Goddard sat nearby at her desk, and with earbuds in, she was oblivious too. "Looks like you all are busy. I won't keep you."

"We really do appreciate it," Caison began. "Director Mobley must've told you where we were located."

"Actually, I asked Director Axell—former Director Axell. He

said it would be fine to stop in because we were all working toward the same goal."

"Please know that we are more than happy to share intelligence with you regarding this situation," Lacy said.

"Thank you, Merrick. Well, if there's nothing else, I'd better head back to WFO." She started to leave. "Don't hesitate to get in touch if you need anything else."

"If you see Agent Fraser, please send him our best," Lacy said.

"He and I don't generally cross paths, but I'll tell him if I see him. Goodbye." She pushed through the door.

Lacy peered at Will. "Is it me or did she seem to be a totally different person just now? Not at all combative."

"Yeah." Will furrowed his brow as he watched the door close behind Balfour. "And why didn't she just email the list? It isn't like we don't have secure servers. Why come all this way to hand deliver it?"

"Don't know. Unless she wanted to check things out here," Lacy replied. "Trevor authorized her, so..."

"He must have his reasons." Caison returned to his desk. "Let's take a look at these names and see what we can drum up."

Lacy wasn't convinced. She joined Will and reviewed the names, but in the back of her mind, she believed Balfour had her own reasons for visiting.

"The names on here aren't much of a bombshell," Caison said. "Maxim Abramov, our resident mobster."

"And the man who initially met with Anton Usenko," Lacy added.

"Right. Then we've got Usenko. I see a few names from the Russian consulate. We should look into them."

"The ambassador," Lacy said. "That's interesting. He's attending an event with a suspected mob boss."

"That could be said about almost every politician at one time or another."

"Good point." Lacy continued to view the list. "I don't see Koslov's name, just like Graybear said."

"Not a chance he'd attend. He's been lying low since Janz was killed. Why expose himself now? And wait, what? Like Graybear said?" Caison turned to her.

"Just that in the initial communications, Graybear indicated we wouldn't find Koslov, so I'm just guessing that's why he's not on this list." Lacy had only revealed to Aaron the truth about her exchanges with Graybear.

"How about we divvy up these names and start digging up some dirt on these people? We've only got two days before the shindig, so there's no time to waste."

"Shindig?" Lacy smiled before extending her hand. "Just give me the names."

————

The screen names appeared after the message had been deciphered with the encryption key. Names that right now meant nothing, but in time would reveal the parties who had participated in the bidding of stolen US intellectual property, giving Graybear leverage.

Once Koslov was let off his leash, new deals would be struck and the operation would continue to grow larger than it had in the past three years. Containment was what Graybear had been working toward and why Daria Liski had been recruited.

The names were again encrypted and stored on a secure cloud server as well as backed up onto encrypted flash drives. There had to be more than one copy because it was very likely that Daria

Liski would be caught, and if that happened, the names would be changed or erased.

The time had come to deliver the message. It was still morning in D.C. and Graybear was about to send Lacy Merrick a message that would shake her to her core. Brevity and ambiguity were required in the event that Merrick's location was compromised. There was no point in going through the trouble just to have the message intercepted by an interested third party. Graybear would make it as difficult as possible, especially hindering anyone's ability to trace it back.

There were ten screen names. All had put in bids, but most had dropped off as the dollars climbed higher until only two remained. Those two were likely the most significant and would need to be prioritized. But handing over all the intel was best in this instance. Because next time, the winning bidder could be any one of these names.

The encryption would have to be sophisticated. Graybear knew Merrick and her partner would be able to decode it in time and that her partner was an excellent cryptographer.

Within minutes, the server was accessed. Graybear wasn't sure if their system had been updated to secure the opening and it hadn't, meaning Merrick wanted to keep open the lines of communication. The message was sent and now the time had come to wait for a response.

———

Lacy studied her monitor as she waited for the background check to come through on one of the names Balfour had relinquished. She turned briefly to Caison. "Are you seeing any red flags yet, because all I have so far is a bunch of irrelevant Russian officials."

"Except for Maxim Abramov. There has to be more, though."

"Maybe not. Maybe it's just Usenko showing off, like Balfour said," she replied.

"Regardless, knowing anything about any one of these people could be beneficial. We learn their weaknesses, we can exploit them. Someone's bound to break."

Lacy noticed an incoming email. She peered at it with some confusion and then understood what it was she was looking at. In a low tone, she called out. "Aaron? Can you come here for a second?"

Her expression seemed to bring caution to him and he walked toward her.

Lacy pointed to the email. "It's encrypted."

Aaron sat down next to her. "Shit. It's Graybear, isn't it?"

Lacy rolled her cursor over the unread message, and before she clicked to open it, she again peered at Aaron to get the okay. He nodded.

"It's asking for a password."

"Do you have one?"

"No. How would I get one?" Her cell phone vibrated. She looked at him with suspicion and checked the message. "Looks like a password to me." She aimed the screen at him.

"Enter it," Aaron replied.

Lacy entered the password and the message appeared, but it was merely a string of letters and numbers. "Okay, now I need the key."

"This is AES, through Google Docs. "You're going to have to copy and paste it to your clipboard. Then let me take it. Gmail has a program to decrypt it too, but I don't trust having this on Google servers."

Lacy copied the message to Notepad and emailed the message to him. "It's Graybear. I'm sure of it. But why the encryption?"

"If Graybear can take over your computer and use an instant messaging program without detection, this would be a piece of cake for him." Aaron walked back to his desk and opened the code.

"Hang on. I just got the key." She showed him the text message. "Are you offline?"

"Of course I am. What's the key?"

"It's a 128-bit, 32 characters." She placed the phone down so he could see for himself and enter the right combination of letters and numbers. "AES is what most government agencies use. Do you think Graybear is government?"

"It's used in the private sector too, so it's hard to say." Aaron finished entering the key and the message was decoded. "What the hell is this?"

"Zero gravity, anonymous blue, what the hell? Sky raider? I don't understand," she replied.

"I was kind of hoping you did because this doesn't make any sense to me," Aaron added.

She continued studying the screen and again peered at her phone. "No more texts. I guess this is all we're going to get. Hang on. There's another email coming. Let me see what this is." She returned to her desk. "It's another one, Aaron."

"Another what?" Caison started toward them. "What are you guys doing?"

Lacy stopped in her tracks. "I received an encrypted email message. Two, actually."

"From who?" He turned his sights to Lacy and then Aaron, neither offering an answer. His expression hardened. "You didn't close the loopholes with Graybear, did you?" He again looked between the two. "Damn it. Why not? Do you have any idea what you've just risked by giving this hacker access to you, Lacy? Hunter, I figured you of all people would've been able to talk her out of communicating with this psycho."

"I tried. Since when does she listen to any of us?"

"That's not fair. I went with my gut on this one. I just wanted to see what Graybear would come up with. Then I could decide if it was worth the risk."

"And?" Caison asked.

"I don't know yet. This message, Aaron just decoded it, but it doesn't make any sense. Graybear just sent me another. I'm going to copy it to my clipboard and send it to Aaron again." Lacy went to work sending the message once again. And once again, the key appeared as a text message on her cell phone.

"Graybear has your cell number now?" Caison asked.

"Appears so." Lacy walked back toward Aaron, who had already applied the program to decode it. "Here's the key."

"And you two know how to decode this stuff?" he asked.

Aaron cast a discerning gaze. "Well, let's see, Lacy worked as a cyber analyst, I've worked in cyber-security for a few years, so yeah, we know what we're doing."

"Don't mind him," Lacy said to Will. "He's pissed that I didn't cut off communications with Graybear. He doesn't think it was the rational thing to do."

"Well, on that point, I would agree with him."

"I had my reasons, and I think they're about to pay off." Lacy waited while Aaron decoded the message.

"Here it is," Aaron said. "It's a continuation."

"More random words?" Lacy asked.

"No. Looks like an explanation for the random words." Aaron pulled back so the team could read the message.

"The names I sent you represent online bidders. I was informed that these bidders participated in black market purchases of illegally obtained US intellectual property. While I do not know who these bidders are, my contact informed me that Sky Raider was the successful bidder of an aeronautics software program developed by

an American company. My contact witnessed this auction firsthand as 'they' were the ones who obtained the IP illegally. My contact works for an organization that employs hackers to steal valuable information and then sell it on the black market. It is now up to you to find these bidders. And the man responsible for running the operation, whom you're already searching for."

Lacy pulled back with a stunned expression. "I didn't see that coming."

"All this time, we thought it was Moscow running Koslov," Caison said.

"Graybear has maintained since our initial contact that Koslov was involved in something bigger. How much bigger can you get than this?" Lacy said.

"Why not come out with it? Graybear doesn't mention Koslov by name," Aaron replied.

"No, but that could be intentional. If this intel were to get into the wrong hands," Caison began. "Koslov no doubt has powerful friends and enemies."

"We need to talk to Trevor about this." Lacy peered around. "Is he coming in today?" She reached for her phone and pressed his contact.

Axell answered the line.

"It's me. Are you coming in?"

"I'll be there inside the hour. Why? Is everything okay?" Axell replied.

"No. It's not."

———

Axell returned to the office, and without delay, approached the team. "Someone mind telling me what the hell is going on?"

"This is Merrick's deal," Caison said. "Better to let her tell you."

She began to relay the information and pulled up the messages for Axell to read.

When he'd been fed all the details, he pulled back and folded his arms. "So you thought you'd keep in contact with the hacker, completely disregarding your safety and that of your team."

"But I thought that if..." Lacy began.

"Doesn't sound to me like you thought at all."

"I screwed up, again, apparently. But, Trevor, I'm telling you, he's talking about Koslov and that's why Graybear sent this over. This was what he's been trying to relay."

"This is a concern the CIA has had in their purview for a long time now. Stealing American property, intellectual or otherwise, is nothing new. We have divisions dedicated to this sort of thing. So all you've done is open the door to a potentially dangerous person who has yet to reveal his or her intentions."

Lacy recoiled but quickly shot back. "Look, I'm sure the CIA has people dealing with things like this, but there's a reason Graybear brought this to me. I have names, Trevor."

"You have screen names."

Aaron cleared his throat. "Um, we can track them back. It'll take time, but I think we can do it."

"That's what you said about Graybear and it's been over a week." Axell glared at him and returned his sights to Lacy. "Regardless, our objective is to tear down Koslov's network and stop the flow of funding to outside groups looking to harm the US."

"This is part of that, I promise you," Lacy said. "I can get more information from Graybear, but I have to develop trust first. Whoever this contact is who sent him this intel, that's who we need to find."

"And the names too. The screen names," Aaron added.

"Exactly," she replied. "We get this and I'm telling you, Trevor, we'll have opened the door to something big."

"Oh, I have no doubt about that. But that's also my chief concern."

CHAPTER
THIRTEEN

THE DOOR to Axell's former office at Langley was open. With his arms folded, he leaned against the frame and peered inside. "Looks like you're settling in nicely. Congratulations on your Senate confirmation. As if there was ever any question."

"Record time for a confirmation hearing." Elizabeth Ward, the newly appointed CIA director looked up at him from her desk. "I am getting settled but did have to change up a few things around here. You know, make it look like a little homier."

Axell entered. "I never was much for settling in. I prefer to pick up on a moment's notice and look like I was never there in the first place."

"Years in the field will do that to a person." She studied him for a moment. "What are you doing here, Trevor? The look on your face suggests this isn't a social call."

"Not exactly. Do you have a minute?"

"Sure. Sit down." Elizabeth gestured to the guest chair. "What's on your mind?"

Axell walked inside and sat across from her. "Don't think I've ever sat in this chair before. Listen, I have a developing situation I think you should be made aware of."

In a tone lined with caution, she replied, "Okay."

"My team is in contact with an alleged cybercriminal, one who has provided us with intel that can't be ignored." Axell went on to tell her about the screen names and Graybear's offer of additional information.

"I am aware of the Russian diplomat, Usenko, and his relationship with Maxim Abramov. We've long suspected Abramov was a go-between for Koslov's money-laundering efforts, and until Koslov was turned over to your task force, we hadn't realized any connections to a European operation. How do the two come together? What evidence do we have that we can use against Koslov?"

"That's a piece of the puzzle we haven't figured out yet. And that leads me to my next question. Merrick is going to attend an event with Usenko tomorrow. It appears Abramov will be in attendance. That said, I would like your help with surveillance and backup, now that we're armed with this new information."

"I think that can be arranged. In fact, I'm still transitioning out of the D.C. station. I'd like to put together a team," Elizabeth began. "And you believe you can get Abramov to track back to this organization we're now assuming Koslov to be a part of?"

"I hope so because right now, I can't see any reason why this intel would come to us now at a time when we're just getting into the heart of Koslov's inner circle."

"And the hacker, what did you call him? Graybear? He's watching you?"

"Yes. Graybear appears to know far more about our op than we realized, which brings about additional concerns for my team's safety, particularly Merrick. But I can handle that end. I just need your resources to help with tomorrow's event."

"Consider it done."

Axell stood. "Thank you, Elizabeth. Enjoy the new digs."

———

The lengths to which Lacy and Aaron had taken to discover the identities behind the so-called bidders were nearly exhausted. They had employed all the resources at their disposal, yet neither had broken through.

"I need to take a break." Her weariness had boiled over as she stood from her desk and turned to Aaron. "You want a coffee or something?"

"I'll come with you." He pushed away from his desk. "I could use a break myself."

The news was always on the televisions in the office, and as the two started into the hall toward the kitchen, Lacy stopped and listened to the broadcast.

"The end of this month marks the one-year anniversary of the Fairfax mall bombing. A ceremony is planned to commemorate the tragic event at the newly completed memorial. Scheduled to speak will be the president along with directors of both the CIA and the FBI, along with some of the survivors. Notably missing will be Lacy Merrick, the woman who uncovered the corruption inside the previous administration after her husband was killed in the blast."

Lacy pressed the remote to turn off the television.

"I didn't know they asked you to attend," Aaron said.

"They didn't. I don't think the new president wants me to be as high-profile a figure as I once was."

"Of course not. That would mean you might constitute a threat to him and maybe someone might come along and convince you to run for office."

"That would never happen," she replied.

"Regardless, you're an American hero. I imagine people will be up in arms about your not being there."

"I'm no hero. I did what I did for incredibly selfish reasons. And I certainly didn't do it alone. So I'm fine with not going. I don't need a day to remember my husband because there isn't a day that goes by I forget." She continued toward the kitchen.

"Hey, you up for some company tonight?" Aaron followed her. "I haven't seen the kids in a while, or Celeste."

Lacy walked into the kitchen and reached for the coffee pot. "Feeling a little lonely, are you?"

"Aren't we all?"

"I guess so. Yeah. Come on over for dinner tonight. I know Liv and Jack would love to see you. I'm not sure about Celeste." Lacy smiled.

"Gee, thanks. And if you want, after the kids head off to bed, we can get back to work. I'll bring my laptop."

"With tomorrow's opening, we should keep at it as best we can. So, yeah, we'll plan on that."

———

Caison was behind the wheel. He pulled alongside the curb about one hundred feet away from the gallery. He turned to Balfour, who was in the passenger seat. "I want you to know that the team appreciates your help on this. I'll touch base with Ward's team after we finish recon and give them the download."

"It's no big deal. We'll all get what we want."

"Hey, can I ask you something?" Caison said.

"Sure."

"Did I do something to piss you off? Ever since I came to you with this, you've been reluctantly cooperative, to put it mildly."

She smiled. "Didn't think you were the type to be politically correct."

"I'm the type who does what he has to do to get shit done. And if that means sucking up to the likes of you, then that's what it means."

"There we go. There's the real Caison I've heard so much about," Balfour replied. "Look, I don't work well with others. I'm sorry if you were told otherwise. And the reason for that is because other people just get in my way. I'm here to do a job."

"We're all here to do a job. And sometimes those jobs require cooperation. Anyway, forget it." He peered through the windshield. "I'm just trying to get to the point where I can actually stand to be near you."

Balfour cast her gaze to the passenger window. "There's a lot you don't know about me, and not that I intend to share, but I don't play nice with others because most of the others think I'm working for the other side."

"What do you mean?" Will asked.

"I mean, my parents."

"I thought they defected to the US and helped our government?"

"They did. But that doesn't change the fact that when I was recruited, I was seen as a Russian. And while that didn't mean much a few years ago, it does now. When other agents find out my parents defected, they just assume their loyalties and mine are still with the Kremlin. Because, of course, my parents worked for the Russian government."

"I'm sorry. I never considered that, even with the way things are today. You work for the Bureau. That should be enough to prove where your loyalties lie."[1]

"You'd think." Balfour continued to look at the nearby gallery. "I think we should walk the perimeter and get a read on where the exits are, the parking, things like that in the event your partner needs to make a fast getaway."

"Finally, something we can agree on." Caison stepped out of his vehicle and approached the sidewalk. He surveyed the area around them, confirming no one suspicious was lingering or watching them. Once Balfour joined him, he began, "So, how did you get in with this crowd? Was it because of your folks?"

"You mean Abramov?"

"Yeah."

"My family's background was a consideration, which was fine. I speak the language. It was a logical fit, I won't deny that. A colleague was already working in the Russian mob scene and I was paired with him."

"Wait. You had a partner?"

"'Had' being the operative word," she replied.

He continued to surveil the exterior of the building as they approached. "I see."

"It didn't last long. He was killed by Abramov's people." She stopped at the rear right corner of the building. "We're going to have a blind spot here. Better let Ward's team know to be sure they have it covered." She continued to peer at the building. "Anything else stand out to you?"

Caison was taken aback by her disclosure. "Um, no. Rear exit on the far north side of the building. Two windows on this side, three opposite, and a picture window at the main entrance. So long as we've got that covered, we should be good."

"Okay. You want to make the call to the spooks, or should I?"

"I'll call Axell and have him coordinate with Ward. Thanks for coming out here with me, Balfour."

"They tell me it's my job." She started back toward the car. "Mind if we get out of here now? I have a lot of shit to take care of."

———

Lacy opened the front door and spotted Aaron, hands in his pockets and a goofy smile on his face. "Hey there. Come on in. Dinner's just about ready." She waited for him to enter and closed the door behind him. "Jack? Olivia? Uncle Aaron's here. Come say hi."

Aaron turned to see them approach. "Oh, man! Is that you, Jack? What, did you grow like a foot or something?"

"No." Jack laughed and reached his arms around Aaron. "I missed you, Uncle Aaron."

"I missed you too, kiddo."

Olivia approached soon after.

"There she is," Aaron said as he peered at her. "How are you, sweetheart?"

"Good." She pushed Jack out of the way and hugged Aaron.

"Hey!" Jack shouted.

"Okay, okay. Let's not smother him," Lacy said. "Why don't you two go wash up? Dinner's about on the table."

"Are you staying for dinner, Uncle Aaron?" Olivia asked.

"Yes, ma'am. Now go on, listen to your mom." Aaron watched as the two scampered off. "They have grown. A lot."

"Yes, they have." She placed her arm around Aaron and ushered him into the dining room. "We're eating at the big table tonight. Just for you."

"Don't I feel special." He sat down at the formal dining table, where a glass of wine awaited him. "I really didn't mean for you to go through all this trouble."

Lacy sat down next to him. "Oh, I didn't go through any trouble. It was Celeste who has been slaving away and making everything perfect for you." She took a sip of the wine in front of her.

"Thanks. That makes me feel so much better."

As if on cue, Celeste entered, holding a dish. "Aaron. I'm so glad you could make it to dinner tonight. I feel like I haven't seen you in ages."

Aaron stood to offer her an embrace. "It has been a while. It's good to see you, Celeste. And thank you for this. I don't get out to restaurants much and I don't cook, so it's nice to sit down to something special like this."

Lacy regarded him with a smile. It was good to have him there. Maybe a social visit was exactly what she needed to get her over the hump about tomorrow night.

"Kids, come sit down now. Dinner's on the table," Celeste shouted into the foyer. "They're probably shoving each other out of the way of the sink."

"We're coming." Olivia sat down.

Jackson sat down next to her.

"Do you always have to sit next to me?" she asked.

"Hey. We have company. Maybe you could both try to act like the young lady and young man you are?" Lacy rested her napkin on her lap.

"She's fine." Aaron winked at Olivia.

"See? Uncle Aaron doesn't mind."

"I can see that," Lacy said to him.

Aaron eyed the young girl. "Now you got me in trouble."

The children laughed and Aaron joined in. Lacy couldn't help but laugh too, and for one sweet oblivious moment, she forgot who she was.

———

The house turned quiet. The kids were in bed and Celeste had retired to her room. Lacy sat in the living room with Aaron. Each had a glass of wine in hand.

"Anything more from Graybear?" he asked.

"No. I would've said something to you. Not since we got the encrypted messages with the bidders."

"Okay. Just checking because, you know, you don't always tell me things."

"You're not going to let that go, are you? How many times do I have to apologize for keeping you out of the loop? And remember, it wasn't just you. I didn't tell anyone. I didn't think I needed to, not at the time. I was hoping Trevor could get whatever Ward had on this unnamed organization too, but, by the sounds of it, she doesn't have anything."

"I guess I can't give you too much grief because I did something I'm not too proud of."

She cocked her head and waited for him to continue.

"Lace, I installed a keylogger on your personal laptop. I—well, I thought you might do something and..."

"And I did. So if those messages hadn't come through on the work computer, you'd have known about it anyway without me having said a thing." She swallowed down the rest of her wine. "So we both lost trust in each other. That's not a good thing, Aaron."

"No, it's not, and I'm sorry. I did it for reasons I thought were right, but it turns out they were really just selfish."

"You're not the only one who behaved selfishly." She reached for his hand. "We can't let that happen again, okay? Not us. The last thing I want is to have secrets between us."

"I don't want to keep secrets from you either, Lace." He squeezed her hand and held her gaze.

"Okay, then. Better get to work if we hope to make any progress before tomorrow night." Lacy pulled away her hand. "I talked to Will earlier. He said he and Balfour did some scouting and cleared the place. By the way, have you met her?"

"No." He turned on his laptop.

"She's a piece of work. Sarcastic, condescending. Kind of feel bad for Will having to deal with her."

"He's a big boy. He's dealt with far worse, I'm sure." Aaron pulled up the list of names again and backtracked where they'd stopped. "I'm still working on the algorithm, but by the look of it, I'm going to need to find another way. Or another algorithm."

"Are you flying blind here, Aaron? How the hell are we going to trace these screen names back to actual people?"

"We don't even need to do that much. We just need IP addresses. Locations. If we can at the very least get that, we stand a better chance at identifying them."

"I have to get in contact with him," she said.

"Who? Graybear?"

"Yes. I have to get him to tell me who his contact is. Where he got this intel. We just don't have the time to whittle this down."

"Initiating contact with Graybear again isn't the solution. In fact, I want you to have as little contact with him as humanly possible. We know who will be at the gallery tomorrow night. You and Will ran checks on all of them."

"Right. And they all came back clean. Even Abramov."

"Well, if they had something on Abramov, he'd be in prison. But the point is, we aren't going to solve this before tomorrow night. And that's going to have to be okay. But we will solve it. Jill and I have been working hard on this. And you." Aaron placed his hand on her shoulder. "We will get there."

The two locked eyes for a moment and Lacy felt a warm sensation in the pit of her stomach. It almost felt like butterflies, but that wasn't possible. This was Aaron, the hacker-geek who'd been Jay's and her best friend in college. Jay wasn't here anymore. But Aaron was.

CHAPTER
FOURTEEN

PROGRESS HAD STAGNATED in identifying the bidders Graybear suggested played a part in a black-market auction, the resulting winner taking home valued intellectual property, stolen property that could be used by any and all criminal organizations and or rogue regimes. As the sun rose and a new day arrived, Lacy had to let Aaron continue to chip away at that work while she focused on her impending date with the Russian diplomat, Anton Usenko, though not any sort of date she'd ever been on before. A key directive was at stake. The goal was to get in with Usenko and win an opportunity to meet with Koslov, the man who helped funnel money that was tied back to her husband's death. Not directly, but for Lacy, there was no distinction between Shen Yang, Lei Jian, Casper Janz, and now Sergei Koslov. They had all contributed to Jay's demise. They had all participated in taking a father away from his children, and a husband away from his wife. This was what drove her to do the things of which she never thought herself capable. But how far would she be willing to go to get what she wanted?

Upon her arrival at task force headquarters, the team was

already in place. Axell had also returned and appeared to be ready for the long haul. The operation rested on Lacy's shoulders and the only consolation was that a single life could be at stake—hers. That was something she could handle. Not like Keith Colburn's death, something for which she still took responsibility, and believed Axell hadn't overcome either.

"Lacy, you're here. Good. Come take a look," Caison began. "I want you to see what we've got planned in terms of surveillance."

She approached him. "As long you guys have my back, that's all that matters to me."

"Balfour and I did some recon yesterday as well as coordinated with a team Ward put together for tonight." Caison continued to describe the plan but stopped short. "Are you okay? You're not saying anything."

"I'm fine. I'm listening," she replied.

At this, Hunter turned away from his desk and studied her. "Did you get any rest last night after I left?"

"Some." Her smile was forced and her eyes held back the truth. "I'm fine, really. Just focusing on tonight. That's all."

Caison and Hunter exchanged troubled glances before Caison continued again. "You know where I'll be and you know we'll have eyes on you. You'll be safe. I'm not worried and you shouldn't be either."

"I didn't say I was worried. I know you all like to tiptoe around me and walk on eggshells like I'll break if something goes awry. But trust me, I'm stronger than either of you give me credit for."

"Lace, no one's saying you're not strong, and definitely not me," Hunter said. "But this is something new—for all of us. We've been chased, been the chasers, and now we're drawing them into our net. It's a different ballgame."

"And I'm ready for it. Will, please, continue." They had it all wrong about her. Yes, this was different, but that wasn't the reason for her outward apathy. In less than a month's time, she would be reminded of what she lost. It was already on every news channel, every social media outlet, and she would have to shield her children from it. That was not going to be an easy task. So now she was dealing with transforming herself into a woman who would feign interest in an ego-driven, one-dimensional man whose only interest in her was her name. But that was the way it had to be.

————

This place was like a Chinese sweatshop, only instead of children, the workers were twenty-somethings. And instead of making clothes, they were hacking into servers all over the world, stealing as much information as they could.

Daria Liski had been chosen to participate in an auction because of the outstanding work she'd done in obtaining high-value IP. Perhaps it was because her boss found her attractive and wanted to impress her or he was genuinely interested in grooming her for a better position. Daria otherwise would be rotting in a Ukraine prison somewhere for the crimes committed prior to being plucked from the pit of despair and plugged into something akin to the Matrix.

So why had she chosen to disclose the dangerous secrets of an underground organization? Because she believed in what Graybear was doing. She believed in a world where the sharing of information should be commonplace and the thoughts and ideas of people should belong to all. It was a utopian viewpoint shared by much of that generation. It all seemed well and good until someone had to figure out how to pay for all this free information. People would eventually stop creating, stop finding cures, and stop making lives easier if they weren't going to be paid for it. How else were they to survive?

Nevertheless, she believed in Graybear and would help even if it meant the destruction of the company that kept her from that prison.

"Daria, might I have a word?" Her supervisor approached.

She followed him to his office, a mild sense of unease crawling down her spine. She'd covered her tracks. She was sure of it. This must be something else.

He closed the door. "Sit down, Daria." On his return to his desk, he began, "I am deeply disappointed."

"I'm sorry? What did I do, sir?"

"Daria." He laced his fingers together. "You must know that we go to great lengths to ensure security here."

"Of course," she replied.

"And yet I entrusted you to observe a highly guarded event that keeps this organization afloat."

She swallowed down the lump in her throat. "Yes, sir, and I appreciate the opportunity. If I could just explain..."

"Then why didn't you come to me with this?" He tossed a file onto his desk and slid it toward her.

With grave concern masking her face, Daria pulled the file near and opened it. Upon inspection, she realized she was not here for the reasons she first believed. This was something very different, and her pulse slowed again. The lump in her throat dissolved. "I didn't realize this was of such importance to you, sir. Please accept my apologies."

"You must come to me with everything, regardless of whether you believe it useful. Do you understand?"

"I do, sir. Yes."

"Good. Then you are dismissed."

She pushed up from the chair and turned on her heel.

"Daria?"

She stopped in her tracks.

"Perhaps we might discuss your future with the organization over lunch next week?"

With a slow turn and a fake smile, she replied, "I would be grateful, sir. Thank you." As she left the office, a wave of nausea surged but only briefly. Remnants of the adrenaline most certainly, but he didn't know. And now he wanted to get closer to her, meaning she might be able to provide Graybear with more information. But she would have to be careful. There was no question in her mind that were she caught, she would be killed. And probably by the man inside that office.

———

In order to avoid running the risk Lacy might be followed, she brought with her a change of clothes. With only an hour until show time, she was ready. The plan was to have several operatives in place, but Lacy, herself, would not be wearing a wire. It was deemed too dangerous.

She emerged from the women's bathroom and entered the bullpen.

Caison stood on her arrival. "You look beautiful, Lacy."

Aaron smiled at her and replied, "What he said."

"Thanks. Where's Trevor?"

"Right here." Axell emerged from his office. "Nice dress, Merrick. Now are you ready to play this game again?"

"You know it."

"Then let's lay this out one more time, then we'll hit the road."

The plan again was put on the table. Two of Ward's CIA officers would be stationed nearby. One at the bench on the other side of the street, dressed as a homeless person. The other would appear to be drunk and sitting in front of a market three doors down from the gallery.

Then there was Caison. His job was to be stationed on the roof of the building across the street, armed with a rifle and a scope. The op would be run by Axell and Ward from a van around the corner. Communications would go through them and Aaron would be there to jam communications with anyone else should things head south.

"And all you need to do is smile and laugh at Usenko's jokes. Take note of the people you're introduced to. Do your best to remember names and positions but don't attempt to use your phone for anything. In fact, I wouldn't take it out at all," Axell said.

"Okay. So when the evening starts to wrap up, what then? How do I get out of there without Usenko offering a nightcap or anything else that would leave us alone together?"

"Well," Caison started. "He knows you have kids. I'd use the old babysitter excuse."

"Great," she replied. "I'm ready if you are."

The team assembled outside where Ward had just arrived. "They're all in place," she said as she approached Axell. "Do we have the green light?"

"Yes, ma'am," he replied. "And here's our woman of the hour."

Lacy approached wearing her black cocktail dress. "Director Ward, very nice to see you again."

"Please. It's Elizabeth. Great dress. You ready to do this?"

"I'm ready to get it over with and earn a meeting with Koslov."

"It'll happen, Lacy. You just need a little bit of time and patience. But remember that you'll have to ensure Usenko thinks you're of value. He has to know that you'll give them what they need before he even considers bringing you to Abramov. And all we can do is go from there to get to Koslov."

"Follow me." Axell started toward the black van and slid open the door. "Hunter, jump in."

Aaron stepped inside the mini communications center. "Very nice. I can work with this." He moved to a seat nearby.

"Lacy, you'll ride down with us, but we'll drop you off a few blocks away where we'll have an Uber waiting to take you the rest of the way." Axell jumped inside the van.

"Perfect." She cast her sights on Caison, who was heading in the opposite direction. "Be careful, Will."

He stopped and faced her with a reassuring smile. "Don't you worry about me. Just focus on you and we'll all be good." With a thumbs-up, he continued until reaching a car that wasn't his own.

Lacy was the last to enter and closed the van door behind her. "At least we're not roaming the streets of Beijing this time," she said to Aaron.

"Not this time." He studied her for a moment. "Everything will be fine. You have a lot of people looking out for you."

"I know." She recalled for a moment the stray thought that breached her psyche in the late hours of last night while Aaron sat next to her. In the haze of war—because there was no mistaking it, this was war—she felt vulnerable, alone. She missed Jay so much she could hardly stand it. And Aaron loved her, she knew he did. And it was in the way that she needed to be loved, but now, the moment had passed and she had come to her senses. There could never be anything between them because it would always be a result of what had happened to Jay. It wasn't organic. Lacy did love Aaron, just not in the way he loved her. And she knew he could see it in her face, even now.

"This is where you get off, Merrick." Axell pulled over to the side of the road. "The white Audi. That's your ride."

Lacy peered through the windshield. "You found an Uber driver who drives an Audi? Guess the side gig pays well."

"He's one of ours, but if anyone needed to check, he's an Uber driver," Ward replied.

"Got it." Lacy opened the door. "See you all on the other side." With a brief nod to Aaron, she stepped out of the van and approached the white Audi.

The man inside rolled down his window. "Need a lift?"

"I thought you'd never ask." Lacy slipped onto the back seat while the man started the engine and pulled away from the curb. She was ready for this. There was too much riding on it for her to fail. Everyone was counting on her and this was the only way to get to Abramov quickly and to understand who pulled his strings, which they assumed was Koslov.

"Here you go, ma'am."

"What do I owe you?" Lacy said half-jokingly. But in the event someone checked, she could at least validate the idea this guy was really an Uber driver.

"It's been taken care of," he replied. "You have yourself a lovely evening, ma'am."

A valet attendant opened Lacy's door and helped her out of the car. "Good evening, ma'am. Here for the exhibit?"

"Yes, I am. I'm meeting..." She began to scan the immediate area and smiled when she spotted Usenko. "That gentleman right there."

"Lacy Merrick." With arms open, Usenko approached. "You look stunning." He offered his elbow.

Lacy linked arms with him as he led the way inside the gallery.

On the opposite side of the street, on the roof of a building, Caison lay on his stomach and aimed a rifle in the direction of the gallery. He peered through the scope. "I've got her. She's inside."

The black van parked around the corner had Ward, Axell, and Hunter inside.

"Roger," Axell replied through the headset. He turned to Elizabeth. "Your people?"

"Mundey, Banks, you copy?"

"In place and eyes on the prize," Mundey replied.

"Stationed and eyes peeled. She's in. Awaiting others on the list," Banks said.

"Copy," Ward replied before she turned her attention to Axell. "It sure would move this along if Koslov decided to show."

"We won't be that lucky. And with her notoriety, it would only spook him. No, this needs to happen through Abramov. We'll have to rely on him to reveal details about Koslov we can use. We don't know how much Janz told Koslov about me or the task force. Maybe nothing, but we can't take that chance. I'm just hoping to catch sight of the folks on the list. We get some high-ranking Russian officials rubbing elbows with a known mafia boss with Russian ties, we got ourselves a party."

Aaron kept quiet, only staring at the monitors where he'd been able to hack into the city's CCTV. There were no cameras inside the gallery he could access, but one that was aimed right at the gallery's entrance. And with its glass doors and walls, he could see her in certain areas.

Back inside the gallery, Lacy started to relax.

"Oh, now this is absolutely beautiful." Usenko stopped in front of a painting. "I have to admit, I don't consider myself an expert, but I do believe this is quite the work of art."

"I would have to agree with you." She sipped on her wine and gauged the room. Several people had now arrived, but she hadn't seen one whose names were on that list provided by Agent Balfour. "You mentioned you wanted me to meet some friends of yours. Have they arrived yet?"

Usenko returned his attention to her. "I don't know. Let's have a walk around and see who we can find. And maybe let everyone see who I have the pleasure to have on my arm tonight."

His smile was completely disingenuous, but she had expected nothing else from a man like Anton Usenko. And as he led her around the room like a peacock showing off his feathers, she believed she spotted Maxim Abramov, the Russian mafia leader from New York.

"Oh, well, here is someone I'd love to introduce you to," Usenko began. "Maxim! How are you this evening? What a wonderful turnout."

Abramov shot a glance at Lacy before replying, "Good evening, Anton. Yes, this artist is a great talent and his art should be well received." He again set his sights on Lacy. "And who is this lovely lady?"

"Ah, this is FBI Agent Lacy Merrick."

She offered a coy smile. "Anton gives me far too much credit. I do work for the Bureau, but I'm not a field agent."

"No?" Abramov replied.

"I work in the cyber division."

"I see. Well, welcome to the gallery. It is a pleasure to meet you, Lacy Merrick." He studied her once again and pointed his index finger at her. "Aren't you..."

"Yes, she is," Usenko answered before she could reply. "This is the woman who brought down a president."

She again appeared modest. "Please. I certainly was not alone in my search for the truth."

Abramov held her gaze. "Truth. Yes. Tell me, Lacy Merrick, did the truth bring you peace?"

Across the street, on the rooftop, Caison jolted. "Oh shit." He pressed on his earpiece. "Hey, anyone seeing what I'm seeing?"

"I've got eyes on Koslov at my eleven o'clock," Mundey said.

"Copy that. I see him at my three. Please advise on how to proceed."

Axell shot a look at Elizabeth.

Aaron whipped around in his chair. "Is he going inside?"

Axell pressed on his earpiece. "Caison, where is Koslov headed?"

"Straight for the gallery. He's approaching the entrance now." There was a short pause and he sounded again on the headset. "He stopped at the doors. I think he sees her."

"How does he know who she is?" Mundey asked.

"Everyone knows who she is," Axell replied.

"Why isn't he going in?" Caison asked again. "What do you want me to do?"

"Nothing," Axell said. "Wait to see what he does."

Caison and the rest of the team kept their eyes glued to Sergei Koslov. No one had expected him to be there tonight. Balfour had all but assured them he wouldn't show, yet here he was right now, less than one hundred feet from Lacy. "He's turning around. Shit. He's leaving. Koslov's leaving. He suspects something. You want me to follow?"

Axell looked to Ward. "Well?"

She pressed on her earpiece. "Follow him. It's our best shot at finding out who he's working with."

"Wait, what about Lacy?" Aaron asked.

"She'll be fine. My men are still out there," Ward replied.

"Copy that. I'm on him."

CHAPTER
FIFTEEN

THE PAIN in Lacy's cheeks grew more intense as the night wore on. It had only been an hour and she had met four other diplomats, a Russian mafia leader, and a hanger-on of Usenko. She couldn't quite figure out where he fit. What concerned her the most was that she hadn't seen or received any signals from the team. The plan had been to let the evening take its course. Let the chips fall where they may and let her do the job she came here to do. But what did that mean for her, exactly? Other than Maxim Abramov, Lacy had met no one of any significance. Had Usenko duped her into thinking he had real connections? Perhaps. But if so, then Balfour fell for his line too. Right now, she was getting a whole lot of nothing from any of these wealthy Russians who liked to throw their weight around.

"Is everything all right, Lacy?" The younger Usenko sipped on his wine as he stood inches from her. "You appear preoccupied."

"Do I? I should apologize, then."

"Your children?" He asked.

It was too soon to use that get-out-of-jail-free card. She needed another reason. "No. Honestly, I was just in awe."

"Really? In awe of what, might I ask?"

"This evening, in general. You—more specifically. You are quite the raconteur. With each piece we approach, you weave a wonderful tale of the artist and history. I have to ask, did you major in Art History?" She hoped flattery would get her somewhere.

Usenko smiled and blushed as though he was an adolescent boy. "You are too kind. I am just a fan of this medium. I did study it, though not formally." He peered around the room. "You know, I should introduce you to a gentleman." He pulled her arm gently forward. "In fact, he approached me while I was getting us another drink. I think he fancies meeting you. And perhaps you two might have something in common."

It worked. She had gotten through to him on another level—appealing to his intellect. This was probably something that few had done, considering his superficial nature. No one had looked beyond that because he had money and prestige. Those were important qualities to certain women, but Lacy was not like those women. She understood what she needed to do to get to the heart of a man like Usenko. And now she was about to meet another in his circle. Lacy could only hope this person would be useful and might lead to Koslov.

"Mr. Mullins," Usenko offered his hand, "as promised, I have come to introduce you to someone."

"Ah, perfect." Mullins turned his sights to Lacy. "Don't keep me in suspense, Anton. Who is this stunning woman on your arm tonight?"

Lacy offered a greeting. "I'm Lacy Merrick. Anton invited me here this evening."

"Lacy. May I call you that?" He spoke the Queen's English with poise and clarity. "I'm Timothy Mullins. How do you know our Anton?"

"We met at a state dinner last week, as a matter of fact," Usenko replied. "We seemed to hit it off nicely, didn't we?"

"We did, Anton." Lacy turned to him. "Timothy Mullins." She considered the name in a purposefully exaggerated manner. "Where have I heard that name before?"

"Oh, I don't think you'd know about him." Again, Usenko answered without being asked the question. "He and I met through a mutual business acquaintance back in Moscow, what, about two years ago, was it, Timothy?"

"Indeed it was." He eyed Anton. "Perhaps Ms. Merrick would like to speak for herself?" He turned his sights to her.

"Oh, it's fine. Anton seems to be right. I thought we might've met in passing, but I can see now that isn't likely. I don't travel to Moscow nor do I do business there."

"No. You don't, do you, Ms. Merrick?" Mullins peered at her with calculating eyes.

"It's Mrs. Merrick," she shot back with a bite in her tone.

Usenko cleared his throat. "Lacy is a widow. She lost her husband in the mall attack last year."

"I see. I'm very sorry, Mrs. Merrick. I meant no offense. I hadn't realized."

Lacy grew suspicious of this man, Timothy Mullins. Something about him was off-putting. But what was it? Did she know him? She couldn't recall seeing his name on the list Agent Balfour provided, which concerned her even more now that she thought about it. "None taken, Mr. Mullins." She followed with a smile. "What do you do for a living, may I ask?"

"Nothing particularly interesting, I can assure you." Mullins sipped on a glass of red wine, his eyes never leaving hers. This man with his velvety British accent had a secret and his face did little to conceal that fact.

"Oh, you might be surprised as to what I find interesting," Lacy replied.

"Lacy works for the FBI." Usenko eyed her. "Cyber division, was it?"

"That's right."

"Now that sounds incredibly interesting. Perhaps we should meet up sometime to discuss the ever-changing world of data proliferation."

Whatever this man did for a living, it wasn't what Anton Usenko believed it was. This man was involved in something else. "Are you well-versed on the topic, Mr. Mullins?"

"I believe so."

"Then a meeting would be interesting," Lacy replied.

Usenko creased his brow. "I'm sure I could set something up for the three of us to sit down for drinks sometime in the near future."

Mullins held Lacy's gaze. "I should think I would like that very much."

———

Caison followed Sergei Koslov at a safe distance, confirming he wasn't spotted. He didn't know where Koslov was going or why he was at the gallery. It threw them all for a loop, and now, as much as he wanted to know where this man was headed, thoughts of Lacy's safety consumed him.

People were looking after her, but not him. Not this time. And while he had every confidence in her ability to pull this off, worrying about her was something he couldn't help.

They'd been after Koslov for months and now was the first time they had a tail on him that could lead to something. He couldn't afford to screw this up. "Koslov is still heading north, out of D.C."

Axell was on the receiving end of the audio. "Keep on him, but be safe. I don't want him picking up on your pursuit."

"Ten-four," he replied through his earpiece. "I'll keep going and see where he's headed. I have plates. Virginia KVE1467."

"We'll run them now," Axell replied.

"We still have eyes on Lacy?"

"She's still inside the gallery. We won't let her out of our sight." Axell handed Aaron the sticky note with the plate number on it. "Run this. Now."

Aaron turned to his workstation inside the van and entered the plates. "Damn it."

Axell approached him again. "What'd you find?"

"These plates aren't registered to that car or him unless he's got another alias we don't know about."

"Keep working it. See if you can find a connection between the registrant and Koslov."

"I'll try."

Axell returned to his station next to Ward. He pressed his earpiece again. "Caison, no luck on the plates. Car's registered to someone else. Hunter's working that angle. You'll have to hang tight until Koslov lands somewhere. Hopefully soon. This is the first time he's gone somewhere besides his apartment and the Russian consulate. This means something."

"I'm on it." Caison continued to follow the Mercedes sedan hoping Hunter could work his magic and get something on this car. But without plates tied to him, it wouldn't be easy. Nothing about this had been easy, though.

He pressed on as Koslov drove. "Where the hell are you going?" He was outside of D.C. now and heading to Maryland. What was in Maryland? They knew he had a place in Manhattan, thanks to Goddard's work hacking into his car's GPS until he'd figured out someone could get access. After a few days, his GPS had been disabled. So much for that. All he could do was follow and keep thoughts of Lacy in the back of his mind.

———

What was it about this man, Timothy Mullins? Lacy thought. This was an important man, that much was obvious. In fact, on a scale ranging from one to ten, Usenko would be a four at best with Mullins most certainly being a ten. "How about next week?" she replied.

"Excuse me?" Usenko looked at her.

"Drinks with Timothy. Next week?"

"I like a woman who follows through. I'm sure I could find a date that would work. I'll get in touch with Anton here and put something on the books. I should continue making the rounds. It was an absolute pleasure meeting you, Lacy."

"And you, Timothy." Lacy watched him walk away. "He seems interesting," she said to Usenko.

"Sure. If you like the James Bond type."

Lacy picked up on his sullen tone and figured she'd better smooth things over. "You know, I don't think I've thanked you for bringing me here tonight, Anton. It has been such an amazing experience. You really are a wonderful date."

His expression softened. "Date?"

"Sure. Why not?"

"Does that mean we can do it again?"

"I would love to." She retrieved her cell phone and checked the time. "I'm so sorry, but I should really be getting back now. The babysitter will need to go home soon."

"Of course." He led her toward the entrance. "Thank you,

Lacy, for a wonderful evening. I look forward to spending more time with you." He kissed the back of her right hand. "Do you need me to call you a cab?"

"That won't be necessary, but thank you. It appears they have several waiting out front. Good night, Anton."

"Good night, Lacy Merrick." He held open the door for her while she stepped outside.

Lacy looked back, confident he would watch her until she got into a cab, which was what she was about to do now. She opened the door to a waiting taxi and slipped into the back seat. It was possible this driver could relay information to Usenko. He was a well-connected diplomat. In that event, it was best to head home because she could trust no one. "Annandale, please."

"Yes, ma'am."

Lacy wasn't wearing an earpiece and the only way she could contact Axell would be on her phone, but that wasn't a practical option right now. She could afford to take nothing for granted as far as Usenko was concerned. So any contact with the team would have to wait until she arrived home, which would take at least forty-five minutes. It would be the longest forty-five minutes of her life.

———

This was it. Koslov was slowing to a stop in front of a row of houses. "Finally." Caison slowed down, dropping back several more feet, but still within eyesight of Koslov's Mercedes.

The headlights were turned off. He was about to lose visual and decided to go on foot from here. He stepped out of his car and tucked his sidearm into his waistband.

When Koslov came into view once again, Caison ducked into

the shadows and watched him. "Come on, man, give me something," he whispered.

Koslov walked up the steps of a brownstone and inserted a key. He stepped inside and closed the door. Caison moved in and tried to catch sight of him inside, but the only window nearby appeared darkened. "Damn it." He noted the address and waited for a sign from Koslov inside. But he would not get one.

He started back toward his car and pressed on his earpiece. "4359 Bunker Street."

"His house?" Axell asked.

"Don't know. He went inside, but I couldn't see in."

"Okay. Merrick is out and headed home. Still awaiting a confirmation. Ward's people followed the cab she entered," Axell replied. "Head into the shop. We'll reconvene there. Axell out."

Caison approached his car and a man was now leaning against it. Wasting no time, he pulled his gun and aimed.

The man raised his hands in defense. "Whoa. Take it easy, Cowboy."

He was Russian, but his face wasn't one Caison recognized. "I suggest you tell me who you are."

"Who I am isn't important." The man pushed off Will's car and flicked his cigarette to the ground. "What's important is that you shouldn't be here."

"I don't know what you're talking about. I'm just out having an evening stroll."

The man laughed. "Of course you are, William Caison."

He turned deadpan. "Who the hell are you?"

"As I said, it's not who I am, but who I represent."

"And that is?"

"An organization that wishes to remain anonymous, but one that has a great many resources and does not like attention. You, Agent Caison, are bringing attention to it."

"I have no idea what you're talking about."

"Perhaps not. Perhaps you still believe this is about the money used to bankroll Shen Yang's failed plan."

"What do you know about that, Mr...." He awaited an introduction.

At this, the man simply smiled. "The time has come for you and your people to step away from this fruitless endeavor. I say this out of deep respect for what you all have done."

"Oh, I doubt respect has anything to do with it. My guess is Koslov sent you to scare me. We must be getting close."

The man took a step toward Caison. "I wouldn't come any closer if I were you."

"Luckily, you are not me, Agent Caison. Because I am in a far better position than you right now."

Another man approached Caison from behind, reaching around his body for the gun he held in his hand.

"What the...!" He twisted from the man's grip and slipped beneath him, gun still in his possession. The odds were against him now and his only option was to bolt across the empty street.

"Let him go," the man said. "I think he got the message."

———

Trust was a fickle lady, and in this business, trusting the wrong person could cost everything. Lacy had seen that first hand. She had trusted her government, her president, and had been let down in the worst possible way. So as she sat in the back of the cab, not knowing if the driver was connected to Usenko or any of his associates, there was a better place to go, one she could easily explain away so Usenko wouldn't know where she lived. And she'd just arrived.

Lacy noted the fare and pulled out the cash, offering it to the driver. "Thank you." She stepped out of the cab and waited for the driver to pull away, standing at the entrance. She arrived at the J. Edgar Hoover building. FBI headquarters. It was almost midnight and she no longer carried credentials because, well, she didn't work here anymore.

But as she entered the building, a familiar face sat behind the information desk. "Lacy. What on earth are you doing here? And dressed all fancy."

"Hi, Pete. Long time no see. I needed a safe place. Hope it's okay."

Pete furrowed his brow and looked beyond her at the entrance. "Is someone following you? Do you need help?"

"I think I'm good now. But I'll need to call for a lift home."

"I'm on it. Don't you worry about it." Pete began to make a call.

Lacy smiled and stepped away to use her phone. She waited for an answer, and Axell picked up.

"Where are you?" He immediately asked.

"I'm at FBI headquarters," Lacy replied.

"Why are you there? Is everything okay?"

"I'm fine. I couldn't be sure the cab driver wasn't with Usenko." She started to speak again but was stopped short.

"Thank God you're okay. We had one of Ward's teams watching but grew concerned when he noted you were making a diversion. I've been waiting for your call. Lacy, we've got a problem."

She peered back at Pete, who didn't seem to be paying attention, before taking a few more steps away. "What's wrong?" As if she didn't have enough to worry about with this Mullins character.

"We expected Caison back fifteen minutes ago. I tried comms again, but we were out of range..."

"What?" She tried to keep down her tone.

"He went after Koslov."

"Koslov? What the hell? How did he…"

"Lacy, I don't have time to explain. You need to get back to the shop. That's where I told Caison to meet at our last communication. I'm hoping he'll find his way there."

"Oh my God." She pushed her hand through her hair. "Okay. I'll get there as soon as I can." She ended the call and marched back to Pete.

"Your ride is on its way."

"Thanks, Pete. I appreciate it."

"Somehow you look worse than when you walked in. Are you sure you're okay? Do I need to call security to help?"

"No. Please. I'm okay. I just have someplace I need to be."

CHAPTER
SIXTEEN

THE TASK FORCE HEADQUARTERS, a dimly lit nondescript building designed to blend in with its surroundings, appeared in the distance. Lacy jumped out of the cab and rushed toward the unlocked doors. Upon making her way inside, she began, "Where is he?"

"He's fine." Axell approached her. "I just heard from him. He'll be here in ten minutes."

She stopped in her tracks and threw her hands over her mouth. After she had the chance to absorb the news, Lacy continued. "What happened to him? Why was Koslov there and why didn't he come in?"

"You have questions," Axell began. "We all do. We're just going to have to wait until he gets here. The point is, he's safe. Now I need to know what happened tonight. You left earlier than I expected you to."

Elizabeth Ward started toward her. "I think Maxim Abramov was watching you, even after you left. Going to FBI headquarters was a good call. You were covered, but my guys had to keep their distance. They're the ones who spotted what they assumed was one of Abramov's men following you in that cab."

"I thought it might be Usenko, but the mobster?" Lacy said.

"Don't sound too surprised," Axell replied. "He runs a huge operation and having a federal agent in his midst probably made him nervous."

"Or he suspected the real reason I was there."

"It's too early to make that call. I'm just glad you're back," Axell replied.

"I wish I could say the same thing about Will."

"What's that you wanted to say about me?" Caison walked inside, drenched in sweat after running from Koslov's men.

"You're back." Lacy rushed to his side and threw her arms around him. "Thank God. I was so worried something had happened to you."

"We all were." Aaron approached. "Glad you're back, man."

"Someone came at me," Caison began. "I waited until Koslov was inside. Got out of my car and started walking toward the townhouse. I couldn't see anything inside, so I noted the address and headed back to my car. Everything went south after that. I was jumped. Managed to get away and hauled ass back here as soon as I could catch a cab."

"Did you recognize the men?" Axell asked.

"No. But the first guy I saw sure as hell knew who I was. Knew I was a fed. Knew all kinds of things about me. Said he represented some organization and that they preferred to keep a low profile. The other guy, well, he came at me from behind."

"That must be what Graybear was talking about," Lacy said. "The screen names and bidders and all that. I need to find Graybear. I have to tell him what happened. He might give me more." Lacy turned to Aaron. "Please tell me you've been able to get some idea of who this person is?"

"Lace, I've been watching you for the past few hours. I don't know any more now than I did yesterday."

"Okay. Before we go too far down this path, I need to know what happened in that gallery tonight. Why Koslov was there, to begin with," Axell began. "Caison, as far as Balfour knew, he wasn't supposed to be there."

"That's right. And he didn't go inside. Something stopped him."

"Or someone." Aaron looked at Lacy. "I think he saw you with Usenko. I think that spooked him."

"Wait. What am I missing here?" Lacy folded her arms.

"Koslov stopped at the door, took one look inside, and left," Caison said. "Axell ordered me to follow him and that's what I did. That's when I came across the Russians."

"That is interesting." Lacy appeared deep in thought.

"And why is that? What happened inside there tonight? Why did you leave so soon?" Axell asked.

"Usenko was showing me off to his colleagues, showing off his art history knowledge, and a man appeared. And he wanted to introduce me to him, which I thought, okay, it's another diplomat. But I was wrong. This guy—his name is Timothy Mullins. He's British. He felt—dirty."

"What do you mean?" Axell asked.

"I mean he was hiding something. He made himself sound as though he was powerful without divulging anything. And he definitely took an interest in me. He said we should meet up again. Of course, this set off Usenko. He felt left out and inserted himself into the plan."

"Mullins," Ward began. "Where have I heard that name?"

"If he gave her his real name, he's no one we should be concerned with," Axell said.

"I wouldn't be too sure. He holds power. I don't think he's

afraid of anything or anyone." Lacy turned to Aaron. "Can you see what you can find on him?"

"On it." Aaron returned to his seat. Within minutes, he turned back. "Timothy Mullins, born in London, 1978." He turned his chair to face the others. "He's a self-made millionaire. Made his money in the tech boom, survived the bust."

"And what does he do now?" Axell asked.

"He's the founder of DataGen," Ward replied. "I thought I recognized the name."

"The data storage firm?" Lacy asked. "I've heard of them. I remember Jay talking about them once a long time ago."

"Interesting. Wonder if he's a part of this so-called organization I was warned about by the Russian." Caison looked at Lacy. "Might be the reason Koslov turned tail. Maybe the two couldn't be seen together."

Axell nodded. "Hunter, find out what you can on Mullins. This whole thing is starting to stink. Sergei Koslov's connections appear to run deeper than we thought. And, he might know more about us than we thought."

"I think the only way we're going to find out for sure is for me to continue communicating with Graybear," Lacy said. "I need you to cut me loose on that, Trevor. He knows a lot more than he's letting on. I don't know why. Unless it's for money. But he hasn't mentioned wanting to be paid. I need to cozy up to him."

"Hunter, Caison, you on board with that?" Axell asked.

"We're getting close to Koslov," Caison said. "I trust Lacy. If this is what she needs to do, then she should do it."

"Hunter?" Axell asked again.

With a deep breath, he answered, "I'll do my best to keep him from getting more than we want him to get. I don't know who we're up against yet, but Graybear is smart and knows what he's doing."

"I'll get you Graybear, whether he wants to be gotten or not," Lacy replied.

"It's late. You all need to go home." Axell started back to his office. "I have a few things to wrap up with Director Ward and I'll be leaving too. We'll start fresh in the morning." He stopped and turned on his heel. "A lot of things went wrong tonight and for that, I'm sorry. But things went right too. You all did excellent work."

"It was good working with you again. All of you. Thank you for giving me that opportunity. I hope I didn't let you down."

"Not at all, Director. We appreciate your assistance." Lacy returned to her desk to gather her things.

"I'm ready to get the hell out of here." Aaron turned off his computer and started toward the door. "You guys coming?"

"Right behind you," Caison began. "Lacy?"

"I'm coming."

The three started out the door and made their way into the parking lot.

"Damn it." Lacy stopped in her tracks. "I forgot something. You guys go on. I'll see you in the morning."

"You sure? I can wait," Aaron asked.

"Me too," Will said.

"I'll only be a minute. Good night, guys." She continued back inside the building and walked toward her desk. Axell's office door was partially open and Lacy could hear him speaking to Ward. She stopped and listened in on the conversation.

"Liz, you can't blame yourself," Axell said. "I would've done the same thing. If you'd let them continue on, Abramov's men would've taken notice. It was a risk you just couldn't take."

"Logically, I get it. But I still feel like I left her hanging out to dry."

"You didn't. What I'm most concerned with is, if these were

his men, and we are in agreement that is most likely the case, then what does Abramov know about us? We suspect he's laundering money for Koslov. Does that mean he knew Casper Janz too?"

"I don't know. If he knows about your team, that could present bigger problems in trying to pin something on Koslov. Lacy could be getting into untold danger by trying to get in with Abramov through the diplomat."

Axell sighed. "What we know for sure is that this operation didn't go as either of us planned. But then, when do they ever?"

Elizabeth nodded. "Almost never. Not in a long time anyway. Probably before Meg was born. By the way, have you talked to her?"

"With everything going on, no. Not yet."

"Trevor, she's your daughter. She wants to talk to you. Don't screw this up by blowing her off."

"Yeah, well, she's your daughter too. Maybe you remind her that it was her decision to cut me off."

"That was a long time ago. A lot's changed since then."

Lacy's mouth fell agape. She quickly grabbed the flash drive she'd left behind and tiptoed out of there before being noticed. As she continued outside, Will and Aaron had already left and she had no one to talk to but herself. "What the hell did I just hear?"

It took a moment before she started into the parking lot again. By the time she reached her car, she turned back, wanting to go inside and talk to Trevor about this admission. Since when did he have a daughter? And Elizabeth Ward was her mother?

She stepped into her SUV and started the engine, still shell-shocked by the news. But telling anyone about this would betray Trevor. He would never trust her with anything. She heard something he hadn't meant for her to. But why? Why keep it a secret?

Lacy drove home almost without thinking about it, her mind consumed with Trevor's secret life. It did explain a lot, though.

How he was with her. The way he protected her like a father would. It was starting to make sense now. But it did hurt that he never told her. After all they'd been through together. He'd held back things from her before and she'd given him the benefit of the doubt. This time was different somehow.

She pulled into her garage and cut the engine. Staring at the wall ahead, her hands gripped the steering wheel, she wondered, "Why didn't you tell me?" Lacy stepped out and walked inside the quiet and dark house. It was almost midnight. She still wore her cocktail dress and her feet were killing her. High heels hadn't been a job requirement in a long time and now she'd had to wear them twice in less than two weeks.

With her cell phone in hand, because she never went to bed without it now, Lacy walked upstairs and peeked in on the kids. She returned to her bedroom, shedding her shoes and too-tight dress, and slipping into a long T-shirt. One of Jay's. His clothes still occupied the dresser and this was her favorite shirt.

Lacy slipped under the covers and placed her phone on her nightstand. Not only did she reel at Trevor's news, but hearing them discuss Abramov and the idea she could be in for more than any of them had bargained for made her head spin. Sleep would not come easy if it came at all.

———

It seemed as though only minutes had gone by, but it had been three hours. Lacy's cell phone buzzed on her nightstand. She opened her eyes and in a half-daze peered at the caller ID. She swiped to answer. "Hey. What's wrong? What time is it?"

"I'm sorry, Lace. I needed to call you. It's 3 am, by the way."

She slowly pulled up on the edge of the bed. "What's happening, Aaron? Are you okay?"

"I'm fine. Listen, I have a lead on Graybear. I'm not positive, but I think I found where the messages are coming from."

At this, she grew alert. "Wait. You found him?"

"No, not yet, but I'm close. I know it's the middle of the night, but can I come over? I need to show you this."

"Yeah. Of course. I'll put on some coffee."

"See you in twenty."

Lacy stood and wrapped herself in a robe. The sun wasn't even thinking of rising yet and Aaron was still wide awake, working away. He was worried for her and he worried enough for the both of them. She headed downstairs and into the kitchen, flipping on the small light over the sink. Coffee was only minutes away and she waited with mugs at the ready.

Her phone lit up with a text message. She picked it up and headed straight for the front door. Upon opening it, Aaron stood wearing shorts and a t-shirt and an overwrought expression.

"I didn't want to knock or ring the bell."

Lacy stepped aside. "Good thinking. Come in. Coffee's ready." She closed the door and walked back into the kitchen toward the coffee maker. After pouring two mugs, she handed one to Aaron and took a sip for herself. "Okay. Tell me what you found."

———

Sergei Koslov had returned to his own apartment after the ordeal with Will Caison. He knew they could be after him, given his association with Janz, but the fact that the agent had gotten that close was alarming. Not to mention spotting Lacy Merrick speaking to his cohorts at the gallery. Had he known she would be there, the entire situation could have been avoided. Someone would pay for that oversight. Koslov had worked so hard to keep a low profile, but he screwed up by going to that exhibit to meet the diplomat. It was a mistake that could cost him his position inside the consortium.

It was morning in Ukraine. He would need to inform his partners of what had transpired, though he feared the solution would be to again put him under what amounted to house arrest. But maybe there was another solution. He recalled as he peered inside the gallery, that Anton Usenko had been speaking to Timothy Mullins. Sergei knew Mullins well, as the two had done business together in the past.

Sergei picked up his cell phone. "I hope I haven't disturbed you."

"Not at all. I have just arrived at the office. How did your evening fare for you?"

"Not as well as I would've hoped. I'd hoped to meet with Usenko and Abramov to discuss the regime change at the CIA."

"And that is not what happened?"

"No. I'm afraid not. As I arrived, I noticed Timothy Mullins inside speaking with Usenko. I thought it best for the two of us to avoid being seen in the same room."

"A wise decision, Sergei. Timothy needs to stay clear of any association with you or your associates. That is vitally important to the operation."

"I understand."

"Then is there something else, Sergei?"

Koslov was silent for a moment, considering whether to reveal the run-in with the task force operative or reveal that Merrick was on the arm of Anton Usenko. Two details that spelled out they were closing in on him. He feared being replaced or worse and opted to omit the evidence. "I was planning on returning to Ukraine in light of the news of a permanent CIA director. And I would like to discuss how Trevor Axell's departure might influence how his task force will operate from here on out." This was a good plan. Inform the board that the problem is Axell's return to his task force, something he had no control over. "And, while I have been wading back into the political waters, I would also like to discuss that I have developed what I think could be a useful partnership."

"I see. And this new partnership. Is this someone I might know?"

"I don't believe so. She is young. In fact, she reached out to me. She is an FBI agent."

"Just an agent? Hardly seems worth the risk."

"She is the daughter of Alexei and Lidiya Yelchin, though her surname was changed." Sergei waited for a response.

"I do believe a trip might be in order, Sergei."

"I thought you might agree." He ended the call but had only postponed the inevitable. The board would be most concerned about the task force.

———

Timothy Mullins stood on the balcony of his D.C. apartment, one of many he owned in the States. Exhaustion wasn't something with which he was generally afflicted. The man only needed a couple of hours a night and had been that way at least since the age of eighteen. It afforded him the ability to get a great deal of work done. But tonight, he wasn't working. He was thinking about her, the woman who had quite the past. And about why she was on the arm of a second-rate Russian attaché who wielded zero clout.

She was exactly as he imagined. Intelligent, beautiful, and with a few rough edges, though she appeared to try hard to conceal that side of her. He spotted it from a mile away in her forged smile. Every time that nitwit spoke, she plastered a grin on her face and nodded. An actress, she wasn't. At least, not good enough to get past him. Reading people was his specialty, among other things.

He wondered if Usenko knew what he was getting himself into. Unlikely. But he could use the kid to get an in with her again. Just as he had proposed earlier in the evening.

Mullins tossed back the remnants of a whiskey sour and returned inside to the much cooler apartment. He sat on the sofa with its sleek gray lines and modern design. And with his laptop nearby, he opened it. "Time to get to work."

CHAPTER
SEVENTEEN

THE SUN AROSE and the coffee was gone. Lacy and Aaron had been at her kitchen table for more than two hours. But Aaron had found something, which was a good start.

Lacy stood from the table and started toward the kitchen sink with the mugs in her hand. "What I still don't get is why Graybear didn't use a VPN to disguise his IP address."

"He did," Aaron began. "But I was able to trace it back through the relay nodes and track down the initial location before the signal bounced to servers around the world. Don't get me wrong, there's a chance I could be tracking back to another proxy server, but I don't think so. And since we've been sitting here, we've uncovered two more possible locations."

Lacy dumped the cold coffee remnants from the mugs and rinsed them out. "Okay. Now that we have that, we need to confirm the physical addresses and go check them out. Today."

"What about this whole Timothy Mullins thing? You seemed pretty anxious to find out more about him," Aaron replied.

"Oh, I am. But I think I'll get my chance with him soon. The way I left Anton, he's going to want to keep me on a leash. I'm his little dancing monkey. He'll want to keep parading me around until he gets bored." Lacy turned at the sound of feet running down the stairs. She smiled. "Well, good morning, you two. Did you sleep well? I'm surprised you're up so early for a Saturday morning."

"Good morning, Uncle Aaron." Olivia approached him and offered an embrace.

He willingly returned it. "Good morning, Liv."

"Why are you here so early?"

"I was just working with your mom on something."

"Oh." She walked to the pantry and retrieved a box of cereal.

"Do you want me to make you something this morning?" Lacy asked.

"No. I just want cereal. Besides, Celeste makes the best pancakes." Olivia continued to pour herself a bowl.

"Well, I can't argue with you there." Lacy returned to the kitchen table. "Listen, why don't you get cleaned up here, and we'll head down to the office and present this to Trevor. You remember where the guest room is?"

"I do. Sounds like a plan."

"Wait, you're going to work today? But it's Saturday." Olivia peered at Lacy with disappointment in her eyes.

"Only for a little while, sweetheart. I promise."

"That's what you always say," Olivia replied.

Lacy turned to Aaron and shook her head.

Aaron appeared unable to offer consolation because the child was right.

———

The red eye to Moscow was heading in for a landing as Sergei Koslov returned his seat to its upright position. The last-minute flight was arranged by his contacts both in the US and abroad. It was a big deal when he returned to Russia. Koslov was always being watched by one government or another. So it was best to take a late, last-minute flight to avoid others knowing about it.

He would meet with his Kremlin official, then travel to Ukraine to check in at the office, putting at ease the minds of those who might otherwise be concerned by the fact that Trevor Axell and his people appeared to be gaining ground on the operation.

The plane touched down and rolled to a stop, where the gangway was pulled out for them. Sergei, sitting in first class, was at the front and exited the plane. As he walked through to the gate, he spotted the man who would escort him to his destination. The Kremlin meeting wouldn't last long and Sergei wanted to get to the office to discuss the important matter at hand. He was going to have to operate carefully and grew concerned the board might want to strip him of his authority. He couldn't allow that to happen. Not after all this time and all the things he'd accomplished. The tide was changing. The organization needed to take full advantage of the social and economic climate and Sergei was the one to lead them.

"Are you ready to go, sir?" the driver asked.

"Yes. Thank you." Koslov followed him to the parking area and slipped into the backseat of the BMW.

As the driver entered and started the engine, he looked through the rearview at Sergei. "The Kremlin, sir?"

"Yes." He gazed out of the rear passenger window at the passing city of Moscow. The Kremlin, the most well-known of the Russian citadels, housed the government of the Russian Federation, much like the White House, as well as several palaces and cathedrals.

Upon arrival, Sergei was escorted inside and toward the man to whom he answered because everyone answered to someone, regardless of their position of power. Sergei was no different, even if the consortium operated autonomously. The government had its hands in it, the same as all the others.

"Sergei. So good to see you. How long has it been?" The member of GRU, or as the Russians call it, the Main Intelligence Directorate, offered a greeting.

They spoke in their native language for a moment before dispensing with the niceties.

"I am here to meet with the board members," Sergei added.

"As I understand it, there have been some concerns that you no longer have the luxury of operating under the guise of another identity. And that the former CIA director is now involved. That could be very bad, Sergei."

"Yes, but I do have a solution that I have already begun to implement. I do not wish for this to be a concern for the government. Nothing will change. That is the reason I am here—to ensure that fact."

"Very well. Then I should let you take care of your business so that you may return to the US." He started toward the door. "Thank you for taking the time out of your busy schedule to meet with me, Sergei."

"It is my pleasure." Sergei left the office. No sooner had the door closed behind him did his face mask in irritation. He hated being their lapdog. And considering they had no real pull over the organization, it seemed futile to continue the diplomacy. However, he knew what could happen if he cut ties or didn't come when they called. It would not end well for him.

But perhaps there would come a time when the organization could exercise its own power and force the Kremlin to bend to its will. Sergei smiled at the idea and knew that if he continued to control the organization, he might someday control the Russian president.

The roughly hour-and-a-half flight from Moscow to Kyiv was departing with Sergei onboard.

Another flight and it was almost over. After placating the GRU, the real work was about to begin. And Sergei was under no illusions that this would be an easy win. Serious people were after him. The same people who brought down a US president and most of his administration. He would need a silver tongue to win over the board. But that was Sergei's specialty.

Kiev was a beautiful city with a rich Eastern European culture and the largest in Ukraine, but the organization was tucked away on its outskirts, in a large complex that was now quickly approaching in the distance.

Sergei's position was to run the US operations, garner partnerships and interest in the goals of the operation. But here in Ukraine, he was only one of many board members who all had important roles to play. Several countries were represented here and all with the same goal: Make money to fund their various interests.

The driver pulled alongside the curb at the building's entrance. A security guard approached while the driver retrieved his credentials.

Sergei waited in the back seat, and when the guard peered inside and recognized him, he nodded.

The driver opened Sergei's door and he stepped out, only to be escorted by another guard into the building. The security was no laughing matter here. Everyone was searched, even board members. Meaning Sergei was patted down and forced to empty his pockets onto a conveyor belt, much like the ones used in government buildings and such.

Finally, he made it through to the other side and gazed up at the floor above. The conference room was on that floor and he started toward the marble staircase. It was approaching late afternoon, but the meeting wouldn't start without him. After all, they had all convened at his request.

Upon arriving on the second floor, he was greeted with smiles and nods. He didn't know most of these people, but they knew him. Everyone here knew him.

"Mr. Koslov, very good to see you, sir. I trust you had a pleasant flight?"

The younger man who wanted to impress a member of the board waited eagerly for Sergei's reply. "Pleasant enough. Has everyone arrived?"

"They have, sir. Please, follow me."

———

Lacy sat across from Trevor, and along with Aaron, waited for a reply from him. They'd relayed the information Aaron had uncovered about the addresses. The question remained of who would be assigned to make the house calls.

"I don't want you to go, Merrick," Axell began. "Graybear already knows you and will spot you coming a mile away. That won't do anyone any good." He looked at Aaron. "You think you can handle it?"

"I worked at Langley and smuggled out intel for what, like a week? Yeah, I can handle checking out some hacker's possible address."

"Don't dismiss this guy as just some hacker. Whoever it is wants something and what worries me most is that we don't know what that something is yet."

"So is that a yes?" Aaron added. "I can check out the addresses. I mean, I did get us this far."

"You did. This is your find. You can run with it. But keep your distance. We have no idea what kind of security this person has."

Axell pulled up close and leaned over his desk. "Do some recon and report back. Do not engage. You understand me?"

"I understand."

"In the meantime, Merrick, I want you to move forward with setting up a meeting to get together with Usenko and Timothy Mullins. Give us a day, at least, to get a team in place to back you up."

"Got it. What about Will?" she asked.

"What about him?"

"He was accosted last night by one of Koslov's men. What are we going to do about that?"

"I'm still trying to work that out. I have a few ideas, but I wanted to run them by Director Ward."

At that moment, Lacy recalled the conversation she had overheard between Trevor and Elizabeth last night. She hadn't said anything to Aaron, even though the desire to was overwhelming at times. But the fact that he now felt the need to run a plan past her didn't feel right. They operated without intelligence agencies' oversight. It had to be that way to maintain political neutrality. After all that had happened over the past year, she realized it was all too easy for political persuasion to enter into every aspect of the government. "Why does Director Ward need to be involved?"

He studied her for a moment. "Because this already involves Koslov, who has been on the CIA's radar for a long time. Since when do we shrug off help from the agency?"

They'd been working side by side with the CIA and FBI, even though they'd run the ops alone. Lacy was coming off as defensive and he clearly picked up on that. "We don't. I'm sorry. Ward has been nothing but helpful to us in the past. I didn't mean to imply otherwise. I'd better get going on setting up another meeting." Lacy started out the door.

Aaron peered at Axell, both seemingly concerned by Lacy's

comments. It was Aaron who spoke first. "I'll pull up those addresses and put a plan in motion to run recon." He started to leave.

"Hunter, keep me posted." Axell watched as Aaron left and Lacy disappeared from view. He pushed up from his desk and went out in search of her.

She had returned to her desk when Axell approached. "Hey, can I talk to you for a minute?"

Lacy already knew what this was going to be about. "Sure." She followed him into the break room. "What's up?"

Axell folded his arms and leaned back against the kitchen counter, peering at her. "Since when do you have a problem with Elizabeth Ward?"

"I don't..." She stopped, knowing he would see through whatever it was she was about to say. "Look, last night. I left something at my desk and I came back inside." She set her sights on the floor. "I overheard you and Elizabeth talking."

At this, Axell pulled away from the counter and stood with his full weight on his feet. "And what did you hear?"

"I heard you two talking about your daughter. The daughter you two share." She glanced up at him only briefly.

"Oh. That must've come as a shock."

"Yeah, you could say that. Trevor, I didn't mean to listen in. I sort of freaked out and snuck out again without talking to you about it. And now..."

"And now you feel betrayed and you're taking it out on her when it's me you should be angry with. I asked her not to say anything to any of you. That when the time was right, I would talk about it."

"I guess the time was never right?" she replied.

"It sure didn't feel like it. With all you've been through, what we've been through as a team. It never felt like the right time to talk about my personal life."

"It's really none of my business. It just feels like I've opened my heart to you. I trust you. I guess I thought you trusted me too."

Axell approached her and placed his hand on her shoulder. "I do trust you, Lacy. I trust you with my life. It's just... my daughter and I haven't spoken in a long time. Things happened when I was a case officer. Things she couldn't forgive me for."

"What changed?"

"Well, I guess you could say she started coming around after I was appointed interim CIA director. She saw all the good things we did. She saw that her mother and I were working together again. And she liked that. But I haven't had the courage to reach out to her, even though Elizabeth asked me to. And I'm a little ashamed of that."

"Were you and Elizabeth married?"

Axell smiled. "For about a minute, a long time ago. Our jobs weren't exactly conducive to nurturing relationships. We parted on good terms, no question. And, a lot of time has passed. We've both gotten over the hurt." He shook his head. "Elizabeth helped clear my name. You know that. We need her—I need her. So I'm hoping you'll be okay when I say that there will still be coordination between us."

"Of course I am. I'm sorry if I implied otherwise. But what about the guys? Are you going to tell them?"

"I don't think the time is right." He smiled. "And I'm hoping we can keep this between the two of us—for now."

"Sure."

"Good. Then let's get back to work. There are people out there we still need to find."

———

Graybear sat at a desk in an office, the computer screen bouncing his reflection. The time had come to send another message reminding Lacy Merrick that there was only one person in charge and it wasn't her. Not this time. This was no longer a game between politicians and rogue agents; this was much worse. It was a game being played by people with far more power. Ones who could, with the click of a button, destroy an enemy, take all they had worked for, and decimate them. And she needed to be made aware of that. Her team was acting too slowly. Sergei Koslov and the others needed to be confronted. So Graybear would have to be the one to provide the information.

A few keystrokes and Graybear was inside once again, ready to communicate with Lacy Merrick. *"Koslov has left the country. He grows concerned by the events of last evening. Your partner was sloppy. He shouldn't have left you alone. But the time has come to press forward. There are a great many things at stake. If you can't act, then I'll have to find someone who can."*

———

Lacy was at her desk while Aaron prepared to leave for the first address on his list, an address that belonged to someone who lived in central D.C. Not the first place he would've considered. But there it was.

She peered at another encrypted message. "Aaron, I got another one." She shot him a look. "It's Graybear. He's back."

"Send it over." Aaron waited for the message as Lacy approached him. "Okay. Got it." Within a few moments, the suspense was over. "Here it is."

The two read the message and Lacy was the first to speak. "Koslov left the country? What the hell? He was just here last night."

"He took off out of here for some reason." Aaron looked at her. "Must be because of what happened with Caison and the skirmish."

"And how would he have known what happened last night? It's like he has eyes everywhere."

"I'm telling you, Lace, this guy is way too close. We need to shut this down."

"And that's why you're going to check out those addresses. We have to find him now. He's threatening to go elsewhere. Aaron, we can't let that happen." She looked over her shoulder toward Axell's office, then back. "You know what? Screw it. I'm coming with you. I want to find this asshole who thinks he can go around us. Koslov is ours. Not his."

"I'm ready when you are."

CHAPTER
EIGHTEEN

A SHIFT CHANGE was underway as Daria Liski entered the offices of the consortium. One of the conference rooms was ahead, and as she walked by, surrounded by glass walls, she noticed the man known to her as Sergei Koslov. While Daria hadn't known his precise title, he was senior management and his grave expression caused her concern. In fact, at this point, anything out of the ordinary gave her pause. But Koslov was an important figure, which made this all the worse.

However, when Koslov caught her in his sights, she sidestepped into an empty office. Daria prided herself on flying under the radar, and being a blip on his screen was the last thing she wanted.

"As I was saying," Koslov returned his attention to the board members. "We must initiate protocols in place for just such occasions. Temporarily suspend bidding..."

At this, the group bemoaned, and with defensive posturing, Koslov continued. "I understand this is an inconvenience. However, we cannot risk further exposure. Director Axell is a formidable foe. We've already seen what his team is capable of.

Our partners in this endeavor will not stand for greater risk to their operations."

"As I see it, this is a problem for you, Sergei, not the consortium. I see no reason to halt our auctions." Lukas Barkov, dressed in a blue suit, with olive skin and thinning black hair, spoke up. "My associates within the Bulgarian government will not stand for this. They have debts that need repaying. And projects that need funding."

Bulgaria's black market was a booming industry, selling everything from nukes to babies. Crime and corruption were rife in the country of roughly 7 million. As a member of the European Union and NATO, its corrupt government relied heavily on the black market operation to provide its officials with economic prosperity. Never mind its people.

"I understand your concern, Lukas, but if the Americans discover what it is we are doing here, it will be the end for all of us," Sergei replied.

"Please. The Americans know. They just don't care," Johanna Wolff replied. "They are so consumed with their politics and their hatred for one another, that they have stopped paying attention to the fact that they have been weakened. Their ideas, stolen from beneath them. We are scarcely a fly on a horse to them, and as long as it remains that way, I do not see a reason to change protocol."

Sergei walked toward the front of the room. "As a member of the German parliament, Johanna, I would expect greater cooperation. I don't believe your embattled Chancellor would wish for further attention to be drawn to him or his party." He surveyed the rest of the members. "I understand everyone's concern regarding this situation. However, I do believe it can be contained. But I will need to have the confidence of all here in this room if I am to proceed as I see fit. Is there any repudiation from other members?"

The room was silent.

"Then as of today, and until further notice, we shall halt our auctions. And I pledge to you, this will be temporary. Please assure those to whom you must answer. Ghost Nation protocol will keep the prying eyes of the United States government trained elsewhere."

———

Will Caison sat alone at a table in the small café, drinking an iced coffee as the day wore on, the rush of caffeine seeing him through. He spotted Anya Balfour through the window. She was right on time.

Upon her arrival, he noticed her expression. She knew the operation last night hadn't gone to plan and appeared to shoulder some of the blame. "Hey, thanks for coming down. Sit." He gestured to the seat across from him. "I have a meeting with Axell and Director Ward in an hour, so I don't have much time."

Balfour pulled out her chair and sat down. "Look, um, I'm really sorry about what happened to you last night."

"Don't be. You know as well as I do, shit happens on these ops. I made it out okay."

"That's not the reason why you asked to meet, is it?" she said.

"No. When you gave us the list, you all but assured us Koslov wouldn't be at the opening, and yet..."

"He was there. Yeah, I heard." She shook her head. "I had no idea. My contacts didn't mention anything about him showing up like that. If I'd known, I would've made sure you were prepared to take him on."

"We don't know each other that well," Caison began. "And frankly, I feel as though you haven't been receptive to having me around, but I'm giving you the benefit of the doubt because Mobley says you're okay. So I gotta think you're okay. That said, I think the time's come for us to put a tail on Maxim Abramov. We're running out of options. Koslov knows we're getting close. He won't linger, and if we lose him now, he'll disappear for good."

"I don't think that's a good idea," Balfour replied.

"And why is that? You already know he's the top dog of a group of Russian mobsters. I don't see the problem here. We tail him. He leads the way to Koslov."

"I can't risk him running off to his cronies at the Kremlin."

"So what if he does?" Caison tossed back the last of his coffee. "Look, what we're dealing with—Koslov—he's dangerous. We can trace him to the alias, Malcolm Ford. Ford helped fund terrorist operations that my team and I risked our lives to prevent. Now, at the time, Ford wasn't on our radar because we were after a member of the Uyghur Separatist Movement."

"I know all about what you guys did with Shen Yang and the Dalian Company. I did my homework."

"Then you know Koslov, aka Malcolm Ford, is still out there, and so are the people he works with, wanting to harm Americans and the American government. I can't let that happen. He has to be stopped and so does his flow of money. And I think Maxim Abramov is probably a large part of Koslov's operation here in the US. We take one out, we get the other. But I need your help. You know Abramov."

"Yeah, I do. I've also seen photos of his victims after they crossed him. Including my own partner. Heads cut off. Eyes gouged out. You think Koslov is dangerous? You haven't seen what the Russian mafia can do."

"Then help me." Caison leaned in to make clear his point. "Help us get Abramov. And in the end, get Koslov." He pushed back again. "Whatever happened last night doesn't matter anymore. What matters is today and what we do to work together to bring down these men."

She seemed to consider his request.

"I followed Koslov to what I assume was a safe house. That's a good place to start. I have the address. Balfour, I need your expertise here. Are you with us on this?"

"We'll both probably end up dead, but sure. Why not?"

"Eh." Caison smiled. "It's not like I haven't had to consider that before."

———

Aaron Hunter's car pulled up to the curb several feet away from the address that he discovered was where the first message originated. "This is it. 1256 Hoffman Street. What do you think? Should we have a look around?"

"It's owned by an LLC., which I suspect is just a shell company. Probably linked back to Koslov," Lacy replied.

"That would mean that Graybear works for Koslov."

"That was our initial reaction. We figured he was an insider or else how would he have known so much about him? And the fact that Koslov's currently out of the country?" Lacy checked her weapon.

"Wait. You're bringing that with you?" Aaron asked.

"We have no idea what we'll encounter and I don't feel like dying today." She started to step out of the vehicle.

Aaron opened his door. "I really hate it when you say things like that." He caught up to her. "What's the plan? Just have a look around? What if we're seen?"

"Take a breath, Aaron. I'm hoping we'll find Graybear inside, wearing a black hoodie, in the dark, with only the light of a laptop on his face."

"You watch too many movies, Lacy."

She smiled at him. "I'm only kidding. No, the plan is to gather as much information as we can about this place. We'll scout it and go from there."

The residential tower was on the outskirts of D.C. in the area of Reston, Virginia. It was located in an older part of Reston, a good distance from the newly developed Town Center.

"This doesn't look like a place where you'd find someone like Graybear," Lacy began. "Unless Graybear was a seventeen-year-old upper-middle-class kid, which I'm not discounting."

"I doubt Koslov, assuming this hacker works for him, would hire some kid." Aaron continued to walk beside her. "This could just be a VPN location, which is what I was hoping it wouldn't be. I'll tell you one thing, Graybear is good, but I'm better. And I'll find him."

The suburban apartment tower rose to twelve stories. It appeared older, slightly outdated but was well-maintained.

"Do you know the occupancy of this building?" Lacy asked as they approached the lobby.

"Right now, it's at 92 percent. Demographics, college-educated, thirty-something, mostly singles or couples living together. Incomes average around $70,000 a year."

"Interesting." Lacy approached the corridor for the first-floor units. "This isn't what I would've expected either. I'm starting to think this could just be one of the VPN locations." She turned to him. "I don't think Graybear is here, but let's keep looking."

"This is definitely one of the addresses, so I say we need to fully vet it." Aaron followed her down the hall. "So I tracked the IP address to this building, but not the unit."

"And how do we narrow down our search?" Lacy asked.

Aaron retrieved his cell phone. "There's an app for that." He smiled. "Just kidding. There isn't. But I can search for current activity on the IP address that brought us here."

"You mean you can tell who's online right now?"

"Yep." Aaron entered the parameters on his phone. "It'll tell us if the person using this IP address is currently online because it's all based on location. Whoever it is could be at work and..."

"That would be a different address. Yeah, I do remember a lot of this stuff," Lacy replied.

"Sorry. I didn't mean to dumb it down for you." He continued to search. "No. I'm not seeing anything active at the moment."

"Okay. Then I think our only other option is to research the residents. One by one. We could find someone tied to Koslov or his associates. I don't think there's much more we can do from here. We should go before people see us and wonder what the hell we're doing out here."

"Got it." Aaron followed her back to the main entrance. "I feel like this was a waste of time."

"Not entirely. Look, Graybear has gone to great lengths to make himself untraceable. But we have resources I doubt he does. This is a start. We know how he's getting messages sent."

"Yeah, well, we might not have the kind of time it's going to take to track him down."

"Then maybe I need to sweeten the pot." Lacy pushed open the door and started toward the car.

"Again, I really dislike it when you say things like that."

———

Upon Lacy and Aaron's return to the task force headquarters, they were greeted by an unexpected guest. Lacy peered at Will before turning her attention to their guest. "Agent Balfour, nice to see you again."

"Merrick, listen. I want to apologize for what happened last night..."

"No need," Lacy interrupted. "I'm not the one who deserves the apology. My partner, Will, does."

"It wasn't her fault, Lacy. She didn't know Koslov would be there. Which brings me to the reason why she's here now."

"Good. I was hoping there would be one." Lacy set her bag on her desk.

Balfour turned to Will. "Caison and I are working on gathering evidence against Maxim Abramov."

"Abramov. We need Koslov," Lacy said.

"Yes, we do. And this was my idea," Caison said. "Abramov was there last night."

Lacy creased her brow. "Meaning?"

"Axell thinks he could be helping Koslov clean his money. I met with Ward and him about an hour ago. He could be the link between Koslov and this organization Graybear is referring to."

"That does sound entirely possible," Lacy said. "When I met him, it was like he knew me. I don't know. He just kept looking at me and talking about trust. Maybe you're right. Maybe he's working directly for Koslov and Koslov knows what Janz knew. If that's the case..."

"We have a whole new set of problems," Caison replied.

"Wait, who's this Graybear?" Balfour asked.

"A source," Lacy added. "Just a source for intel on Koslov."

"You're telling me you all have an asset and you didn't mention that to me?"

"Until now, we didn't realize you were a part of this team," Hunter said, appearing to defend Lacy.

"Okay, I think we're all getting off on the wrong foot here," Caison said. "Here's the deal. Balfour has far more contacts in that world than we do. We all need to work together to bring down Abramov. If we can do that, we stand a good chance of getting him to turn on Sergei Koslov. Which, if I remember correctly, is our ultimate goal, dismantling his organization."

"Right. An organization that appears to be stealing IP from US companies and selling it on the black market for the potential use against us later," Lacy replied.

"Is this what your asset is telling you?" Balfour asked. "Do you have a way of reaching out to him? It would be a good idea to get him onboard."

"It isn't exactly like that," Caison began. "He's only been in contact with Lacy. And it's been touch and go in terms of cooperation."

"I see. Then what does Merrick need to do to change the terms of their relationship? Because as I see it, that needs to happen if we are to move forward. Your asset could be the key to everything."

"Then what do we need you for?" Hunter asked.

Balfour smiled. "I like you, Hunter. I only just met you, but I like you." She turned to Caison. "If you want evidence on Abramov, then we start with Anton Usenko." She then turned to Lacy. "And I believe he's taken a liking to you, Merrick. Seems you might be the one who holds the key to this entire operation."

Axell entered the bullpen. "Agent Balfour. To what do we owe the pleasure?"

"I asked her here to help," Caison said.

"I'm sorry about the failed op last night," Balfour replied to him.

"It happens to the best of us. Wasn't your problem. Glad to have you here. With your background, I think we stand a better chance of moving this thing along." He turned to Will. "Caison, when you have a minute?" Axell started toward his office.

"Sure. I'll be right there." He placed his hand on Balfour's shoulder. "You'll excuse me for a minute?"

"Of course."

Lacy noted the exchange with suspicion.

"Lacy, we should get back to it." Aaron turned in the direction of his desk.

"Right."

"What is up with you?" he whispered.

"What?"

"Um, Balfour. Sounds like she wants to help. Do you have something against her?"

"No." Her tone softened. "I guess I'm just angry about what happened and what could've happened to Will last night. I need someone to blame. But it shouldn't be her. She just rubbed me the wrong way when I first met her. And Will too. He dislikes her more than I do."

"Doesn't look that way to me. Looks like he might have a thing for her if you ask me," Aaron replied.

"I'm not asking. Let's just get back to the business of Graybear."

"Balfour thinks you should continue working Usenko to get to the Russian mobster."

"That's what I've been doing and this isn't her call. It's ours. And I'm going to offer Graybear a chance to meet. Screw this trying to track him down bullshit."

"How are you going to get a message to him? We can't find him."

"I won't need to. I'll meet with Usenko tomorrow. I have a sneaking suspicion Graybear will be watching. And maybe I need to get with Mullins too. If Graybear thinks I'm getting close to either of them, he'll act."

Aaron held her gaze. "That's what I'm afraid of."

CHAPTER
NINETEEN

THE MEETING HAD BEEN ARRANGED and Anton Usenko seemed more than happy to again have an opportunity to see Lacy. She had ignited a spark, pressing forward on a relationship that could become an inferno whether she wanted it or not.

"I'm seeing him for lunch and he assured me Timothy Mullins would be there too." Lacy retrieved her cell phone and keys from her desk.

"Balfour suggested you bring up Maxim Abramov and see what reaction you get," Caison said.

"Are you sure about that? Given what we know right now, that it's possible he suspects we're after Koslov?"

"She's the expert. If Balfour thinks this is the way to go, I don't think we can argue the point."

"I'm glad you've put so much faith in her then. All right. Can you give me something on him? It won't play well if I suddenly start dropping names for no reason."

Aaron, who stood at Lacy's desk, nodded. "She does have a point."

"Ask him about Abramov's art collection. I don't know. Mention you were impressed with his knowledge of the artist the other night. Find out how he and Usenko met or if they work together."

"Great. So you want me to wing it?" Lacy closed the lid of her laptop. "I need to get out of here if I want to be on time."

"You're taking your own car?" Aaron asked. "Do you think that's wise?"

"It'll be fine. It's not like I'm showing him to my house or anything. Besides, how hard do you think it would be for him to find out my registration information online?"

"Not very."

"Exactly. I don't want to give the impression that I'm hiding anything. And as far as any of them know, I still work for the FBI. I've also reached out to Michelle Vogel in the event any calls come in asking for me or anyone asks about me. She knows what to do." Lacy turned to Will. "You ready to go?"

"Right behind you. I'll be parked on the next block, so I won't have eyes on you. But you know what to do if something doesn't feel right."

"I do. I'm to head to the ladies' room and call you." Lacy started toward the door. "It's starting to feel like this is old hat. Spies have it easier than I thought."

Axell stepped out of his office. "Caison, Merrick."

They stopped just short of the front door and turned to him.

"Stick to the plan and don't do anything stupid. We don't have backup this time."

"Copy that," Caison replied.

"I'll make sure he doesn't leave me hanging in the wind like he did last time." Lacy grinned at Will and preempted his remarks. "Relax. I'm kidding." She patted his shoulder. "Come on. I don't want to be late."

Axell watched as the two left the building and started toward Hunter. "What do you think about all this?"

"About her trying to egg on Graybear?" He shook his head. "I don't like it. I think Graybear has an agenda. He's doing this for no one but himself as far as I'm concerned."

"Maybe. But we're mired in the shit right now. We need something to break loose."

"What happens if Maxim Abramov does know about Lacy and what she's up to? Do you think he'll relay that to the diplomat?"

"I think the only one who will know if Usenko has caught on is Lacy. She'll have to read him to make that determination. And I think this could be our best shot at getting to Koslov. I know you're worried about her. But she's not the same woman she was a year ago. And to be honest, you're not the same man."

"No. I don't think any of us are the same. Not even you."

"Better get back to work," Axell said. "We need to know when Koslov will be back in the country. Have you made progress?"

"I'm still searching the airports, but I'm getting there."

———

The restaurant in downtown D.C. was just ahead. Caison pulled curbside behind Lacy as she stepped out and inserted her card into the meter. A glance and she noticed Will turn the corner.

As she arrived at the entrance, she spotted Anton Usenko inside but didn't see Mullins. "Damn."

"Pardon?"

She whipped around at the voice behind her. "Timothy."

"Lacy. Looks like we've arrived at the same time. Must be on the same wavelength." He pulled open the door. "After you."

Her heart jumped into her throat, not because she was afraid of Mullins; quite the opposite, in fact. But because she was afraid to screw up.

They approached the table where Usenko sat alone. He stood on their arrival. "Lacy. How fortunate I am to see you yet again and so soon." He eyed Mullins. "Timothy, so glad you could join us." It appeared he tried hard to believe his own words.

Mullins pulled out a chair for Lacy.

"Thank you." She felt uncomfortable because neither man would sit until she did. Once they did, she began. "I don't know about you two, but I could use a drink."

Usenko took the lead and summoned the waitress. He placed the order.

"I'll be right back with your drinks."

"So, now that that's taken care of," Lacy began. "I believe we left off on the topic of my profession, such as it is."

"Indeed. You work in the FBI's cyber division," Mullins replied.

"I do."

"And of course, we all know how that led to the complete and utter destruction of a powerful presidential administration."

"Timothy, is that really what you wanted to discuss? My discovery of the truth of the mall attack?"

"Forgive me, but I find it most fascinating."

"Because I'm a woman?" Lacy began. "Or because of the corruption I exposed?" Usenko had been completely left out of the conversation, and when Lacy glanced at him, she spotted his irritation and quickly changed course. "Anton, what are your thoughts on the state of cyber security in the world? Or would you also prefer to discuss the tragedy that had befallen my family?"

"I'm here to spend time with you, Lacy. I do not wish to be a reminder of anything so unfortunate that has happened in your life." He eyed Mullins. "Perhaps we should discuss something more appropriate?"

"I meant no disrespect, Lacy. Please forgive my intrusion. Quite honestly, I'm in awe of you, your strength, perseverance. Never before have I met a woman who possessed those qualities in such abundance."

Lacy turned her sights to the table for a moment. "It is I who means no disrespect. Please accept my apology. I wanted to sit down with you again—and Anton." She revealed a demure smile. "I am working hard to cast away the troubles of this past year. It hasn't been easy for my children or me. I would like to start fresh. I would like to meet new people with new and interesting ideas, which is exactly the reason I'm here today. I am the one who is fascinated by both of you. So how about we start fresh?" She offered her hand to him. "I'm Lacy Merrick. I work in the cyber division at the FBI. And you are?"

Mullins flashed a charismatic smile. "Timothy Mullins. I work in a similar field. I believe we have much in common."

Finally, she felt the meeting was back on track. Her own anger nearly derailed it altogether. But now with parameters set, she could proceed and get the information she needed to learn more about Sergei Koslov. And this time, not alienate the one man who could tie them all together, Anton Usenko.

"I think another drink might be in order." Mullins waved over the waiter. "Good afternoon. I would very much like another whiskey sour." He regarded Lacy. "And you?"

"I'll have another white, thank you."

"And I'll have what he's having," Usenko replied. "I actually enjoy a good whiskey now and again."

"I figured you for a vodka man," Mullins replied. "Glad to see you venture out once in a while. You know, it has been some time since we've crossed paths. And now I hear you've been assigned to the consulate here in D.C.?"

"I have. Only just arrived a couple of weeks ago. I look forward to my time in Washington. I have always loved this city."

"And what is your primary responsibility?" Lacy asked.

Usenko paused a moment. "I suppose you could say I am a liaison between your government and mine. Among other things, my responsibility is to facilitate meetings and discussions regarding the policies already set forth between the two nations."

"I'm sure that must be very interesting. A fly on the wall, so to speak," Lacy replied.

"Oh, I'm afraid I don't have the privilege of attending said meetings. That would be the business of those who hold higher positions than I."

So he didn't have a high level of security clearance, that much he had just made clear. "But you do get the privilege of attending state dinners and such, which was how we met."

"Ah. I see now. Clearly, my invitation must've been lost in the post." Mullins took a sip of his drink.

Lacy flashed a sultry smile. "You have a wonderfully dry sense of humor, Timothy."

"Yes, he does," Anton replied. "Tell me, Timothy, what is it that you're doing in D.C. right now? With your schedule, it seems very rare you would remain in one city for more than a few days."

"That is generally the case, however, I am in the process of opening a new office and am currently overseeing that. So I will be in D.C. for the foreseeable future."

"Well, aren't we lucky?" Lacy thought that might have been a little over the top. Flirting was one thing, but throwing herself at a man was another. And she had begun to feel like she had accomplished the latter. Still, she couldn't dismiss Usenko. Playing off the both of them was growing difficult. Lacy couldn't recall the last time she was required to flirt for any reason, let alone to expose a ring of cyber-thieves operated by Koslov. "I have to say, though going back to issues of cyber security, it has become increasingly difficult to protect information online." She turned again to Mullins. "In your line of work, did you say you were in the data storage business? Is that the new office you're opening? Before I joined the Bureau, I worked at a cyber-security firm."

"I don't believe I mentioned the type of business I run. Perhaps you read it somewhere? No matter. I see that you and I can relate. Yes, I am opening a new operation, not entirely dedicated to storage, but also to providing broader information access to those who don't have any due to the region of the world they might inhabit."

She screwed up. Ward had mentioned the name of his company. Mullins hadn't. Lacy felt her cheeks flush but only for a moment.

"Yes, this is a problem I see in Russia. Not in Moscow or St. Petersburg, of course, but in the rural areas. Access is almost non-existent," Usenko replied. "There are very poor regions of our country which have suffered as a result. I grew up in one such area."

"And look at how well you've done for yourself, Anton," Mullins began. "You now have wealth, power, influence. And all because you pulled yourself up from the dregs of society and hoisted yourself onto the shoulders of those who came before you."

Usenko appeared slightly confused by Mullins' comment. Even Lacy couldn't quite decipher if it was a compliment or a dig. She turned to him. "I assume you, too, are a self-made man, Timothy?"

"As a matter of fact, I am, coming from a background not dissimilar to Anton's. Though the rough streets of London aren't quite the same as communist Russia."

Anton's cell phone buzzed. "Excuse me for a moment, I must take this." He stepped away from the table and walked outside.

Lacy turned back to Mullins once Usenko was out of earshot. "Can I ask you something?"

"Of course."

"You don't think much of Anton, do you? May I ask why that is? He seems to be nothing but cordial toward you."

"There are a great many things you don't know about Anton Usenko. He is not all he portrays himself to be."

"And you know this for a fact?"

"I know enough. You should be careful around him, Lacy. His acquaintances are many and quite powerful. I suspect you have caught his eye because he believes he can use you to his benefit, I'm sorry to say."

"Is there anything else I should know?" Lacy added.

"Just that I would very much like to meet with you again. Perhaps on a personal level and without a chaperone."

"I think that can be arranged."

"I do hope so." Mullins peered beyond Lacy's shoulder. "Ah, you're back. I trust everything is all right?"

"Yes, all is fine." Usenko returned to his seat. "Where were we?"

———

Caison still waited in his car around the corner and ended the phone call. He wanted to move along this little luncheon and so he called the Russian consulate and summoned Usenko to the phone. Rather than speak to him directly, which he couldn't risk, he asked to leave a message but asked it to be relayed as soon as possible. And so his office made the call to Usenko. Getting Usenko out of the way momentarily would give Lacy a chance to speak to

Mullins directly. From what they knew of the man to date, he was rich and powerful and likely had a great many contacts, only one of which was Usenko. He hoped Lacy was able to get more intel from him. Mullins might become more useful than they initially believed.

He peered through the rearview in search of her. Not that he should see her coming from that direction anyway, but instinct left him no choice. Caison didn't like leaving her on an operation alone. Axell already had this discussion with him, but it wasn't something he could turn off. He'd been with Lacy since the beginning. He had worked on helping her find her husband's belongings after the attack. And he was one of the only people who believed her about the Dalian company. Hell, he even convinced Axell to come on board with the crazy idea of a Chinese plot against the US. Turned out, it wasn't so crazy after all. But their work wasn't finished. Not by a long shot. They might not be looking out for rogue Chinese agents anymore, but Malcolm Ford, aka Koslov, had a lot of money to throw around at pet projects. That had to end. And if what Graybear believed was true, that Koslov headed some international ring of IP thieves, then they had entered a new realm of crimes against humanity. God only knew what these thieves had sold to rogue regimes or terrorist organizations. Even foreign companies stealing patented ideas to make a product themselves and sell it for less money on the American market. All of it served to again undermine what the American worker and citizen had set out to accomplish for himself.

Sometimes Caison believed it was a losing battle, much like the fight against terror. Strike down one snake, another would rise in its place.

————

The lunch plates had been cleared and the past thirty minutes had seen little in the way of fruitful conversation. It was merely witty banter at this point, or at least what these two men considered witty banter. Lacy felt it had become more like two dogs vying for territory. The proverbial pissing match and it was time to call a cease-fire.

"Well, I really enjoyed the meal. Thank you so much for setting this up, Anton. It was—enlightening."

"I'm glad you enjoyed yourself. As did I, although I suppose I really ought to get back to the office. It appears I've missed several calls already." He retrieved a credit card. "This one is on me."

"That's very kind of you, Anton," Mullins replied.

"Yes, thank you very much," she added.

"Can I walk you to your car, Lacy?" Usenko asked.

She cast a brief glance to Mullins, who appeared to hold a smile, which was thinly veiled for the truth it held behind it. "Yes, of course. I'd like that. It was a pleasure seeing you again, Timothy."

He stood. "And you. I do hope our paths will cross again in the near future. Anton, it was a pleasure. Enjoy the rest of your day."

"You too." He began to usher Lacy with his hand on her back. "Will you be headed back to FBI headquarters, then?"

"I have another meeting, but then after that, yes."

"You do lead a very exciting life, Lacy Merrick."

She chuckled. "Not as exciting as you might think. But again, I want to thank you for the opportunity to learn more about you and Mr. Mullins. He does seem fascinating."

"You have no idea." Usenko opened the door for her. "He has been known to find himself in a bit of hot water at times."

"I imagine it must be so with the ladies. He appears to hold women with little regard."

"You did see through him, then," Usenko said. "I knew you

were smart." He stopped when they approached her car. "Earlier, you mentioned Maxim Abramov."

"Yes." She had mentioned him only in passing, and she thought he had skirted a reply, so she didn't dare mention him again. But it appeared he had taken notice.

"As an agent of the FBI..."

"I'm a civilian worker, not an agent."

"Of course," Usenko replied. "As an employee of the FBI, I'm sure you've heard the rumors surrounding Abramov and his connections."

"Honestly, I don't believe I have. I work in the cyber division, so unless he's a hacker, I wouldn't know much about him. But it seems you know a lot about him."

"I do. And while he is a very interesting man, Lacy, he is not a man with whom you should wish to become acquainted."

"But you are."

"Hazards of the occupation. I should say no more. However, my goal is to see that no harm comes to you."

"Harm? Well, now you have my attention." She pulled him aside. "Anton, do you fear Mr. Abramov? Are you in danger?"

"I am not in danger. And I do not fear Maxim. He is, however, a very powerful figure not only here but in my country. He has the ear of very important people. So I will just say that any further dealings with Maxim Abramov should be avoided at all costs."

"As a member of the FBI, I am compelled to ask, because we do enforce federal laws, should I inform an agent of this?"

"That, Lacy, is the last thing I would want you to do. I am simply asking that should you wish to continue spending time with me, any talk of Maxim Abramov will need to be off-limits from here on out. I do hope you understand."

"Of course I do. I certainly didn't mean to encroach upon the topic."

"I know. I can see it in your eyes. You are an honest woman, Lacy Merrick, and I do enjoy spending time with you."

"And I enjoy spending time with you too, Anton."

"Then it's settled. I would like to set another time to meet, but I must check my schedule as I am due to fly home next week."

"I will wait to hear from you, then. Have a very safe flight, Anton, and I look forward to seeing you again very soon." She leaned in to kiss his cheek.

His cheeks flushed the faintest shade of pink. "Good day, Lacy." He opened her car door and she stepped inside.

Lacy pulled away and turned the corner, approaching Will's car. She parked behind him and walked to his car, stepping inside.

"Finally. I was wondering when your lunchtime soiree would be over." He noted the expression on her face. "What is it? What happened in there?"

"You remember what Balfour said about mentioning Abramov?"

"Yeah. What about it? Did Usenko say something?"

"He warned me about Abramov. He said I should do my best to steer clear of him."

"Okay." Will furrowed his brow. "So he didn't offer evidence?"

"No. Of course not. They're on the same side, by the look of things. He warned me because I brought him up, like you said. And well, after the lunch, he walked me to my car and told me about him."

"I'm not really sure what you're getting at. What is it that you want me to do here?" Caison asked.

"I think, if we can get something on Abramov, if Balfour can do her job, then I can use that with Anton."

"Use it how?"

"I can warn him. The two of them are working together in some capacity. That much is clear. So if I tell him I got word the feds have something on Abramov, he'll take me into his confidence. And if I get that, he'll lead me to Abramov and then to our target. I'm certain of it."

"That's a dangerous game, Lacy. These Russians, and especially the mafia, they don't screw around. You get that, right?"

"You're going to talk to me about danger? Really? Will, I think we've been through enough to understand that our safety is not guaranteed. I knew that when I signed on with Axell. I thought you did too."

"I do. I just don't like it when you're the one in the crosshairs."

"I've been in the crosshairs since Day One," she replied.

"And what about your plan to draw out Graybear? How does that fit into what you're now proposing?"

"Funny enough, I have a feeling it'll all tie together better than we expected."

"And why is that?"

"Because I think I might know who Graybear is."

CHAPTER
TWENTY

THE FBI'S Washington Field Office was a place Will Caison knew well. He'd worked with Agent Adam Fraser, who had been an integral part of their team virtually since the beginning. And then there was Kate Reid, a woman with whom he had shared an intimate past, though it hadn't lasted long. Now she was at Quantico, a rising star inside the Behavioral Analysis Unit.

Caison had given up his job as a counterterrorism agent at the Louisville office to come back to D.C. His title now didn't really matter. In fact, he wasn't sure he had one. Regardless, the work he was doing still resonated and he was happy to be under Axell's charge and working with Lacy Merrick. She meant a great deal to him, and so when she said Balfour would need to step up her game with regard to Maxim Abramov, that was what he was here to do now because the only thing he wanted was to keep Lacy safe, and while she had taken her own path before, now he could help guide the outcome.

"Hey." Caison stood in Balfour's doorway. "Sorry to drop by unexpectedly. Can we talk?"

Anya Balfour was at her desk and appeared surprised to see him. "Yeah, come in. Don't you believe in calling before just dropping by?"

"It's important and I was in the area." He continued into her office and sat down. "We need to step up our timeline on Abramov."

"What do you mean?"

"I mean, there's a plan in place that involves Abramov and Anton Usenko. But without something on Abramov, the whole thing falls apart."

"Okay. Hang on. You and I talked about getting something solid on Abramov. That's what I've been working on for, oh, I don't know—ever. So to have you come in here and demand that I expedite this case for what? So you can get to Koslov through that weasel Anton Usenko?"

"Look." Caison could see he had once again set Balfour off and it wasn't that hard to do. "I'm just saying that we've been messing around with finding Koslov and now we have a legitimate in with Usenko."

"You mean Merrick has a legitimate in," she replied.

"Yes. And we want to take advantage."

"Okay." She folded her arms and peered at him. "What do you want me to do? Pray that evidence against Abramov just materializes from thin air?"

"Like you said, you've been working Abramov for a long time. What can we do, you and me, to get something that will stick to this guy? He's a Russian mafia thug. He has to be dealing in drugs, money laundering, gambling, you name it. You know more than you want to let on. So why don't we start there? What is it you know about Abramov that you're not telling me?"

Balfour laughed. "Who the hell do you think you are?" She

walked around her desk to tower in front of him. "You come in here like you own the place and start demanding I provide you with intel to help your case? You're a real dick, you know that?"

Caison stood to meet her and was only a few inches taller. "I can't believe you've made it this far in the Bureau with an attitude like that. Do you ever look beyond the nose on your face or are you always looking out for yourself?"

She stared into his eyes, refusing to back down when she finally reached around his neck and pulled him toward her lips.

Caison tried to withdraw, but as her lips pressed against his, he gave in. He wrapped his arms around her waist and held on tightly.

When the moment passed, she pulled away. And just as quickly as she had kissed him, she returned to her desk and sat down. "Okay. I have a few ideas as to where we can start. If this works, we'll have something tangible in the next forty-eight hours. I don't know if any of it will stick, but it might be enough for Merrick to get the warning to Anton Usenko. From there, it's a short distance to Koslov."

Stunned by her unabashed behavior, Caison dropped into his chair again. "Where do we start?"

———

Upon Lacy's return, she sat at her desk, and almost as if by command, Graybear had also returned. The prompt on her screen appeared. She darted a glance to Aaron, who was busy with his own tasks, but it wouldn't take long for him to be notified that the servers had been breached once again. She had a single shot at a reply before Aaron would shut it down.

While Lacy couldn't be one hundred percent sure of Graybear's identity, she knew he was watching her today, as he had every time she met with Anton Usenko. That was the first clue. And upon reading the message that appeared on the screen, her theory appeared to hold water.

"Did you enjoy your lunch with the wolves today?" Graybear had asked in the message. *"Your path is a treacherous one. I hope you are prepared. Because if not, the wolves will rip you limb from limb."*

The short but on-point message impelled a quick response. Another look to Aaron and it appeared she would have a moment to type her reply.

That was when Aaron approached her. "Hey, you haven't said how the lunch went. You okay?"

She stopped and turned to him, attempting to shield the work on her laptop. "It went well. Sorry, I was just checking my emails first. But yes, Will is meeting with Balfour to discuss their options. Any idea when Koslov will be back in the country?"

"He's covered his tracks very well. I'm still running through the manifests in the CIA database. His name is on the list."

"How did you get your hands on those?"

"We have friends in high places." He started to walk away. "Let me know if you need anything."

Lacy recalled their conversation about trust only days ago and now felt guilty, but the time for caution was over. Now they had to jump in with both feet because pinning down Graybear's identity was paramount to understanding if he was friend or foe.

Lacy returned to finish the message. *"You underestimate me. Have you forgotten what I'm capable of doing? Maybe the time has come to end this cat-and-mouse game. If we are truly working toward the same goal, then a meeting is in order. Name the time and place and I will be there."*

She pressed enter—and waited.

Caison returned and headed straight toward Lacy's desk. She closed down the screen as he approached. "You're back. I hope you come bearing happy news."

He leaned against her desk. "I think I do. Hunter, you should hear this too." He waved him over.

"We could use some good news right about now," Aaron replied.

Caison surveyed the bullpen. "Where's our illustrious leader?"

"He's with Ward, still turning things over. Must be a big deal when you have to brief your replacement on the state of intelligence gathering around the world," Aaron replied sardonically.

"I just came back from Balfour's office. She has something that just might work for us regarding delivering a message to Usenko." He eyed Lacy. "If you get the message to him and it passes muster, we stand a decent chance at him running it up the flagpole to Maxim Abramov."

"And if that happens before Koslov returns from wherever he's at?" Lacy began. "Don't you think there's a chance he might just stay put?"

"It's possible, but let's work on that timing. You're right, I don't want to risk scaring him off so he'll be in the wind before we get the chance to confront him."

"And this organization he supposedly operates," Hunter said. "What about Graybear?" He turned to Lacy. "Any messages from him lately?"

"No. Radio silence," she replied.

He appeared to accept her reply and began again, "What exactly has Balfour come up with, Caison? She's been working him for how long and only now has a plan in place for us? Don't you find that concerning?"

"Believe me, she's not happy about any of this. She's afraid we'll spook Abramov and he'll be gone. I can't say I blame her, but we're out of time and I didn't give her an out. That said, she has assets inside who relay intel on Abramov's operation."

"Then why hasn't she pulled the trigger on him before? Why wait?" Lacy asked.

"She's working the long game. There's a strong possibility, an almost certainty, that Abramov is tied to the Kremlin and that's what she's been trying to prove."

"But now with this, does it put her investigation in jeopardy?" Lacy asked.

"It might. But Mobley has asked her to help us and that's what she's going to do," Caison said.

Lacy noticed his air as he spoke about Anya Balfour. It had changed dramatically. The hint of disdain in his tone was nowhere to be heard. The look of irritation had all but vanished. "I'm surprised she's come around. You must've worked hard to convince her to help."

"She knows what we're doing is important. I think I was able to get through to her on that aspect." He looked away almost as if embarrassed, but soon continued. "So here's the deal. She's meeting with one of her informants this afternoon after he's met with Abramov. From there, she's hoping to get new intel on their proposed endeavor to hack into casino slot machines. Their latest in a slew of activities ranging from drug trafficking to importing stolen confections."

"I had no idea there was a black market for sugary treats," Aaron replied.

"There's a black market for everything," Caison added. "Point being, if she gets what she needs, it will provide us with something."

"That's it?" Lacy asked. "Hacking into slot machines is what we're going to use to get to Abramov?"

"Lacy, it's a much larger operation than you know. Trust me on this. These Russian mob guys don't screw around. They're all still connected to the Russian Federation and who knows who else. This is the quickest solution to our problem. We can take it or leave it."

"I guess we don't have much choice. I need to go to Usenko with something worthwhile, something with a modicum of truth behind it, or else I'll lose him."

"You'll lose him and you might lose your life," Hunter replied. "If this is the best we have, then so be it." He returned to his desk.

"What's up with him?" Caison asked.

"He's just getting anxious. We all are. I feel like we're chasing our tails with Koslov. He's out of the country, apparently running some underground cyber theft ring. Still able to finance whatever the hell he and his cohorts want to fund and we're sitting on our thumbs waiting for other people to do something for us."

"I get it," Caison began. "But we decided this was the best plan of action. And I know Axell agrees. Balfour and I get this deal done, you go to Usenko, and we're golden."

"Right. Well, at least she has come around. You sound as though you're getting along better."

"I guess so."

Lacy noticed Will's cheeks flush. Something had definitely changed.

———

The Ghost Nation protocol had been implemented and was so named because of the clout the operation possessed. The board members were comprised of several government representatives from Eastern Europe as well as wealthy corporate entities. They were essentially a nation unto themselves, driving economies, controlling politicians, and changing public policies. But all that had to cease under this practice. The black market auctions that raised funds would halt until such time as Sergei Koslov and the other board members could reassess the risk coming from the U.S. intelligence community. It would cost the organization hundreds of millions of U.S. dollars, but the move was necessary, according to Koslov. "I have to get back to Washington." He began to pack his laptop. "You will take care of things until I can again make contact?"

"I will, Sergei. It will be difficult to stem the tide of anger that will surely arise from this, but I will see to it that we cease operations for the time being."

"And the other situation?" he added.

"Yes. I will see to that as well." The gentleman escorted Sergei through the building and back toward the entrance. "Please, as soon as you know something..."

"I will be in touch. Rest assured, this is a necessary step to securing our future." Sergei walked through the doors and stepped into the waiting BMW.

The gentleman, who was also the head of auctions for the Asian market and Daria Liski's supervisor, headed back inside. There was something he would have to see to before anything else. And it was not something he relished.

He approached the young woman, whom he considered the best of the best, and his heart sank. "Daria, do you have a moment?"

She pulled away from her laptop. "Of course, sir."

He waited for her to approach and led her out into the corridor.

"Where are we going, sir? I was right in the middle of an acquisition," Daria said.

"There are some people we need to see—downstairs."

Downstairs was a place few ever returned. She wore fear in her expression as she followed him. Her eyes darted into the other offices as she walked by. No one looked at her. No one acknowledged her existence. She swallowed down the lump in her throat. What had she missed? Who found out what she had done?

The manager walked on without another word. The elevator was ahead and he held the door for her. "Daria, please, we must go."

She stepped over the threshold and as the doors closed and the elevator descended, she had to find a way to escape because she would not be coming back up—ever.

Daria opened her stance just a little as the doors parted, revealing concrete walls and exposed pipes. They were in the basement.

"Daria." The manager stepped out and waited for her. "It's time."

She appeared to move forward, but in a last-ditch effort, she shifted her stance, slammed down on the emergency elevator button, and while the man was distracted, she bolted past him through the halls in search of an exit.

"Daria, come back!" He was a good twenty years her senior and not in the best of shape. He pulled a two-way radio from his pants pocket. "She's trying to escape. I need help in the basement!"

Daria pushed on, running in search of an exit. She had never been in this part of the building before and hadn't even considered she might need an exit strategy when she started this little espionage game of hers. How naïve to think she could get away with it, but who could she call now?

Her eyes widened as a door came into view. It looked to be an exterior door, but what awaited outside? She could hear people running down the emergency stairwell. They were coming for her. "Shit. Shit." The door was closer. "If I can just get outside."

People yelled for her to stop; large men with even larger guns who wouldn't hesitate to fire upon her given the chance. She couldn't give them that chance. "You're almost there. Run, damn it!"

Inches from the door, a shot was fired. It ricocheted from the metal on the side of the door but missed her. With her arms outstretched, Daria pushed the bar on the emergency exit door. As fate would have it, it was unlocked.

A burst of late afternoon sunlight shone in her eyes, temporarily blinding her. When her vision cleared, she realized she was in the parking lot. Her personal belongings remained in her office, including her mobile.

The massive building was tucked into a wooded, obscured forest. She had no choice but to make her way through the woods and pray she would come out on the other side before they caught up.

Voices sounded in the distance. The security team was gaining on her. Daria's legs grew tired. Her breath was labored not only from the physical exhaustion but from the adrenaline the fear pumped through her veins.

"Over here!"

Someone was there. She slowed to listen and the voice again reached her ears. "On your left. Run, Daria!"

It was someone who knew her name. But how was that possible? There was no time to think, only act. Daria ran in the direction of the voice and, in the distance, she spotted a man standing next to a car. Smoke billowed from the diesel engine's exhaust.

The car was running, seemingly ready to whisk her away. But to where? And for what reason? Was this a trap?

"Graybear sent me. Get in!" He opened the door.

Daria slipped into the passenger side, and as the man returned to the driver's seat and started the engine, she stared at him. "Who are you?"

He began to pull away through the brush and out into the open, where a dirt road was just ahead. "I'm here to help you. You helped Graybear and the time has come for the debt to be repaid."

CHAPTER
TWENTY-ONE

IT HAD BEEN MORE than twenty-four hours since Lacy replied to Graybear with an invitation to meet. Perhaps he wasn't as eager to help as she expected, or he had overstated his powers. Regardless, time was running out on her end. Agent Balfour had moved forward with her plans, and according to Caison, her informant returned with the intel they needed. Soon, it would be up to Lacy to approach Anton Usenko about an impending raid on Abramov's warehouse where the slots were stored. That, they all assumed, would result in word reaching Koslov. But no one knew for sure if he was back in the country or if this plan would actually work. No one had yet been able to track down Koslov.

A text message arrived on Lacy's phone, which rested on the kitchen desk as she finished putting away the dishes from dinner. After viewing the message, she walked to the front door, and upon opening it, she reeled back. "Jill. What are you doing here? Is Aaron okay?"

"He's fine. We need to talk." Her eyes darted left then right. "Outside."

Lacy stepped out into the hazy summer-esque sky. "What's going on, Jill?"

"I have a message for you." She handed Lacy a slip of paper.

She opened the folded paper and began to read. "Wait a minute. I—I don't understand. Who gave this to you?"

"I think you know the answer to that already, Lacy. You're a very intelligent woman." Jill began to leave.

"Wait. Where are you going? Jill?"

She stopped and turned back to Lacy. "This has to stay between us. If the others find out, I don't know what will happen to me."

"Are you working for him?" she asked.

"Him? I don't know who you're talking about. But if you want me to continue helping you, I'd recommend keeping Aaron out of this." Jill walked away until she disappeared beyond the end of the road.

Lacy stood outside, staring at the road in the gray light. "What the hell just happened?" She knew but was afraid to acknowledge it because if what she now believed was true, that meant that Jill conned all of them.

She returned inside and continued to hold the paper in her hands. He wanted to meet and didn't want to leave an electronic trail, so he sent a courier, one who had access to some of the most sensitive information the task force had acquired. If she worked for Graybear, which seemed an almost certainty, then this was how he got in. How he got to Lacy. But that still didn't answer the question of who he was, or why he was offering to help. Her theory about Graybear's identity was still intact, but this had thrown a wrench in the works.

The instructions on the paper were for her to drive to an address and to be there in the next half hour. That alone should have been cause for her to call Axell and ask for backup. But she knew he would nix the entire idea. And he would be right, but that didn't mean she wasn't going to follow through on her own. So much of what she'd done this past year involved putting others in danger. Her friends, her colleagues. And while her own life had been in danger plenty of times, this time, she had the chance to leave them out. Let them stay safe. And there was something in the back of her mind that still maintained Graybear wasn't in this to hurt her. She had to go with her gut.

Lacy quickly stepped to Celeste's room and knocked. She heard Celeste's approval to enter. "Hey, I need to run out for a little bit. Can you keep an eye on the kids and make sure they get to bed on time?"

"I think that's something I can handle. I won't bother asking if everything is all right."

"Thank you. I won't be long." Lacy returned to the kitchen and reached for her purse and keys before heading through to the garage. She started her SUV and backed out, pulling onto the road that led to the guard gates of her community.

They swung open and Lacy pulled through and onto the main road. She was familiar with the destination in Woodbridge but had never been to this particular address.

This was the moment for which she had waited, confirmation of Graybear's identity. But the greater problem seemed to be the fact that one of their own, Jill Goddard, had been working for him all along, meaning this plan was put in place virtually since the moment they were informed of Malcolm Ford's true identity. This breach would send Axell beyond anger. He would be furious and the ramifications of that were unknown.

The address was just ahead as Lacy double-checked the slip of paper. "This looks like a great place to meet someone at night—alone." She peered at the abandoned building, which looked as though it might have once been a restaurant but had clearly shuttered a long time ago.

She killed the engine and stepped out onto the curb fronting the building. There were no other cars, and before she closed her door, Lacy placed her gun inside her purse.

A path leading to the front of the building lay ahead. As she approached the doors, ready to open them, a light flickered on inside and illuminated a small corner of the entrance.

"Hello?" Inside was what appeared to be a waiting area. It reminded her of an old Red Lobster that had closed down. The smell of seafood lingered and not in a good way.

"Thank you for trusting me enough to come here." The figure of a man emerged from the shadows. "I'm sure you must've been worried about who you would come across. I admire your resolve."

Lacy had been validated; her gut was right on target. "You're Graybear?"

"In the flesh." Timothy Mullins bared a diabolical grin as he approached her. "We need to talk."

Lacy studied him, and with a slow and deliberate nod, she replied, "I'd say so."

———

The road on which Daria traveled was by appearances, leading to nowhere. Of course, the man who had come to her aid must have had a destination in mind. But in the growing darkness, she could scarcely see a path ahead and her thoughts turned to whether she had made the right decision getting into this car. Her choices were limited. She could wait on the grounds of the consortium to be recaptured and probably murdered, or jump in with a man she didn't know because he said Graybear sent him.

"Where are we going?" she asked the stranger who sat behind the wheel.

"To a safe place. A place where you can offer your information without recourse. Isn't that what you've wanted?"

"That depends on the cost to me personally. I hope I haven't misread Graybear."

"There are many reasons he has chosen to do what he has. However, you'll get the chance to see for yourself. We'll arrive in short order."

"He will be there?" Daria asked.

"No. He is otherwise engaged, but his representative will be." The man continued to drive.

She regarded the stranger once again. "How did you know I would be where you found me?" This was probably a question she should have asked early on, but when being chased and offered an escape route, looking a gift horse in the mouth was ill-advised.

"Trust is a valuable asset to Graybear. And while you provided crucial information, there was no way to verify if you were planting the intel."

"You thought I was setting you up for a trap?" Daria replied. "Then why did you come for me?"

"We had to be sure your intentions were honorable. We have operators inside the consortium. And if you check your own cloth-ing, you'll see how easy it was for us to keep tabs on your location."

"What?" She began pulling at her shirt and pants. "Where? What did you plant on me? How?"

"Calm down. Be grateful we did. Otherwise, you would be tied to a chair and beaten until you had no choice but to speak. Graybear saved your life."

She continued to search her clothing until she found it. A small, decorative button on her blouse had been replaced with what appeared to be a tiny camera.

"We're here." He pulled onto a long concrete driveway flanked by large trees that appeared to lead up to a home.

Daria's eyes widened. Never had she seen anything so opulent. She was just a hacker. A low-life, according to her own family. And if this was Graybear's home, then she was wrong about him too.

"This is it?" she asked. "Does this belong to him? Graybear?"

"Did you think he didn't have such luxuries? There is more to him than you know. But maybe now you will get your chance to learn."

———

Lacy's fears had been abated, but perhaps she was being naïve. Mullins was a powerful and wealthy man, but he had an interest in her she picked up on almost immediately. And her confidence grew.

"Why try to hide your identity?" Lacy began. "You obviously knew what my team and I were working on. Why didn't you reach out to one of us? Would've saved us valuable time."

"I did." Mullins ambled inside the empty space. "I reached out to you. I couldn't very well come straight out with it, now could I? I am a man running a dubious enterprise and had you looked into me further, you would have seen that. So I had to earn your trust and vice versa. I had to know that your efforts weren't going to be in vain."

"And what about Jill? How did you get to her? Has she always worked for you?" Lacy asked.

"Yes. I do feel somewhat guilty for inserting her inside your team and forging her C.V. She is a close confidant of mine and I trust her. Just as I know you do, and Mr. Hunter."

"Yes, he does trust her, but I don't know that it will hold water after this. She had access to a vast amount of sensitive intel, top secret, in some instances. She could be put in jail for that."

"You won't do that. And certainly not if you want my continued help."

Lacy moved near him. "Speaking of help, what is it that you plan to do to get us to Koslov? Seems you're the man with the plan. Makes me wonder why you haven't chosen to act before now."

"Fair question." Mullins lit up a cigarette. "You don't mind, do you?"

Lacy shook her head.

"Thanks." He leaned against the host podium with his elbow and inhaled deeply on the cigarette before continuing. "It wasn't until the Shen Yang incident that I realized what Koslov was doing." He exhaled and a plume of smoke rose into the air. "And I'm afraid even I have a line that mustn't be crossed."

"And that line is?"

"It's all a good laugh when the only ones hurt are the massive conglomerates too stupid to pay enough dosh for decent cyber security. By all rights, they deserve what they get."

"I can't say I agree with you on that point, but please, continue," Lacy replied.

"When Koslov talked to the board, most of whom I know, about how he would like to invest in ventures that would make it possible for even greater gathering of information, I grew concerned. And then, of course, his arrangement with the dearly departed Casper Janz came to light." He flicked the cigarette butt to the ground and stamped it out with his shoe. "That was when I knew even I could not stand for something so horrific as aiding in terrorist activities."

"I still don't understand why you didn't come out and speak to our team. Why you sidestepped all of them to get to me. You frightened me in my own home. That is an unforgivable act, espe-cially after what my children and I have already survived."

Mullins approached her and gently took hold of her hands. "Lacy, I am terribly sorry for bringing any sort of fear into your home. It was not my intention. I hope you can one day forgive me for that."

"I suppose that depends on you now, Timothy."

"How so?"

"You're a wealthy man. You have the means and apparently the contacts to bring down Koslov. My team and I have been working on a plan to go through Usenko, which could work. But I imagine you might have something more effective at your disposal. And that something we will need to implement immediately."

"I am at your service."

———

Aaron opened his apartment door at the late hour, surprised by who stood on the other side. "Lacy, what are you doing here?" He stepped back. "Come in. Is everything okay?"

"Everything's fine. I'm sorry to just stop by and especially so late. I didn't wake you, did I?"

"No. I'm just working." He closed the door behind her and started toward the kitchen. "You want something to drink? A beer or water or something?"

"I'll take a Diet Coke if you have one, thanks." She sat down on his sofa. "I haven't been here in a while. Still like the place?"

Aaron started back with the drinks in hand. "Oh yeah. Haven't been chummy with the neighbors or anything, but everyone seems really nice. Here you go." He sat down next to her. "So what brings you by?"

"I know you're going to be pissed..."

"Again, I really hate it when you say things like that."

"Sorry, I do that a lot, don't I? Aaron, despite what you and Will and Trevor have been telling me, I took it upon myself to respond to Graybear yesterday. He accessed the system and sent me an instant message. And before you chastise me, I did it because I had a hunch about his true identity."

He opened his mouth.

"Just listen for a second—please. I'll get right to the point. I just met him—live and in person."

"You what?" He jumped from the sofa. "Alone? What the hell, Lacy? Are you crazy?"

"I'm alive, aren't I? Sit down. I need to get this out without you flying off the handle."

"Okay, okay. I'm sorry." He returned to the sofa. "Go ahead."

"You know I had lunch with Anton and a man named Mullins?"

"Timothy Mullins, the rich guy. Yeah." He eyed her with concern. "Please don't tell me Usenko is Graybear. I think my head would explode."

"He isn't. Mullins is."

"Timothy Mullins is Graybear? Are you serious?"

"I am. It's him. And I just met him—tonight, at some abandoned building."

"Well, that makes me feel better, you alone with a rich criminal hacker. Thanks for sharing," Aaron replied.

"I wasn't afraid. Look, he wants to get Koslov, same as us. I knew I was right about Graybear. I knew he wanted to help."

"Why would he help us? Something must be in it for him. A man like that doesn't get that wealthy by helping others. Sorry to burst your bubble, Lace."

"He didn't like what happened with Koslov and Casper Janz.

That was when he knew he had to do something. And there's one other thing."

"Can't wait to hear this."

"Aaron, Jill works for him." Lacy watched as Aaron's expression hardened. "He planted her with us to find out if we were for real. If we had the means to get Koslov. I'm sorry. It's a betrayal and I told him that."

Aaron turned away and cupped his hands together as he rested his elbows on his knees. "I can't believe this shit. We ran a background check. She was clean. I mean, what the hell?"

"I know this is a shock. Mullins has more money than he knows what to do with and he is involved with Koslov and this company he talked about, the one that's selling intellectual property on the black market."

"Upstanding guy."

"Yeah, I know. But he wants to help and that was why he sent Jill."

"Lacy, what the hell are we supposed to tell Axell? He's going to flip his lid. You know that."

"Then we'll need to talk to him and explain the situation." She reached for Aaron's hand. "This is our chance. We can get Koslov with Mullins' help."

"We don't need his help. He's a damn criminal. Besides, we have Balfour. She and Caison have a plan that you agreed would work."

"I do think it could work. At least to bring down Abramov, which is crucial to Koslov's operation here in the US. Abramov helps him funnel money to various causes. We will still need Balfour for that. But you and me, we can run on this thing with Mullins. I need your help, Aaron."

He eyed her hand on his. "Okay. I'll keep my mouth shut

about Jill until this is over. Then Axell can decide what to do with her. But how do we get him on board with Mullins?"

"Let me work on that. I have an idea."

CHAPTER
TWENTY-TWO

THE RISE of a new dawn brought Lacy to the task force headquarters at an early hour. She and Aaron had to be ready to confront Jill about last night's meeting and conceive of a plan to keep Jill's employer under wraps until such time as they could develop an appropriate response to the questions to which Trevor Axell would surely demand answers.

Upon her arrival, Aaron was already there. "Thanks for coming in early," Lacy said.

"As if I had a choice."

"Please remember that we need Jill right now. I know how pissed you are about Mullins planting her here and I am too, truthfully. But like we discussed last night, it has to be this way in the short term. We'll sort the rest out after we get our hands on Koslov."

"Yeah, I got it. Just like I got it last night," Aaron began. "But that doesn't change the fact that she betrayed us. I still can't believe I didn't catch it first."

"None of us did. Not even Trevor."

"That's because he entrusted me to do the hiring." Aaron caught sight of the entrance. "There she is. I'm surprised she showed up after facing you last night."

"I'm sure Mullins gave her the all-clear." Lacy pulled up in her chair.

Jill walked into the bullpen. "I suppose you two have a lot of questions for me."

"You could say that," Aaron replied. "First of all, what gives you..."

"Aaron." Lacy raised her hands. "Let's not jump down her throat right now." She eyed Jill. "We need your help and I know Mullins must've filled you in on the plan."

"He did." She turned to Aaron. "For what it's worth, I am sorry. You're a good guy, Aaron, and I wouldn't have wanted things to be this way if I had had a choice."

Her apology appeared to fall on deaf ears as Aaron shifted his gaze back to Lacy. "First on the agenda is to let Caison and Axell know what you discovered with Mullins last night. And what he wants to do to help."

"We'll have to ease them into it," Lacy began. "Like you, no one wanted me to contact Graybear without them."

"You made the right call," Jill said. "I told Mullins you would. You're a good person, Lacy. Much better than what this government deserved."

She glossed over the compliment, angry at what Mullins and Jill had done to put her in play. "As I was saying, we've got Balfour's strategy relating to Abramov. Do we even need that at this point?"

"Hang on. That means you're going to have to run Mullins?" Aaron asked.

"No one runs Timothy." Jill turned to Lacy. "We have a lot on

Koslov and the consortium, but the more we can tie him to people here in the US, like the mobsters, the better our case will be to shut down the entire operation."

"Yes, but our goal with regard to Abramov was simply a means to an end," Lacy started. "It was a way for me to get an introduction from Anton Usenko to Abramov. A way for me to get inside the operation itself. But now, I'm not sure that's the way to go. With Mullins, we might be able to bypass that entire plan. Especially considering there's a strong possibility Abramov could be aware that we are after Sergei Koslov. We just don't know."

"And with that loose end dangling, I'm hesitant to continue that pursuit at all," Aaron said.

The front door opened once again and Caison entered. "Am I late for something?" He peered at the three huddled in conversation. "Was there a meeting I didn't know about?"

"No, good morning," Lacy said. "You're right on time."

"On time for what?" He set his things down on his desk. "Is Axell here?"

"Not yet, but he will be soon. We need to wait for him."

"All right. If you say so, but I don't like where this is going. I'll grab a coffee, then." Caison regarded them with some suspicion before walking into the breakroom.

"Well, he doesn't seem at all concerned," Lacy said wryly. "I see Trevor walking up." It wasn't until she noticed someone coming in behind him that Lacy sat up and took notice.

"What is it?" Aaron turned swiftly in the direction of the entrance. "Who's that with Axell?"

"Timothy Mullins." Lacy eyed Jill. "Did you know he was coming here?"

"No. I swear, I didn't know."

Axell walked in and held the door for Mullins. "Good morning, all. Glad to see you're here. There's someone I'd like you to meet." He eyed Lacy. "Actually, Merrick, I think you might already know him."

"Yes. Timothy. I'm surprised to see you this morning," Lacy replied.

"Lacy, pleasure to see you again. I hope you don't mind, I thought it best to get in touch with the head of your team, Trevor Axell. We had a rather interesting conversation earlier."

"Yes, we did." Axell patted him on the back. "How about we all go into the conference room and have a nice little chat?" He looked at Jill. "Don't suppose you would mind bringing in some coffee?"

She peered briefly at Mullins before turning back to Axell. "I don't mind at all." She made her way to the kitchen, dismay masking her face.

Lacy rose from her chair. "Trevor, can I have a quick word with you before we get started?"

"I thought you might want to. Let's go have a sit down in my office." He eyed the others. "If you'll excuse us for one moment. Please, go ahead into the conference room. Hunter and Caison can show you the way."

Axell held open his office door as Lacy walked inside. He closed it and moved to his desk. "Boy, I bet I caught you by surprise." He sat down.

"You could say that. Mullins came to you?"

"He did. Lacy, I thought we knew each other better than this. Why would you keep me out of the loop on something like this? You once again risked your safety and that of the team."

"After Beijing, I thought I should handle it myself. I caused most of the heartburn in that situation and it almost cost you the rest of your life. Not to mention Agent Maddox's and Agent Shaw's. I needed to make amends..."

"And you thought getting mixed up with Timothy Mullins was the right way to do that?"

"Trevor, I didn't know he was Graybear. I suspected it, but I didn't know until I was face to face with him." She hesitated to bring up Jill because she didn't know just exactly how much he was aware of. "But that doesn't answer my question as to how you got in touch with him."

"I didn't have to. He came to me. After the two of you met."

"He lied."

"Did you expect a different outcome from a man like him? He's a black-market trader who suddenly had a jolt of conscience strike him. He's not the man you think he is. He's done things— bad things. And just because he wants Koslov as much as we do, doesn't mean we should trust him."

"Trevor, he explained everything to me last night. He reached out to our team, to me, because he wants to do the right thing."

"Maybe. Honestly, it's too early for me to gauge. But I'll use his sources, his intel, and we'll work together to get Koslov. I will guarantee you one thing. When this is over, he'd better be prepared to go into hiding because I won't let him get away with what he's done for the past several years."

"And did you tell him this?" Lacy asked. "Because I would be surprised if he wanted to help with you threatening him."

"It wasn't a threat. It was a promise. And yeah, he knows. And he stuck around anyway."

"So do you trust him? With this, at least?" she asked.

"With Koslov, yes. But we'll be keeping him at arm's length. And I need you to remember that. He's a very powerful man. And if we didn't need him, I sure as hell wouldn't use him." Axell stood. "We'd better not keep them waiting too long." He walked back around and opened his door.

Lacy started through.

"Hey," Axell said. "You don't owe any of us anything and especially not for anything that happened in Beijing. At some point, Lacy, you have to realize that everything doesn't happen because of you. It happens despite you."

They arrived in the conference room where the others waited.

"I apologize for the delay. Let's get started," Axell said. "First, I want to say that as a result of the information we have received from Mr. Mullins, we should consider the idea that Koslov is well aware of our operation, which in turn means Maxim Abramov is aware. So any more ideas that Merrick should convince the diplomat to bring her into his confidence, at this point should be scrapped."

"So we don't need Balfour anymore?" Caison asked.

"Let's not make her aware just yet. She could still be useful, I just haven't figured out how. Can you keep her in the loop without giving away the farm?"

"I think so. I don't know for how long. She's pulled strings to deliver the intel on Abramov's operation as it now stands. She's going to wonder why we aren't acting on it."

"I think I can assuage your concerns in that regard, Mr. Caison," Mullins said. "I don't see a reason why Lacy can't still get chummy with the diplomat and perhaps persuade him to believe she has something to offer to help Abramov. I have seen how Anton is when Lacy is around. There is no doubt in my mind he fancies her quite a lot."

Will appeared irritated at his casual reference to Lacy as if he knew her well. And the fact that Usenko had taken a liking to her. "We already believe Lacy can use the intel derived from our FBI contact that will make Usenko a very popular man with Maxim Abramov. So you're bringing nothing new to the table."

"You're missing my point, sir."

"Then by all means..." Will replied.

"My point is Anton Usenko doesn't see the big picture. I have worked with him in the past. He is a single-minded individual. If she plays up to him, which she will most certainly have to do, he will take her word as truth. And if she says she has something that could help Abramov, he will be more than willing to bring that information to him."

"Our concern then would be understanding whether Abramov would believe she essentially turned," Axell interjected. "Do you think that's possible, given your knowledge of him?"

"Yes," Lacy stepped in. "I can convince him. I just need the opportunity."

————

The private jet touched down on the corporate airstrip and skidded to a stop. It was a hairy landing in the dark and fairly isolated area in the farm fields of upstate New York. That was the way it had to be, though. While flight plans were still required to be registered per FAA regulations, humans were fallible and easily bought off. It was how Sergei Koslov was able to land in New York, where he had just arrived at the late hour.

"Sir?" The flight attendant opened the door. "Your car is waiting, sir."

"Thank you." Sergei continued off the plane and walked to a waiting car. He slipped into the back seat and checked his cell phone.

"Where to, sir?" the driver asked.

"Home, please."

The driver pulled out of the hangar and headed toward Battery Park, where Sergei's luxurious penthouse condo awaited.

In just over two hours, he had arrived back home. Sergei stepped out of the car and approached the entrance of the high-rise tower. Inside, he spotted a man whom he had not expected to see, but who appeared to be expecting him.

Maxim Abramov noticed him through the glass doors and began his approach.

"I did not expect to see you here and so late. Am I to take it that word has already reached you as to the board's decision?" Sergei started toward the elevators with Abramov in tow.

"This is not a decision that should have been made lightly and without regard to our operation here."

As the elevator doors parted, Sergei stepped inside. "If you believe this decision was taken lightly, then you don't know me as well as you think you do." He pressed the button to the penthouse floor. "The former CIA director's team is getting close and we had a breach in the system. Those two combined left the board with no choice."

"So I heard. A breach that, by our standards, should never have occurred."

"Which was exactly the reason the decision was made. A decision the board has supported."

The doors opened to the penthouse unit and Sergei continued inside. "You might as well have a drink with me."

Abramov followed him in. "And what about the breach? Is it taken care of?"

"I have only just arrived. I am unaware if it has been contained, but I will find out." Sergei poured each of them a shot of vodka. "We may, however, have a more pressing concern."

"And that would be?" Abramov accepted the drink.

"The information obtained by the breach and who it was intended to serve."

———

Lacy pulled onto the street where her home lay ahead. It had been a long and tiring day working to convince the team she could take on the task. She too felt Anton Usenko had a myopic view of the world, his world, and who he could use to benefit himself. But it appeared someone had new plans for her as she pulled onto her driveway. Someone was already here, sitting inside a black car parked in front of her house. Lacy reached for her weapon and eyed the front door before stepping out of her vehicle.

The driver's side door of the mysterious car opened at the same time. It wasn't until she moved closer and the man approached that she realized who it was. "For God's sake. Do you have any idea how close I was to blowing your head off?"

"My apologies." Mullins tugged on his suit jacket. "I needed to talk to you."

"Ever hear of a phone?" Lacy put away her gun. "What are you doing here? Wasn't spending the entire day at my office enough?"

"I know you're upset about the way I handled things. Meeting with Director Axell and all that."

"You think? After all the cloak and dagger, you come forward anyway? You made a fool of me."

"I did have my reasons. Mostly selfish, I can assure you. Can we talk inside?"

"No. My family is in there. I don't even want to know how you got my home address. But I think you should leave and we can talk tomorrow."

"I'm afraid I can't do that, Lacy. It is imperative we speak. There's been a development." He walked back toward his car. "Can we please go somewhere, then? I won't keep you from your family for long."

Lacy eyed the front door again, guilt bearing down on her for not going inside. It would only upset the kids and it was too late for tears right now. "Fine."

Mullins opened the passenger door for her. "I won't keep you. I promise."

Lacy slipped onto the passenger seat and peered at him as he entered. "Don't worry. I won't let you."

CHAPTER
TWENTY-THREE

AS MULLINS DROVE along the streets illuminated by the city lights, he briefly cast his gaze on Lacy. "I'm sorry about taking you away from your family. I wouldn't have chosen to do so were it not critically important."

"So you keep saying. I really hope you aren't wasting my time because I should be with them tonight."

"Yes, of course." He cleared his throat. "After we parted ways earlier this evening, I was informed of a flight coming into New York, more specifically, a private jet that was scheduled to land on a corporate runway I frequently use myself."

"Of course you do."

"The flight had one passenger on it, Sergei Koslov."

At this, her attention was piqued. "Koslov's back in the country?"

"He is, indeed. But that is not the reason I made the uninvited visit to your home. You see, I have help. Several people who I pay handsomely to provide me with information on the consortium." He paused a moment before continuing. "Unfortunately, one such person was discovered. I was, of course, protecting her, and she has escaped, but it set off alarms within their ranks. Koslov and the board members have initiated the Ghost Nation protocol. Partly because Koslov saw you at the gallery and was then confronted by Caison, but then when my informant was exposed, that sealed the deal, as the Americans say."

"What exactly is Ghost Nation?" Lacy asked. "And how does this affect our plan?"

"Greatly, I'm afraid," he replied. "Ghost Nation essentially calls for the ghosting, for lack of a better term, of the operation. The auction sites will be shut down, the office emptied of all who work there, including those who obtain the stolen intelligence that is put up for sale. And the members scatter. They return to their own governments. The entire operation is dismantled until such time as the board deems it safe to reestablish operations."

"I don't understand the term, Ghost Nation," Lacy began. "I mean, I get the ghosting part, but the nation? What does that mean, exactly? Who are these people, Timothy?"

"They are the corrupt. Corporate and government officials, mainly. Many of whom hold high positions in their respective countries. Bulgaria, Ukraine, Russia, even Germany. All of whom use the money to finance their own black market operations and projects inside their own countries. These people are essentially unelected officials of a secret nation. This organization serves to exercise global political influence and power by lining the pockets of those who can help them achieve their own personal goals. Stealing intellectual property, among other things, is how they fund their operations. The United States has been oblivious to this fact for so very long. They have no idea it has been happening right under their noses for decades. Well before the term 'cyber' was even used. Now it's just easier to get what they want."

"And you were a part of all of it, weren't you? You took part in the auctions. You used your money to buy influence elsewhere around the world. So why the change of heart? Things not progressing as you had planned?" Lacy said.

"As I stated previously, I have become an unwitting participant in something the organization has devolved into. It has become nothing more than a terrorist fund-raising mechanism. And Sergei Koslov is the one responsible for that."

"Is your informant safe now?" Lacy asked.

"Yes. For now. She is under my protection and I will keep it that way until I know she will not face retribution from her country or yours. This is partly the reason I approached your team leader, the former director, Trevor Axell. The time has come for me to negotiate on behalf of her and the others I protect."

"And yourself, I'm sure." She paused. "Why am I here? We are already working to stop Koslov. We have the aid of the CIA and FBI along with the unfettered resources with which our own task force is provided. I get why you're helping now, though I can't say it will afford you the privilege of immunity. That will be up to the US government. But you have yet to show me, apart from offering information that Koslov has returned, why you have brought me with you."

"I wanted to show you something." He pulled onto a driveway that wound its way through a narrow opening of an otherwise heavily wooded area. "Something you need to see first-hand." He stopped the car with its headlights shining upon a stunning modern home with sleek lines in black and accented with cedar wood. "This is my home. Well, one of them."

"Lucky you." She stepped out into the black night. "No abandoned building this time?"

"I had to be sure you could be trusted first before bringing you here." Mullins started toward his front door.

A twinge of angst shot through Lacy as she followed him. Just a subtle warning in her gut, but she ignored it and continued to the door.

With his keys, Mullins opened it and held it for her. "I know what you must be thinking and please rest assured that if I wanted you dead, you would be dead. And I most certainly do not want you dead, Lacy."

She stepped over the threshold with some residual reluctance. "I hope whatever this is, it's good because you picked a hell of a time..."

"It is." Mullins switched on the lights and the living room, more of a loft area, really, brightened in an instant. "So, as you have already guessed, I am monitoring Koslov through various resources. And tonight, I know that Maxim Abramov met him at his flat when he arrived home from Kyiv." Mullins continued into the home, turning on the rest of the lights while he approached what appeared to be an office.

Lacy followed him, and when he stopped, she asked, "Are we going in there?"

"Yes. This is my command center, you could say. This is where I track the comings and goings of those involved in the consortium, including Koslov."

"It's a shame you waited so long to decide to do the right thing."

"As you say, I'm likely to never receive immunity from this country. Yet I still maintain a degree of morality. And I can safely say that after this, you won't see me again."

"We'll see about that." She peered around the room. "What is it that you want me to see?"

Mullins continued inside and began turning on the computers and monitors.

"This is quite the setup you have here," Lacy said. "Don't suppose any of this is legal."

He smiled as he looked at her from over his shoulder. "Unlikely." He pulled out a chair. "Come, sit down."

Lacy dropped onto the chair, where several monitors were positioned.

"Hang on. Let me just get this up and running for you." Mullins continued to boot up his systems while she waited. "This is from about two hours ago. After Koslov returned home and after he met with Maxim Abramov." He loaded a video file of what appeared to be Koslov's apartment.

"You have visual inside his home?" She spun around. "We've been tracking his whereabouts for almost two months, trying to decipher who he's working with and where he goes and you had this all along? Are you kidding me?"

"Please. I really need for you to see this." Mullins eyed the screen. "Here it is."

The video played, showing Koslov opening his front door. Lacy couldn't see who was on the other side, but it only took another moment and the worst possible outcome had happened. "Oh my God. What the hell is she doing there?" She whipped around to him. "This happened tonight?"

"Yes. Just a short while ago. That was when I decided to come to you with this directly. And, since we have a history now, I reckoned you might be the only one who would trust me."

"We have to tell Will." She started to rise.

"No. Just wait. I need you to listen to the audio." He turned up the volume.

"They're planning to use Anton Usenko to get to you." Agent Anya Balfour stood in the middle of Koslov's living room. "I made up some intel I thought they would buy and they did. Caison ate it up."

"So you've garnered his trust," Koslov replied on the video. "Good."

"I played hard to get for a while, but then it was easy after that. I just gave him what he wanted."

Koslov approached her and stroked her hair. "As long as you remember who you really belong to."

"How could I forget?" Balfour raised on her tiptoes and kissed Koslov.

Lacy appeared stunned. "She's a double agent."

"And it seems she used your friend and colleague quite resourcefully. It even seems as though she has Director Mobley and Trevor Axell fooled as well. Not an easy feat. I almost admire the woman."

Lacy furrowed her brow. "Well, I'm glad she has the qualities you look for in a woman." This time, Lacy stood. "I need to leave. I have to warn Will."

"You're missing the most important aspect of this entire situation," Mullins added. "I'm not worried about Will Caison. It's you who should be worried. You're the one who will be walking into the lion's den with Usenko."

———

It was almost 2 am before Lacy walked through her front door. Her head reeled and her pulse quickened to the point that she was lightheaded. She knew something had changed in the manner in which Will spoke to and about Agent Balfour. Lacy had to assume they'd slept together and that was what Balfour had alluded to during her rendezvous with Sergei Koslov, a man she now knew had Balfour in his back pocket.

Mullins had sent Lacy back with a driver, and along the way, she texted Will and asked him to come to her house. She needed to be back home before the kids awoke in the morning, but this conversation couldn't wait until then. She had to warn him now and then they could figure out how to take Balfour down along with the rest of them. Her unlikely ally, Timothy Mullins, was confident he wasn't going to let himself be taken like the rest of the organization. He was just a player anyway, not an operator. But there would come a time when Lacy would seek him out again for his crimes and he wouldn't get away. However, that would have to be tabled for the time being.

She spotted headlights through the front curtains and walked to the door, pulling it open partially just to be sure it was Will coming up the street. It was and she waited for him to approach.

"Must be important to bring me over here at this time of night. Are you okay?" Will stepped onto the porch.

"Come inside." She locked the door behind him. "Let's go sit in the kitchen. You want a water or something?"

"Sure. Thanks." Will pulled out a stool at the breakfast counter, the place where he had had conversations with Lacy many times before over the past year.

Lacy set down a bottled water on the counter and stood poised opposite him. "I just got back from Mullins' home. One of them."

"His home? What the hell were you doing there?"

"He wanted to show me something, Will." Lacy pulled out the thumb drive from her pocket and placed her laptop on the bar. She inserted the drive and waited. "I need you to see this. Then we can talk about how to handle it."

Will regarded her with worry. "What is this, Lacy?"

"Just watch." She waited while the video played and watched Will's expression turn deadpan. Anger arose in his cheeks. He appeared to feel exactly how she knew he would—pissed off and used. Just as she had felt after discovering what Owen Ballard had done to Jay and her family.

She stopped the video. "I'm sorry, but I had to tell you."

"And Mullins volunteered this information?"

"Yes. Look, I know he's shady as hell and he'll get his, but right now, we're after Koslov and now we know who he has working for him." She touched his shoulder. "I'm sorry. It seemed like maybe you and Balfour were starting to get along."

He pulled away, his chest heaving. "No. I was using her the same as she was me, by the looks of it."

"Will, it's okay to let yourself care about someone..."

"I don't care about her. I care about you. I care about our team and about doing what we set out to do."

He was hurt. His face couldn't hide the emotions and Lacy noticed it clear as day. "Our options have been severely limited. Mullins figured if I went to Usenko now, it would put me in danger. Abramov would be ready for me."

"Lacy, we're on our own. You and me, Axell and Hunter. It's just us again." Will stood. "Playtime is over. This ends now."

———

Axell rubbed his stubbly chin and eyed his team. The 5 am hour didn't seem to have fazed any of them. If they shared an hour's rest between them, he would've been surprised. They'd all been kicked in the gut, even him. "We can't let on that we're aware Balfour's a double agent. We still need her."

"What's the point?" Lacy began. "Everything we tell her will go straight to Koslov."

"Yes it will, but here's what I'm thinking. You convince Usenko that information has made its way to you regarding a certain FBI agent—Balfour—who you now know has been playing both sides. He'll run that up the flagpole because he trusts you. And that's how you'll get in with Abramov."

"You're saying I need to convince him to relay this news to

Abramov? That I'm warning him Balfour will take down his mafia organization to get to Koslov."

"It's the only way I can see that we can still use Usenko to work in our favor. He has feelings for you, Lacy. I'm sure you can see that. I think this could work."

"And then what?" Caison began. "She somehow convinces Usenko that she'll help him and the entire Koslov operation?"

"I don't think you're seeing the big picture," Axell said. "She'll only need to provide evidence Balfour has been helping us, which we can deliver. They'll trust her after that. She'll offer an exchange program, so to speak. Quid pro quo. However, Caison, you'll need to keep Balfour occupied. She can't know we're onto her. So whatever you have going with her, you'll have to keep it up. We can turn the tables, but Lacy's going to have to be the one to do it. After everything is said and done, Balfour will go to jail."

Will looked away, appearing embarrassed and angry he let himself be manipulated by Anya Balfour.

Lacy knew he felt deceived. Though no one had come out and said what exactly had gone on between the two, it seemed pretty clear they'd started a physical relationship. "Will, it'll only be for a little while. Just until we can get hard evidence on Abramov. That's what we'll use to bring down Koslov."

"And what about you, Lacy?" Aaron asked. "This game is far too dangerous. I don't agree with it. There has to be another way to deal with Balfour and keep Usenko close."

"Now that we know the truth," Axell began. "We can protect ourselves. We have to circumvent Balfour and convince these people Lacy wants to work with them. We're too damn close to throw this away. I don't see another solution. This is how Lacy gets in without Balfour's knowledge. She gets in, gets them to turn on Balfour, we get our man."

"I'm supposed to meet with Anton tomorrow afternoon. I can

present him with this newfound intel regarding a spy in their midst. He'll then relay that to Abramov. I know this kid. He wants respect from these people. He'll think he's helping them."

"What about our problem child?" Aaron thumbed behind him, pointing into the bullpen. "What do we do about Jill?"

"She's our primary link to Mullins, besides Lacy," Will said. "I don't know how you feel about this, Axell, but I say we keep her onboard, if for nothing else than to keep tabs on her, then we cut her loose when this is over."

"Agreed." Axell straightened in his chair. "Once again, there are forces out there who have sought out our team to use for their own gains. We've been through this before. And we've come out on top. This time will be no different. We get Koslov through his mafia ties first. Balfour and Mullins will fall like dominos."

CHAPTER
TWENTY-FOUR

THEY ALL HAD PLAYED this part before; keeping the enemy close was a means to an end. And keeping FBI Agent Anya Balfour close had now become a priority. It would be up to Will Caison to do the bulk of the work.

Lacy studied Will as he held the small recording device. "No way. If I go in there with Usenko wearing this, I'm done."

"You have to. It's the only way we can ensure you stay safe," Caison said.

"Trevor, come on. There has to be another way," she pleaded.

"I understand your concerns, Lacy, I do. But if we don't keep tabs on you, and Usenko sees through this, we can't get you out of harm's way."

"I don't think it will come to that. I'm telling you, Anton Usenko is easily manipulated. And especially by women. I've seen it. He's like a lost puppy and all he wants to do is please me." She raised her hands. "I know how that sounds, but it's the truth. He wants more and he'll keep trying to impress me, but he won't hurt me. Unless he sees this." She held the device between her thumb and forefinger. "I go in with this, I won't be coming back."

"Fine." Axell shook his head. "Let her go."

"What?" Aaron's mouth fell. "Are you serious? How the hell are we supposed to know where she's at? Why can't we send Caison like before?"

"Because Balfour could be watching if Caison doesn't keep her distracted long enough. She has no idea about this meeting and we need to keep it that way. Besides, Lacy's going to be at the same restaurant as before. It's a public place in the light of day. She can handle this, and if there's anyone on this team who feels otherwise, then maybe it's best you remove yourself from this situation." Axell eyed the two. "Any takers? I didn't think so." He turned to Lacy and in a hushed tone began, "You keep your eyes peeled, speak your piece, and get the hell out of there." Axell returned to his office.

Lacy gathered her things and started to leave. "I know what I'm doing and I need you both to get that." She stopped and turned back to them. "You know as well as I do that if this were either one of you, the issue would never have come up. Remember that." She pushed through the door.

"She has a point." Jill, who had remained at her desk, chimed in.

Caison shot her a look. "You don't know anything about her or the rest of us. Better for you to keep your mouth shut."

———

Lacy drove to the FBI headquarters and entered the building. She stepped onto the elevator and started toward her old floor at the Cyber Division. "Knock, knock." She peeked into Michelle Vogel's office.

A broad smile appeared on her former supervisor's face.

"Lacy." She pulled off her reading glasses and approached with her arms open. "How are you? I wasn't expecting you today."

"I'm doing well, thanks for asking. And you?" She stepped back from the embrace. "How are you doing here?"

"Same. Nothing much has changed since the new president was sworn in. With Mobley still the director, I suppose it wouldn't change. But I hear Trevor Axell declined the permanent CIA position."

"He did. He wants to stay with the team and I really couldn't be happier."

Michelle started back toward her desk. "Well, come in, sit. Let's catch up."

"I wish I could. I'm only just stopping by."

Michelle stood with her arms pressed straight against her desk. "Let me guess, you're working on something right now?"

Lacy used her index finger and touched the tip of her nose. "I need to ask for you to continue to give me some cover."

"That is something I can handle. Still working on Koslov?"

"Yep. And people think I still work for you. Do you mind if we keep it that way for a while longer?"

"That was the plan. I'll keep it that way."

"I appreciate the help. How about I give you a buzz after this is over? We'll meet up for drinks."

"I'd like that, Lacy. Be safe out there."

"You know I will." Lacy smiled before walking away. She missed Michelle and how easy things used to be. How black and white things were to her. Now there were so many shades of gray, she had lost count. Her entire job was operating inside those shades. And telling friend from enemy wasn't easy. At least in her job before, she knew who the bad guys were. Who the terrorists were and where they came from. Not anymore. Her enemies hid in plain sight right now. Including the elusive Sergei Koslov, a man who was running some underground operation to generate money to distribute to his own personal terrorist buddies. That was the reason she had to succeed. That was the reason she couldn't wear a wire or anything that might put the plan in jeopardy. Because catching Koslov was in view now and she would not be the one to screw it up.

The time had come to meet with Usenko. And pray for the best. She sent a brief text to the team. *"Leaving FBI HQ now. Heading to restaurant."* It was the best she could offer for the time being. Now it appeared as though Lacy had made it ahead of Usenko. She walked inside. "Two, please."

"Right this way, ma'am."

Lacy followed the host and was seated at a table next to the window. It was the optimal place for her to ensure she was not secluded and could keep watch for anyone else who might enter.

She noticed Usenko arrive and the host pointed him to her table. With a smile plastered on her face, she waited for him to approach. "Anton, so nice to see you again."

"And you." He kissed the top of her hand before taking his seat.

Lacy conjured a look of flattery. "I appreciate you meeting with me. I do think we need to discuss something very important."

"Why don't we enjoy our meal first and then you can tell me what it is that you know about your FBI friend."

"Of course." Lacy didn't like where this was going. He didn't seem concerned at all. Was it possible he already knew she was about to lie to him?

When their food arrived, it was Usenko who brought up the topic. "This information you wish to share. You say it could be the catalyst intended to bring down Maxim Abramov?"

"And his higher-ups. I believe it could be—yes." Lacy sipped from her iced tea. "I think he needs to know about it, which is why I'm here."

"Yes, I suppose it is the reason you're here. You do seem to be looking out for my interests, Lacy Merrick. That is something I truly appreciate. And I do hope I can repay you at some time in the future."

"I just want you to be safe and this would no doubt keep you from harm's way as well."

"Your concern for me is kind." Usenko wiped his lips with his napkin. "Perhaps we should finish here and then I think it should be safe to discuss your concerns as I walk you to your car."

"Yes, I think that would be a good idea."

The delay was concerning. Lacy began to feel as though he was waiting for something or someone. However, her only way to handle it was to continue with the pleasantries until the lunch was finished. And that time was drawing near.

Usenko placed a credit card on top of the bill that had arrived.

"Really, you don't need to keep paying for me. I do have a job." Lacy smiled as she pushed out her chair.

"And a good one at that, I'm sure. But please, my treat. I insist." Usenko fell in behind her as she started toward the exit.

Lacy led the way with a measure of strained confidence. She was afraid he wouldn't buy the story and he might not yet fully trust her enough to take it to the mobster. Either that, or he figured out he was being played. Neither was a good scenario.

Her SUV came into view as it sat curbside at a metered spot. "Here I am." She pulled out her keys and surveyed her surroundings. "So, as I was saying..."

"You know, perhaps it would be best to sit down, inside your car, if that is all right with you?"

Her pulse hastened. "Yes, you're right, that would be better." Lacy unlocked the door and walked around to the driver's side before stepping in at the same time as Usenko.

He closed the door, signaling she should do the same.

"As I was saying, my sources at the Bureau have informed me that there is a double agent in your midst. I recall your insistence that Maxim Abramov should remain a topic off-limits between us. And while I respect that, it does bring to mind that maybe your relationship with him is directed by those who hold positions of authority. It is those people who should be made aware of this information." She paused to gauge his reaction, which he seemed to reveal virtually none. "I would recommend you get word to Abramov and then he can do with it as he sees fit."

Usenko appeared to contemplate her warning. He nodded. "This could indeed be problematic, Lacy." He regarded her. "I can't tell you how much I appreciate the warning. But I must ask, why? Why are you telling me this? I know you to be nothing if not a patriot. A seeker of truth. This seems to contradict all I have seen or been told about you."

"I understand why you would think that. And, this is not easy for me. However, I have grown fond of you, Anton." She reached for his hand. "I wouldn't want you to be ensnared in something that frankly means little to me or to the work I do."

"Indeed." He eyed their hands that were now laced together. "You are right. We should get a warning to Maxim and he can disseminate the information to the people who matter. I think you should do that with me. You might not know this, but I am, how do the Americans say it, 'low man on the totem pole.' My words might fall on deaf ears, but with you there, the one and only Lacy Merrick, how could they deny the truth?"

This wasn't part of the plan. Get in and get out. That was what Axell said. "Don't you think my presence might cause concern for them? This might be better received were it to come from you directly."

"Perhaps it would be advantageous for you to establish connections outside of the US intelligence community." He squeezed her hand. "I can offer you things, Lacy. Things that might, in turn, help you to reach your goals. You never know what information could exchange hands as a result of a mutually beneficial relationship."

A mutually beneficial relationship, she thought. It had sounded as though Usenko may already be aware of her intentions, but perhaps because of his feelings for her, believed he could convince her to reveal more valuable information. The tables were turning. Usenko wanted to prove his worth to his people and using her was a way to do that.

But what she hadn't counted on was going anywhere with him. And now she cursed herself for not wearing a wire. Lacy would be on her own. However, denying him now would almost certainly raise suspicions. For a brief moment, she ran through a variety of scenarios and the only feasible one was for her to go with him to see Abramov. It could work. "I think that would be the best possible outcome, Anton."

"Good. We should waste no more time. As we are already together, should we leave now?"

"What about your car?" she asked.

"I had a driver." Usenko peered through the windshield. "We should go now. I know where he is."

———

Caison turned up at Balfour's door and knocked. "Hey, you have a minute?"

"Sure, come in." She pushed away from her screen for a moment. "I wasn't expecting you. What's going on?"

He walked in and sat down across from her. "Just wanted to know if you had word from anyone regarding Koslov's return to the country?"

"No. I haven't. I've been pretty busy keeping things going with Abramov."

"Sure." Caison eyed Balfour, trying to read her intentions, but she was unreadable. And now, he had to be too. "Any more movement from Abramov?"

"Not that I'm aware of. Then again, I do have a lot on my plate right now."

"Sorry, I know you're busy. Forgive the interruption." He pushed off the chair.

"No, wait. I'm sorry. Please sit." Balfour stood and walked to her door, closing it before approaching Will. She leaned over him and kissed his lips. "Been wanting to do that all day."

"Have you now?" He grinned but felt sick to his stomach. This woman was betraying her country and lying right to his face. Will should've trusted his gut at their first meeting.

She held his gaze. "How about we sneak away for a little bit?"

"You know what, I should be getting back to the shop. I'm sorry to drop by. I know how you dislike that." He began to rise.

"You care a lot about her, don't you?" Balfour asked.

"Excuse me?"

"Merrick."

Maybe he wasn't as unreadable as he tried to be. "Of course I do. We're part of a team and she's been through more than anyone should."

"Ah, but I can see there's more to it than that. You feel guilty about what happened between us. That was my first clue." She approached him. "Will, I like you. And I think you like me. I just hope that if you want something more from whatever this is between us, then you'll treat Merrick like a colleague and not your wife."

He was annoyed by her remarks, but he couldn't raise his voice or set her off to the fact that he knew who she really was. "Look, you haven't known me for very long. And yes, I would like to change that. But you should know something about Merrick and me. I was there when she lost her husband. So I do have a certain level of accountability to her. She wouldn't want it to be that way, but that's just the way it is. I don't want you to think there's anything more to it than that, because there isn't." Will grabbed her waist and pulled her close. "I'm not the person you think I am. I look after my team. We have each other's back. That's all." He pressed his lips hard against hers before pulling away again.

Balfour appeared surprised by his sudden burst of passion.

"I hope one day we can do the same for each other. Whether on a professional or a personal level, because I'll tell you one thing, Anya." He stepped back. "People have tried to peg me my entire life, in the military, in the FBI, even now. But what no one realizes is that I do what's necessary to get the job done. And I think that's how you are. So if you really want things to move forward between us, then you need to put your petty jealousies away. I don't play those games."

"I see I had you pegged wrong. I'm sorry. I guess I was wrong about a lot of things. But there's one thing I'm never wrong about."

"And that is?" Will pressed on.

"I know men. And I've been around enough men like you, Will. Men who are willing to cross the line to get what they want, if they think it's the right thing to do. I think that's the man you really are. And if that's the case, then you and I will get along just fine."

Will held her gaze for a moment longer before finally breaking away. "I have to go."

"Hey," Balfour started. "Come over tonight."

Will cast his sights upward, as if considering the request. "I can do that." He opened the door. "Just as soon as I make sure my team doesn't need me." He closed the door behind him.

Balfour started back to her desk. "I figured you'd say that."

CHAPTER
TWENTY-FIVE

WITH HER EYES fixed on the road ahead, Lacy continued the drive to see Maxim Abramov. According to Usenko, he had a home in a suburb of Maryland, which was about an hour away from where they were now. Abramov stayed there when he had business in D.C. Otherwise, he was in his apartment in Manhattan, overseeing a multi-million-dollar illegal operation.

Lacy was fearful about how Abramov would take her unexpected presence. Usenko seemed to believe he could convince him that she could offer legitimate intelligence and didn't appear concerned, but then again, he might have reason not to be. Like maybe this was a set up and she was about to become the prey.

"We must be getting close now," Lacy said. "Are you sure he's good with this? Meeting me on short notice?"

"I informed him this would be an advantageous meeting. I have his trust, I assure you."

There was no way to contact anyone on her team. Maybe on arrival, she could find a way to get a message to one of them, but not right now and not in front of Usenko. They would have no idea where she was headed. For that matter, she didn't really know either. She had to trust the man sitting next to her. Trust wasn't her strong suit anymore.

"You're a remarkable woman, Lacy." Usenko continued to gaze through the windshield of her SUV. "Since we were first introduced, I learned a little about your history and your run-ins with governments, both foreign and domestic."

"As I said, I'm only interested in the truth," she replied.

"I do hope that applies to all instances."

She creased her brow. "Of course it does. I don't pick and choose which truths I reveal. This is the only reason I agreed to go with you today. I want to help keep you out of harm's way."

Usenko pointed his finger at the road ahead. "Make the next right."

This was it. She was going to meet Abramov, the east coast Russian mob boss with ties to Sergei Koslov. The loose end she needed to cut. He was the last of the ties to Casper Janz and the Dalian Company. Take him down, take down his entire organization. That was her goal. But this was an unplanned expedition and if she couldn't pull this off, there was no chance she would get out alive.

"You can stop here." Usenko unbuckled his belt. "Someone will be out in a moment. They'll have seen us arrive."

Lacy stopped the car. *Just convince Abramov of what I can give him and he'll take me into his confidence,* she thought. Right now, all she cared about was getting home to her kids. Whatever happened after that, getting Koslov and all the rest didn't matter. Not right now. She made a mistake getting into the car with Usenko. Now she had to find a way out.

She spotted two men approaching her car. One of them opened her door and she smiled. "Good afternoon." But before she could continue, Usenko spoke up.

"Mr. Abramov is expecting us."

"Of course, sir." The man stepped aside and allowed Lacy to exit her car.

Usenko followed and both were led to a grand entrance of the elegant home. "It is best if you let me lead the conversation until such time as I ask you to elaborate on what you discovered."

"I understand," Lacy replied. No weapon, a cell phone in her purse that would most likely be confiscated at any moment, and she was about to enter the home of a dangerous mafia leader to relay valuable news in hopes of gaining his trust. Piece of cake.

The door opened and the two were escorted inside the massive foyer. Maxim Abramov, in his bespoke suit and expensive shoes, approached them. He appeared as a hackneyed character from a bad gangster movie.

"Welcome." Abramov opened his arms wide. "I can't tell you what an honor it is to see you again, Mrs. Merrick. May I call you Lacy?"

"Of course. Mr. Abramov, pleasure to see you again too. Our previous meeting was all too brief."

"Please. No need for formalities here. Call me Maxim." He turned to Usenko. "Anton, good to see you, my friend. Both of you, please, come in. We should have a drink." He led the way to a sitting room that was overly stylized to look like something out of *Downton Abbey*.

Lacy looked on as they entered the room. But what she searched for was an escape route.

"Lacy, you look nervous." Abramov stood at the bar and poured drinks. "Don't be. From what Anton has told me, you are an ally. And I should be grateful you are here."

"I don't know if grateful is the right word." She peered at Usenko. "As I mentioned to Anton, my interests lay beyond petty crimes."

Abramov's expression hardened and he stopped in his tracks. "You think what I do is simply petty crimes?"

"No. Of course not. Forgive me. I mean no offense."

Abramov smiled as he grabbed the shot glasses and handed them to Lacy and Anton. "I like you, Lacy. We should toast." He raised his glass. "To a new and interesting friendship with the formidable Lacy Merrick."

———

"Balfour's placated, for now. I'm supposed to meet her later, too." Caison leaned against Axell's office door with concern masking his face. "It's been too long, Axell. I should've gone there with her."

"After what happened with Koslov, if you had been there and were marked, it would've been over. All of it." Axell pulled upright in his chair.

"We haven't heard from her." Caison held a measure of guilt in his eyes. "It's been almost two hours. We need to track her cell to get a location."

Axell's expression mirrored Caison's. "I already had Hunter try that. Her cell's been turned off. The only logical assumption is that she's with Usenko and he led her somewhere, possibly to Abramov, which could mean she convinced him..."

"Or she didn't," Caison moved in and sat down.

"We're going to have to act. I'm not getting a good feeling about any of this."

Hunter appeared in the doorway. "Still no word?"

Axell shook his head.

"I did say this was a bad idea, especially letting her go without a wire. But I can tell you that her car has been located." Hunter continued into the office and sat down next to Caison. "With Jill's help, we just got a track on her car's GPS. She's in

Maryland. I have an address. It's a house owned by a shell company."

Axell appeared relieved by the news. "If I were a betting man, I'd say that must be where Abramov is holed up. Usenko took her straight to him."

"Son of a bitch," Caison said.

Axell turned to Hunter. "Keep your eyes glued to that GPS. I want to know when she leaves if she leaves. No one's going to harm her. She's far too valuable and Abramov wouldn't take the chance." Axell sounded as though he wasn't convinced of his own words. "If we haven't heard anything from her in the next 30 minutes, let's roll out."

"Finally, a plan I can get behind," Caison said.

"Not you, Caison. You need to stay close to Balfour. Hunter and I can follow Lacy if it comes down to that. I know you want to be there too, but if Balfour gets a whiff of what we're up to, or finds out we know all about her, she might unleash hell on Lacy."

Caison appeared ready to argue the point but conceded. "Fine. I'll keep her occupied." He began to leave but stopped at the doorway where Hunter now stood. "Don't you dare lose track of her car."

"As if I need you to tell me that."

The two exchanged rivalrous glances as Caison left.

Hunter soon returned his attention to Axell. "There's something else. I have a current location on Koslov."

"You found him?"

"Mullins did. He just contacted Jill while we were tracking down the GPS coordinates. Koslov is in New York, at an apartment in Battery Park. Now that we know where Lacy is, are we worried he'll join Abramov? And what do you want to do about that?"

Axell leaned back in his chair and folded his arms across his chest. "We can't take our eyes off Merrick. Koslov, if he was told that Abramov has her, there's a chance he'll want to take action."

"Do we need to ask Ward or Mobley for some backup?" Aaron asked. "We have no idea how many people Abramov has at his place. And I'm telling you, Axell, it's a damn compound. I'm sure it's heavily guarded."

"Here's what I'm thinking," Axell began. "The address Lacy's at is Abramov's, is that correct?"

"I'm almost certain. He's listed as a managing director of the company that owns it. So it's a logical assumption."

"Okay. So she's there, with Abramov, relaying the news of a double agent at the FBI." He paused to consider the options.

"Axell, even if he believes her, what guarantees do we have that he'll let her go?"

"There's no guarantee, except we have to believe he'll take her at her word if she's proven right. Then he'll let her go. We'll worry about what happens after that once she's back with us."

"We have to trust she's already relayed the intel and he bought it. He may not have given her the chance to tell her story," Hunter said.

Axell looked at him with anger hardening his features. "Keep eyes on her car. I'll give it 30 minutes. No news, then we're going to Maryland. We'll enlist Mullins's help and it'll be part of the deal we make with him if he wants to remain a free man."

———

Maxim Abramov was the type of man who used intimidation as a scare tactic. The personality trait didn't come as a surprise to Lacy. He was a mob boss. But he didn't appear to use the same tactics with her. As their conversation progressed, he appeared to soften in her presence. Still, she had yet to reveal the purpose of her visit. That would be the true test of her mettle.

"I suppose we should get down to the reason why I'm here." Lacy looked to Anton for confirmation.

"Yes. Lacy comes with vital information regarding the FBI."

"I see," Abramov replied. "And you do work for the FBI, is that correct, Lacy?"

"I do."

"Then what is in this for you? Why would you deliver news that could hinder your own organization?"

"As I mentioned to Anton, and he seemed to agree, my current position entails work mainly outside the US, working inside the parameters of foreign nations that have sought to propel a rise in terrorist activity. What the FBI does internally has no bearing on my job, however, should we come to an agreement, maybe there could be something in this for the both of us."

"Ah, I see now. What is it you Americans say? Quid pro quo?"

"Something like that," Lacy added. "I give you information, you, in turn, give me information."

Abramov tossed back another shot before returning to the sofa where Usenko and Lacy sat. He licked his lips and tugged on his suit jacket. "Do you know exactly what it is that I do, Lacy?"

She cast her gaze briefly at Usenko before finding her confidence again. "I believe I do. At least so far as the intel I've received suggests."

"I don't believe you do, but tell me, what is it that you think I should know?"

This was the moment Lacy had to pull off. And for a split second, she was reminded of Beijing, although she felt confident this time would end much worse should she be unable to pull it off. These were not Chinese police. These men were Russian mafia and a shot to the head would mean nothing to them. Killing a federal agent, or in her case, a presidentially appointed task force agent, was meaningless.

"I've been informed through a contact at the Washington Field Office that an agent who has befriended someone in your organization is playing both sides of the coin. She is relaying information intended to help you, but in fact, has plans to use that information to destroy your operation."

"A spy? In our ranks?" Abramov asked.

"I don't know any more than that except I do know her identity. That information I can offer once you and I have reached an agreement."

Abramov turned to Usenko. "She is quite the find, Anton. This could prove beneficial. However, there is one thing I must ask." At this, he turned back to Lacy. "I have learned through my own resources that you, Lacy Merrick, are not who you appear to be. And this valuable information is actually designed to bring you into my confidence. Well played, but there are many cogs in this machine. And I'm afraid, Lacy Merrick, you are not one of them."

———

Caison held his phone to his ear. "Axell, I need to be there. I've done as you asked. In fact, I'm here at WFO now and I just met with Balfour again. She suspects nothing. I gave her nothing. I asked Fraser to put a team on her in the event Koslov's people come because we've just put a huge target on her back. Please. There's no more time to waste. You and I both know what will happen if Lacy blinks first. If you think there's even the slightest possibility she did, we need to get her. Now."

"Then get back here because the time's come to bring her home." Axell ended the call.

Caison returned his phone to his pocket and marched through to the lobby of the WFO.

There was no doubt Abramov would have security everywhere, which presented another set of problems. This whole thing could have been avoided had Axell listened to him in the first place. He should have made Lacy wear the damn recorder. At least they would know if the deal was going south. Now all they knew was that they had to get to her before Balfour figured things out. Or Abramov, for that matter.

He drove back to the shop where Axell and Hunter prepared to leave. Upon arrival, they had a plan in place. Caison approached them while Axell relayed the details.

"So far, we have no idea if Lacy's in trouble. But enough time has passed to suggest something has gone awry. That said," Axell eyed each of them, "it's best if we extract her now."

"And how do we plan to do that without putting her at risk?" Caison asked.

"With Mullins' help," Hunter replied. "Axell's already been in contact with him and he's agreed to provide surveillance and help with a distraction for the security around the building where Abramov is holed up."

"And are we meeting with Mullins?" Caison asked.

"Yes, you are." Mullins entered the bullpen. "Are we ready? We're going to lose daylight if we don't leave now. We don't know what her situation is and it's better to get her out of there before dark." He thumbed over his shoulder. "I have arranged transport. We should leave now. But not before I make something clear. I did warn you this could happen."

CHAPTER
TWENTY-SIX

THE BEADS of sweat that gathered at Lacy's neckline were the only indication of her distress at the present situation. Fortunately, it was not visible to anyone else, including the man who sat next to her, Anton Usenko. He appeared confused by Abramov's statement and both men set their sights on her, waiting for her to clarify her position or face the consequences. She had always been a quick thinker, now it seemed her life could depend on that talent.

Lacy revealed a calculated smile. "I'm afraid I'll have to disagree with you, Maxim. I may not be a cog in your machine, but I am the fuel that will help keep your machine running. Without my efforts, it will only be a matter of time before the Bureau will have the evidence they need to file charges with the help of the agent. And, in fact, I have the ability to expedite such efforts, should I feel the least bit concerned that I am not being treated fairly after our arrangements are made."

Abramov laughed. "I do appreciate a confident woman. Perhaps I should have sought you out much sooner. I suppose I do have Anton to thank for bringing you to my doorstep." He eyed the young Russian attaché before turning back. "Lacy, I would love to give you a tour of the house." He placed his arm around her and ushered her into the corridor. "It isn't much, but I like it."

Usenko was left behind. And as Lacy peered over her shoulder, she spotted two men flank him. Her heart dropped into her stomach as the look of fear masked his face. Something had gone wrong. It seemed Abramov hadn't believed her after all, and now Usenko might pay the price for making the introduction. However, she had to continue to play along and figure another way out.

———

Timothy Mullins opened the door to the home where he had shown Lacy the critical footage of Agent Anya Balfour side by side with Sergei Koslov. He led them inside.

"We don't have much time," Axell began. "Do you have eyes on her?"

The men walked into the modern home carved into the woods on the outskirts of Metro D.C.

"As a businessman, I have kept close relations with the partners associated with the consortium. Maxim Abramov's ties to the Russian mafia aren't important to me. What is important are his ties to Sergei Koslov. So my interest in Abramov only extends to his dealings with that end. Meaning yes, I have satellite imagery on Abramov's home, however, I have nothing inside."

"When did she go in?" Caison asked as they stood inside the foyer.

"About ninety minutes ago. Usenko accompanied her and she was driving her own vehicle. It still sits outside Abramov's home."

"We have to leave now," Hunter began. "How long will it take us to get there and how many people can we get to assist?"

"I'm not sure what sort of operation you think I run, Mr.

Hunter, but I have no need to employ hired hitmen. Nor have I amassed some sort of army. We are, in fact, on our own."

"What can you offer us then, Mullins?" Axell began, "Because you are wasting our time at present."

"I can offer continued surveillance of the exterior of the property. Activity coming and going, and if you give me enough time, I can get something set up on the interior. I can hack into the CCTV, though it will only be temporary so as not to be detected. It will allow you to gather enough information on his security detail that will enable you to plan your extraction. Which is why, I assume, we're all here."

"How long?" Caison asked.

"Ten, perhaps fifteen minutes."

"That's too long." He turned to Axell and Hunter. "Look, I think we're just wasting time if we all sit here and wait for Mullins to hack into Abramov's system. I'll go now and we can maintain radio contact. You can let me know what I'll be up against." Caison started toward the door.

"Wait," Axell demanded. "We are going there as a team. I won't see any one of us try to be the hero, including you, Caison."

He whipped around. "Too bad you didn't think about that before you sent Lacy on her own. You said she could handle it."

"There was no way of knowing Usenko would insist on taking her to Abramov. That wasn't how it was supposed to go. We don't know what's happening and we're going there because there's a chance her cover could be in jeopardy. We're going there because she's been there too long. And I'll be damned if I'm not prepared to get her out of there." Axell turned his attention to Mullins. "Do what you need to do and be damn quick about it."

Mullins nodded and pressed a button on the wall that unlocked the very room Lacy had been shown, the surveillance room.

"What the hell is this?" Hunter started inside. "Who the hell are you watching?"

"Anyone who could be a threat to me or my company," Mullins replied before casting a wary glance at Axell. "Is there any chance you could forget you saw this?"

"So long as Merrick comes back safely, I didn't see anything," Axell said.

Mullins sat at one of the desks and got to work. "Mr. Hunter, this is your profession too, am I right? If we're in on this together, then we should do this together. The quicker we detail what type of satellite he's using, the quicker we'll gain access."

Hunter approached and sat down next to him. "I couldn't agree more."

―――――

Lacy continued until Abramov reached a room that appeared to be his office. She hadn't heard any sounds coming from elsewhere in the house, meaning she had to assume those men had taken Usenko outside to take care of whatever it was they were to take care of.

"Lacy, come and have a seat. We have much to discuss." Abramov walked inside and to his ornate cherry wood desk.

Lacy followed along, still maintaining an outward calm, but it was getting harder to achieve. She sat down. "Will Anton be joining us soon?"

Abramov sat in his tufted leather chair. "Oh, I don't think so. This is something only you and I should discuss."

"You should know that Anton has been nothing but loyal to you. If this is about me, and my intentions, then it should stay that way."

Abramov laced his fingers together in front of his chest, his elbows resting on the arms of the chair. "I admire your concern for Anton. However, I have found his interest in you appears to have outweighed his common sense."

"How is that?" Lacy wanted to keep him talking. Because if they were talking, she was alive.

"Now the last thing I believe you are, Lacy Merrick, is ignorant. And certainly not in the ways of men—men who have taken a fancy to you, as I'm certain Anton had."

Had. Abramov just used "had." This wasn't a good sign. "Regardless of whatever perceived feelings you think Anton might have toward me, I can assure you, from what I've seen, he aspires to be more like you."

"Well, maybe it no longer matters. What matters now is that you are here and the time has come for me to decide what it is I should do."

She was going to have to again be quick on her feet. "As I said before, I have zero interest in your business activities. That said, I do believe there could be a benefit to both of us if you choose to accept a working relationship between us. I have access to information I don't think you do."

"I imagine that is true. The problem I see with that is, I would be asked to expose those people who hold far more power than I do. How long do you assume I would last after that? Do you truly believe the Russian government has no interest in my activities? And yet that doesn't seem to appeal to you."

"Not unless they're funding terrorist organizations. In which case, I would be more than happy to take them down," Lacy replied.

At this, Abramov laughed whole-heartedly. "For a woman, you have great big balls. I like that."

Lacy grew tired of the back and forth. She needed to bring this to a conclusion because, one way or another, she had to know if she was going to get out of here alive. "Do you want my help or not, Maxim?"

———

Caison eyed the time first and then turned to Axell. "We need to go."

"Just hold tight," Hunter began. "We're in. We just need to get the layout."

Axell approached them. "You're in?" He leaned over Aaron's chair. "How many guys they got? What are we looking at?"

"Hang on," Aaron said. "I'm just getting a good look around now." He turned to Mullins. "You seeing what I'm seeing?"

"I am. It appears as though they have security at all the entrances, which stands to reason."

"And is also going to be our biggest hurdle," Caison said as he joined them.

"Indeed. However, as I said, a diversion is what's needed in this instance, and that, my good man, is where I can be of assistance."

"What kind of diversion are we talking about?" Axell asked.

"I can kill power to the home. That would cause quite the scramble."

"And it would force his security detail to shuttle Abramov elsewhere to keep him safe. And that may or may not include Lacy," Caison replied. "Let's try again."

"Fair play. I could initiate a coordinated outage within the area that would create concern along the exterior of the property. They aren't completely isolated and the disturbance could bring out the looky-loos."

"I'd like to look at something with a little more impact." Axell eyed Mullins. "What can you do to his facilities? Particularly something near his home, if there is one. Something that would warrant his security's attention."

"There is something else I hadn't considered, but that along those same lines could be quite effective." Mullins typed on his keyboard until it seemed he had reached his destination. "Here." He pointed to the screen.

The team congregated around Mullins and stared at the monitor. He continued. "This transformer here and this one here. Blowing these should make a considerable noise, kill the power around the area, and be a big enough diversion to attract the attention of his security."

"I like it. That's what we need to do, then," Axell said. "Now that we see what we're up against, the time to act is now." He turned again to Mullins. "Can I ask one last favor?"

"I assume you'd like a lift?"

"You do have air support on standby," Axell replied.

"I do. I can have you there in under thirty minutes."

"Then what are we waiting for?" Caison asked.

———

Lacy waited for Abramov to say something, but he only stared at her—through her, as though he was waiting for her to crack. But she wouldn't. Not in front of this man, not in front of anyone. There was no going back to the woman she was only one short year ago. That woman would have crumbled under the weight of a terrifying man like Maxim Abramov; a killer, a mafia boss, and a man she knew was linked to Sergei Koslov, and he was her target. Lacy would stop at nothing to get to Koslov and that meant her resolve could not waver. Not now. Not ever.

"This name and this help you are so willing to provide, what guarantees can you offer me?" Abramov asked. "And what do you want in return?"

"I can guarantee this agent will never again see the light of day. And I can guarantee you will be able to continue your operations, unaffected, so long as it doesn't involve foreign funding.

"Terrorist organizations, I assume you mean."

"Yes. And as far as what I want in return, I want Sergei Koslov. I want to end his black-market support of terrorist activity. I want to end the theft of US intellectual property." She leaned in to make clear her point. "You give me Koslov and I'll give you guaranteed freedom."

Abramov pulled back in his chair and crossed his arms. "You want Sergei Koslov."

"I do."

The door to Abramov's office opened. Sergei Koslov stepped inside. "Lacy Merrick. I was wondering when our paths might cross."

Abramov eyed her. "You see, I do not need the help of a former FBI employee. And now you work for a task force led by former CIA director, Trevor Axell? Sergei knows all about you and your little tiny task force and how you've been after him for some time. He also knows this agent of which you speak is very, very loyal to him." He turned to Koslov. "Isn't that right?"

"That is correct, Maxim." He approached Lacy and stood only feet from her. "Casper should have done his duty and eliminated you, Lacy Merrick. You and your task force were a thorn in his side and now you have become a thorn in mine."

"We killed Casper Janz." Lacy's eyes captured his firmly. "We brought two governments to their knees. You and Mr. Abramov are the thorns and the time has come to rip you from our sides."

Abramov turned to Koslov. "I told you she had big balls. I assume you have a plan?"

A thunderous boom sounded in the very near distance. The three people in the room whipped around in the direction of the noise. Lights flickered inside. Shouts came from beyond the office door.

Abramov shot up from his chair and brandished his gun. His security guards rushed inside. "What the hell is going on out there?"

"I'll radio now." One of the guards pressed the button on his two-way. "What was that?"

The radio crackled and sputtered while the voice on the other end began. "I think the power."

Another boom, like a detonated bomb, shuddered the room before it went dark.

"We lost power! What is happening out there?" The other guard appeared ready to pounce.

The radio sputtered again and a faint voice came through. "Transformers. Power's knocked out."

In the darkness, a guard looked at Abramov. "It's okay. It's just a transformer. I'll go kick on the generator." It was then the lights returned. "Someone must've beaten me to it."

"Go. Find out for sure!" Abramov turned to Lacy, who stood frozen in place. "Maybe we underestimated you." He looked to his second in command. "Take her and put her in the safe room until we know what happened."

Lacy shot a glance at the men. "No. I don't know what's going on out there, but it has nothing to do with me."

The guard gripped Lacy's shoulder.

"Let go of me!"

"Somehow, Lacy Merrick, I believe you might have everything to do with this," Abramov said.

Koslov walked past Lacy but stopped and turned back to her. "You think I am afraid because you killed that insignificant bug,

Janz. Lacy Merrick, governments are simple to bring down. They are filled with greedy and vulnerable politicians who are so very easily swayed by money. I, on the other hand, am swayed by nothing and no one. The most powerful of men have tried to stop me. I doubt a woman such as you can."

Lacy watched as he and Abramov left the room, the guard's grip on her arm tightening. "You don't know me very well, then."

CHAPTER
TWENTY-SEVEN

THE CORPORATE HELICOPTER landed about one hundred yards away during the time the transformers blew. Mullins' plan had been effective in hiding their arrival, which could mean their plan stood a decent chance of success.

Axell was in the co-pilot seat of the single-engine rotor wing. Mullins was also a pilot and insisted on flying the aircraft. "I'm going to need you to stay here and be ready. I don't know what condition Merrick will be in and we won't have time to sit around. Abramov's men will figure out what happened and there's a good chance they'll take it out on her before we can find her." He turned to Hunter. "Caison and I will go in and extract Merrick. You'll stay here with Mullins, is that clear?"

"No. I need to be there too. I can help. You know I can, Axell."

Axell peered at Caison as if in search of an agreement. "Fine." He nodded to Caison. "Get him a gun."

"Is there anything more I can do?" Mullins asked.

"Just stay here and be ready." Axell opened the door and jumped out. The blades had stopped spinning, but he kept his head down as he jogged away from the helicopter toward the road.

Caison and Hunter joined him and the three could see Abramov's home in the distance.

"They'll be looking for a reason the transformers blew," Axell began. "No winds and no storms will raise their concerns."

"Then we need to get in there now." Caison pushed ahead.

"Damn it." Axell turned to Hunter. "Come on. Keep up with him."

Under cover of darkness, they started toward the home where they knew Lacy to be. Generator lights scarcely illuminated the inside.

Axell pulled to the right. "He wasn't supposed to kill the power inside."

"We thought we isolated the transformers," Hunter began. "We got it wrong."

"Over here," Axell continued. "Remember that blind spot on the exterior from Mullins' satellite. That's where we need to be."

They reached the blind spot, which was on the right side of the main house structure, near the front.

"Axell, these guys are going to be heavily armed. There are only three of us." Hunter shifted his gaze between them. "How are we going to make this work?"

"We've seen the layout of the house. We should assume with the commotion, that Abramov would want to take Lacy and Usenko someplace where they could keep a close eye."

"What are you talking about, like a guest house or something?" Hunter asked.

"No," Axell said.

"A safe room," Caison replied.

"That's what I'm thinking, but we can't be sure right now. Best thing to do is to find an unguarded entrance and go inside."

"What about Usenko?" Caison asked.

"I couldn't care less about him. We get our woman and we get out." Axell again started, this time toward the back, where he figured would be the first place a stationed guard would leave. If for nothing else, then to go around front to find out what happened to the power.

And he was right. "See? I haven't been out of the game that long." He turned the handle and the door opened. Once inside he stopped and regarded the others. "Caison, you go there, I'll head in this direction, and Hunter, I want you close to me."

"I can do this, Axell."

But he wouldn't let Hunter finish. "That's an order. You're with me. Caison has military and Quantico training. He knows what to do. Will, go."

"Copy that." Caison started in the direction in which he was ordered.

"Hunter, we're going down here." Axell started along the corridor, which for the moment was still abandoned.

"Where are all his guards?" Hunter whispered.

"Probably trying to figure out what the hell happened. We need to work fast. I need you to listen for the sound of her voice, or Abramov's and Usenko's. We have some light, but I can't say that will be the case for the entire house."

"What about Caison? How are we going to know what's going on?"

"Don't worry about him. Worry about us."

———

Caison moved on to the east wing of the sprawling home. A voice sounded and he had to assume it was security and darted inside what appeared to be a small office. It couldn't have been Abramov's. Probably head of his security. As soon as the coast was clear, he started again and didn't stop until his foot caught on something on the ground and he nearly tripped over it. "What the...?"

Caison turned his sights to his feet, and even in the dimly lit room, he knew what he was looking at. He had reached a sitting room where a fireplace stood in the center and chairs were placed in front of it. One of the chairs was down and that was where the body must have fallen.

He kneeled for a better look, and upon gazing at the man's face, he realized who he was looking at. "Oh shit." Caison picked up his phone and texted Axell. He couldn't risk a phone ringing or buzzing loudly. *"Found Usenko Dead."*

————

Lacy was returned to a room where a mob boss and the head of a dangerous black-market organization had waited. She had no idea what was happening outside of this 15 by 15 room in which she had been placed.

There was power inside the room, however, so at the very least, she would be able to see her killers. Although she hadn't given up yet. What Abramov alluded to could be correct. Whatever was going on outside of these four walls could well have been the work of her team. They must have grown concerned by her radio silence. Trigger number one. And if they realized Koslov was heading her way, that would've been trigger number two. And Axell wouldn't have waited for a third trigger. He would've pulled it before that happened.

If it was them, she had no idea how they would get out of this mess, or find her. She had no weapons, no way to communicate with anyone else. Lacy was in the worst situation she could possibly have imagined. And that was saying something.

What she needed now was nothing short of a miracle. And in

her experience, they were usually in short supply. "How long are you planning on keeping me in here?"

Abramov turned to her. "I'm happy to set you free if you admit this is your team's doing."

"I have no idea what you're talking about. I came here to help you and you're the paranoid one."

Koslov approached her with anger masking his face. He raised his hand, and with the back of it, slapped her across the cheek. "How you have made it this far is beyond me. But you will make it no farther, Lacy Merrick."

She winced in pain but would not shed a tear. Instead, she pulled back upright and wiped the spot of blood from her cut lip. "I've suffered worse at the hands of men much stronger than you." She was really pushing her luck now. Pissing him off would only cause him to hit her harder next time. But if she dared show any weakness, it would end in her demise.

"That's enough." Abramov stepped in between them. "What the hell is the matter with you?" He eyed Koslov. "She could still be of use, but not if she's dead."

Koslov tugged on his shirt. "How do you mean?"

"I mean, if we are being surrounded by CIA or FBI, then we can use her as leverage."

"You don't know what's going on out there, Maxim. Perhaps you should find out before you overreact. This could be nothing and we are simply wasting time."

Abramov regarded them both. "Fine. I will learn what has happened. Then we will find a solution to this problem." He pressed keys on a keypad next to the door. It opened, and outside, the hall was illuminated with pathway lights in the ceiling. He started out the door and it closed behind him.

"Good. I was hoping to get you alone." Koslov approached her, using his height to intimidate her.

"You think you can scare me? Why don't you just hit me again? I'm sure that must've felt good for you."

He chuckled. "Well, this is going to be fun, isn't it?" He grabbed both her arms and yanked her close. "You're a widow now. I bet it has been a long time since you've felt a man's touch."

She recoiled, but only for a split second. "Is there a man in here? Funny, I don't see one."

He slapped her again.

The sting on her face forced a stray tear to fall from her right eye, but she would not relent. Lacy turned back to him, spitting in his face.

That was enough to bring him to a level of anger she hadn't yet witnessed. Koslov threw her against the wall, and her back struck the light switch. He forced his tongue down her throat and held her arms against the wall.

In a moment of desperation, Lacy had to act. She bit down as hard as she could on his tongue and his blood spilled into her mouth. And with her knee, she raised it with might into his groin.

Koslov stumbled back, his mouth oozing blood and the tip of his tongue dangling by a thread. He tried to talk but could only make a growling sound.

Lacy had to make her move now. She began pounding on the door, praying someone on her team was out there. She hadn't seen Abramov key in the passcode to open the door and there were no windows. If someone didn't hear her, Koslov would regain his strength and he would kill her.

———

Caison stopped in his tracks. A faint sound reached his ears. Was it security rushing toward him? He couldn't say; it was still too distant. He started again, but this time, he heard it more clearly.

He peered into the corridor where he believed the sound was coming from and continued until it sounded again. And this time, it was unmistakable. Someone was pounding on a door. "Lacy!" he half-whispered and half-shouted. "Are you in there?"

Through the door, she spoke. "Will? Get me out of here now! Koslov's here!"

A sudden realization struck him hard. Koslov was inside with her, meaning he wouldn't hesitate to kill her. "Jesus!" He tried the door, jiggling the handle, but it was locked. "Shit. Shit. Lacy, how do I get you out?"

"The keypad!" Her tone sounded more panicked through the door. "Will, now! Open the door now!"

He heard her struggling inside. "Son of a bitch! Lacy!" Will drew his weapon and fired on the keypad, then fired on the door lock. He heard a click and again tried the handle. Upon opening it, he spotted her, hunched over near the floor. "Lacy! Oh my God! Are you okay?"

It wasn't until he spotted what she was looking at that it had occurred to him what happened.

"I killed him." Lacy slowly turned her head to Will and then back to Koslov. Blood shrouded his face as his nose had been pushed upward with enough force to pierce his brain. "I killed him."

"Lacy, we have to leave now! Usenko's dead. Hunter and Axell are here somewhere. We have to get to them." He began to pull her up. "Come on. You can do this. We need to go now, Lacy."

She nodded and stood, following him back out into the corridor.

Caison reached for his phone, this time calling Axell. He answered, "I got her. I got her."

"Then let's get the hell out of here!" Axell replied.

"Where can we go?" she asked.

"Mullins is waiting for us outside a couple hundred yards away. We need to get to Axell and Hunter."

"Aaron's here?" Worry filled her voice. "He doesn't have the training for this. Why is he here, Will?"

"It wasn't my call."

They both turned at the sound of footsteps approaching.

"Axell?" Caison shouted.

Lacy followed but stopped short. "Trevor! Oh my God. Where's Aaron?"

"I'm here." Hunter pulled up from behind Axell. "How the hell do we get out of this place?"

"Follow me." Axell started with Caison and the others following closely behind.

The generator still hummed and lit up the halls but only enough to get through them. And now they had to worry about running into Maxim Abramov and his security detail.

"Koslov's dead," Caison began. "Lacy took him out." He continued to keep pace with Axell.

"He's dead?" Axell asked.

"He was coming after me. I didn't have a choice," Lacy added, struggling to keep up with them.

"There's a door. That's where we entered. Let's hope no one's on the other side," Caison said.

Upon approaching the door, Caison pushed it open and the night sky concealed any threats that might still linger.

"Is that Mullins up ahead?" Hunter asked as the chopper's outline appeared.

Two men were quickly approaching, shouting and with their guns aimed at them. One of the men fired.

"Shit!" A bullet whizzed by Caison's ear. "Take cover!" He pulled Lacy behind what appeared to be a storage shed. "Axell, over here."

Axell stopped and turned sharply toward him, dragging Hunter behind. "There's a guard gate ahead. We have to take them out if we stand a chance of clearing the path." He turned to Lacy. "Are you okay, because we need all hands on deck right now."

"I'm okay. Will, give me a gun." She held out her hand.

Caison pulled out a nine-millimeter. "You sure you're okay?"

She snatched it from his hands. "I'm fine. Let me do this."

At this, Hunter retrieved his own weapon. "It's four against two. We can do this, but it'll get harder once the power's back on. It's now or never." He aimed his weapon at the men who still charged forth.

From the side of the outbuilding, the team set up a perimeter of defense with Axell leading the command. Caison was a close second and Hunter and Lacy operated as backup.

"Caison, I need you to flank my right. We're going out." Axell started to emerge from the corner. "They're at our five o'clock."

"Roger."

Shots rang out once again. Lacy pulled back at the sound, but when she turned to Aaron, he forged ahead. "Aaron! No! Stay back."

He either wasn't listening to her or hadn't heard her and continued ahead with Axell and Caison. With his gun at the ready, Aaron pulled the trigger. The kickback startled him as he lost a step. "Shit!"

But he'd done it. One of the men collapsed, taking a bullet in his side. The other man continued to fire and draw nearer.

"He's coming." Axell moved in closer and again fired.

The man fell. They were both down and the team could press on.

"Move now!" Axell started ahead toward the location of Mullins' chopper.

As they neared the helicopter, the lights on the property illuminated again. And behind the team, more security rushed toward them.

"Get it running!" Axell shouted and used his index finger, swirling it around in hopes Mullins would see the signal.

He did. Mullins started the engine and the blades turned. Dust and debris on the ground pulled up and whirled around it. The sound of the chopper reached the team as they approached.

Bullets continued to slice the air, narrowly avoiding their targets. Axell pulled open the door and helped the others inside. "Go now! Get in!"

Caison lifted Lacy from her feet, almost throwing her petite frame inside. Hunter jumped in behind with some help. Finally, it was Caison and Axell who got into the passenger side.

"Mullins, we need to get off the ground now!" Axell peered through the window at the oncoming men. "Go!"

Mullins pulled up the yoke. "Hang on!"

The chopper ascended rapidly as the men approached, firing on the airship. Bullets ricocheted as Caison pulled the door shut. "Go, go, go!"

They were in the air and out of reach. They'd made it. Lacy peered at Aaron. "Are you okay?"

"I'm fine. You?"

"Fine." She gazed at Will and waited for him to nod, then called out to Axell, "Abramov's still alive."

He turned back. "I know. This isn't over yet."

CHAPTER
TWENTY-EIGHT

THE CHOPPER DESCENDED onto the grounds of Mullins' lavish home, where the team had departed only a few hours ago. And plenty had happened during that time. The most substantial being that Lacy had fended off and killed Sergei Koslov, a fact she had yet to accept.

She was slow to step off the helicopter as Mullins shut it down. Axell stood on the ground in front of the open door, hand extended, ready to help her out.

"Lacy?" He waited. "It's okay."

She held his gaze, but she wasn't ready to believe him. The feeling of being trapped inside that room with Koslov's hands around her throat and his tongue inside her mouth wouldn't escape her. Bile rose the more she considered what had happened.

"Lacy, come on." Caison's hand pressed against her back.

She finally stepped off the chopper. The others emerged and Mullins approached and Lacy peered at him. "How did you know I was in trouble?"

"I didn't." Mullins pointed to Axell. "He did. Or rather, he assumed you could be in trouble and it appeared as though his assumption was in fact correct. Are you all right?"

Aaron pushed in between Mullins and Lacy. "She's fine. She just needs to clear her head." He ushered her toward the home while the others fell in behind. "I can't believe what you did back there. I thought we weren't going to get to you in time."

"I thought I was on my own," she began. "I got in too deep this time and I wouldn't have made it if you hadn't shown up."

"You did it, Lace. Koslov's gone. It's done."

She was silent as they approached Mullins' home. And it wasn't until he opened the door that she turned to Aaron to speak. "It's only Abramov and him now." She trained her sights on Mullins.

"Let's not forget Balfour," Aaron replied. "I guess we aren't finished here."

"No. Not yet."

Inside the home, Mullins turned on the television and began flipping the channels. "Nothing on the news yet. That's a good sign."

"How long do you think it'll be before Abramov gets word to Koslov's organization?" Axell asked.

"You mean, if he hasn't already?" Mullins replied. "I'm quite sure they've been notified and are likely preparing a response."

"A response?" Hunter asked.

"That's right. They'll send a team to finish the job Abramov and Koslov started." Mullins turned to Lacy. "And that will mean ending you first and foremost. The rest of you, well, we'll have to see what happens. Axell's a high-value target. Possibly too risky to remove him. I can't say as much for you two, Caison and Hunter."

"And what about Balfour?" Lacy asked. "We have enough to charge her, assuming you'll provide us with the video. She was working with him. She knows exactly the type of operation Koslov ran. If they think she'll flip, they won't make a move."

"That is a valid point." Axell turned to Mullins. "From here on out, you're working for us."

"Sorry?"

"You're working for us now, Mullins."

He laughed. "And if I refuse? You understand that I have more money than you could scarcely imagine. And with that, politicians in my pocket. You might wish to reconsider your demands."

"I'll reconsider nothing. You're working for us because if you don't, you won't have a country willing to take you in, not Ukraine, not the US, and not even your own. You have money—yes. But I have the backing of the FBI and CIA. If you don't help us, I'll make sure you end up in some shit-hole detention center, maybe even Guantanamo. Don't fuck with me, Mullins."

Mullins eyed the rest of them. "And here I thought we were friends."

———

Lacy walked up the steps to her front door with Will accompanying her. She inserted her key and turned to him. "I'm okay. Really. You didn't need to follow me home."

"You can say that, but Lacy, I know you. Maybe not as well as Hunter, but I know what you went through tonight and no one could come out of that without being a little shaken up." He paused a moment. "I'd like to stay. I'm happy to sleep on the couch. I just don't think you should be alone. First of all, because Abramov is still out there. And second, because I think you need someone around. I know you'd never admit to it, but I think you do."

She regarded him. "Fine. But we should still be there with the others tracking down Abramov."

"Let them handle it. Aaron knows what he's doing and so does Mullins, as much as I hate to give him credit for anything."

Lacy walked inside and held the door for him. "He led us to Koslov. He led you all to Abramov—to me. I think Trevor was wrong to threaten him and it could come back to bite us." Once inside the kitchen, she opened the refrigerator door and retrieved two bottles of water. "I handled myself tonight. Regardless of what could have happened to me. I killed Sergei Koslov."

"And he attacked you, Lacy. I think that scared Axell more than anything. Because if we hadn't shown up when we did..."

"I'd be dead. Maybe not at Koslov's hands, but Abramov wouldn't have let me out alive." She swallowed down almost the entire bottle and held his gaze again. "I'm so tired, Will."

"You should go to bed."

"No. Not just that. Every time we think we're ahead of the game, something goes wrong. Someone else comes after us. Is this ever going to end?"

Will got up from his stool and walked around the kitchen island, standing in front of her. "This is the deal, Lacy. This is what we signed up for."

"I know we did. I know." She cast her gaze into the foyer and the staircase. "What if something had happened to me tonight? What kind of mother risks her life this way when her children only have one parent left?"

He took hold of her arms and pulled her close. "The kind of mother who wants to make a better world for her kids. The kind of mother who will hunt down everyone she possibly can who intends to do harm to her family or her country."

"That's going to amount to a lot of people in my cross-hairs." She smiled half-heartedly.

Her eyes reddened around the edges and her smile fell. Lacy moved closer. "I've never killed anyone before. What does that make me?" She raised slightly on her tiptoes as their eyes locked, gripping the back of his neck before pressing her lips against his.

At first, she felt him resist, but it lasted only a moment when he pushed into her, returning the kiss with feverish passion. Her mind was hazy and all she could feel was desire and she pushed aside everything else that tried to get in the way. Will had been there for her. From the very beginning, he had believed in her. And there was no baggage with him. There was no history like she had with Aaron. It was easy—this feeling.

"Come upstairs with me," she whispered.

Will looked into her eyes and she was as confident of her decision as she was the moment she decided to ask him for help one year ago. Nothing else mattered.

"Are you sure?"

She smiled because he wanted her too and his attempt to verify it was gallant and that was who he was. Never one to take advantage of her, but wanted her badly just the same and there was a part of him, she was sure, that was hurting too. He'd been used by Balfour. And maybe he needed this as much as she did. "I'm sure." She started toward the staircase, pulling him through the darkened house.

When they reached her bedroom door, Lacy pulled it open and stood before her bed. The one she shared with Jay and one that no other man had ever occupied. Perhaps this was a betrayal, or maybe it was just Lacy being human, with all her faults. She was not perfect and trying to be had been exhausting.

Will pulled off his shirt before taking hold of Lacy's and gently pulling it over her head. It was too late to stop it now and she didn't want to. It had been so long since she felt her skin tingle this way. And this was Will, a man she trusted and a man she cared for.

She lay bare before him, vulnerable yet confident, defying all she was supposed to be and being the woman she was. A woman who needed this man right at this moment. And tomorrow didn't matter. Only now. There was only now.

———

The cell phone buzzed on her nightstand, rousing Lacy from sleep. She reached for the phone and answered. "Hey. What's going on? What time is it?" She then peered at her alarm clock and pulled up onto the edge of her bed. "What? Okay. I'll be right down."

Will stirred and was soon awakened while Lacy stood and pulled her robe from the bench at the end of her bed. "What's going on?"

"They're downstairs."

"Who?"

"Trevor and Aaron." Lacy started toward the door and turned back to him. "Maybe you should stay here."

"Is that what you really want?" He'd already begun to dress. "If they're here, something's happened. And how am I supposed to explain it when they call me?"

"You're right. I don't know what I was thinking."

He approached her. "Please don't tell me you regret..."

"No. No, of course not. Come on. We should get down there."

The two started down the stairs as the morning light appeared through the windows. Lacy, wrapped in a robe, answered the door. "Come in."

Axell entered first before Hunter and the two stopped in their tracks at the sight of Will standing behind her.

Aaron turned his sights to Lacy, appearing confused and hurt and everything she hadn't wanted him to feel.

Axell picked up on the awkward and tense silence. "We need to talk. You got any coffee?" He immediately started into the kitchen.

"I'll put on a pot." Lacy walked past Aaron without a word.

But before Will could continue, Aaron thrust his hand out, stopping him in his tracks. He couldn't seem to find the words, only regarded him with betrayal imbued in his eyes.

Will opened his mouth and struggled to form any words at all. Instead, he shook his head and walked into the kitchen.

Axell poured himself a mug before the pot finished brewing. "Mullins has a line on Abramov. He booked a ticket to Kyiv, probably to see this board of directors Mullins mentioned. That's where we need to go."

"Us?" Lacy asked as she sat on the stool. "Why not ask Ward to send a team? She's already got people there in play. And what's the plan anyway?"

"The plan hasn't changed. Koslov might be dead, but the consortium lives. And Abramov will go there to warn them of what happened. Our job will be to shut them down—for good."

"Trevor, we need Director Ward for this. We can't get there without her and we certainly can't get to them without her."

"Mullins said there was a contact there who helped him. Her name is Daria Liski. She was discovered, but he was able to have her extracted safely and now she's holed up in one of his compounds." Aaron looked at Lacy but turned away. "She knows the place inside and out and he thinks she can get them in."

"Who?" Lacy began. "Get who in? Us?"

"Us or Ward's people. Whoever. I don't know. I'm just telling you what we know right now and why we're here." Aaron shot another glance at Will.

"And where is Mullins now?" Will asked. "After you threatened him, he's going to help us?"

"Yes. We made a deal. After I cooled my jets, I knew I screwed up. So I cut him a deal, so long as he comes through," Axell replied.

"Okay, but Trevor, I still don't think it's us who should be going."

"I have to agree with her," Will replied. "This is the CIA's job. I know we've been after Koslov, but going to Ukraine, and especially after what happened in Beijing, I think it's a mistake. We'll be putting our task force at risk—again. Ward has the people there."

Axell seemed to consider the advice of his team. "Let me get Ward on the horn and find out who she has there that she can rely on. Our team will run the op from here. Mullins will get us access to this Liski woman and she can get them in." He looked at the time. "Abramov is still out there. So for now, I want us all to look out for each other. I'll get a team in place with Mobley's help and we'll take Balfour into custody too. She might yet be useful. Caison, you'll need to play nice with her."

"Yeah, I can work on her too."

"Then it's settled. Get dressed. We'll all meet up at HQ in thirty minutes. Hunter and I will head back now after we pick up Mullins. We'll reconvene there." He eyed Will. "Maybe you'll want a fresh set of clothes too."

Axell started toward the foyer with Hunter in tow. "See you down there."

When they both left, Lacy shut the door and looked at Will. "That's not how I would've preferred things to go."

"Me neither. I'm sorry, Lacy. I should've left after..."

"No, you shouldn't have. But you should go home and get cleaned up. I don't want the kids..."

"Right. I'll see you back down at the shop."

————

Another excuse poured from her lips as Lacy tried to explain to the kids at breakfast why she had to leave so early, and before she knew it, Lacy was once again out the door. She didn't know what would happen today with regard to Abramov or the consortium, but it seemed Axell was receptive to the idea that Ward's team should handle it. They weren't equipped, nor did they have any legal authority to arrest anyone or shut anything down. The task force wasn't law enforcement. It was intelligence gathering and it appeared Axell might've forgotten that, calling on his days as a case officer. He wasn't one anymore.

She arrived at the shop bearing the uncomfortable sentiment that carried over from this morning when Aaron peered at her. He was hurt, that much was painfully obvious. Right now, however, a Russian mafia boss was sending people after her and her team while Koslov's operation awaited news. And no one knew the forces that backed them.

"I'm here. Sorry it took me so long." She walked into the bullpen where Mullins and the rest of her team were already working.

"Good morning, Lacy. How are you? I trust you slept well?" Mullins asked.

"No, I didn't. But then, I think you knew that." She eyed Axell.

"Perhaps. Come. See what your team and I have been working on whilst you've been catching up on your beauty sleep."

For a man she believed had a faint if not measured interest in her, his tone had changed markedly. Had word gotten around already? Unlikely, but it felt that way to her. "What is it?"

Aaron peered at her with the same betrayal his eyes held this morning. "Axell's been in talks with Ward. She's getting word to a team already in play in Kyiv. And Mullins here is having Daria Liski brought to us so she can guide them in."

"Wouldn't it be better to have her there?" Lacy asked.

"No. She'd be dead in a day. I removed her from Ukraine the day she was extracted. The consortium has tentacles that reach far beyond anything you could possibly imagine. Eastern Europe is completely entangled in their web and the resources of several covert operatives could be utilized on a moment's notice."

"I see. So she'll be here, running the op with us."

"That is correct, my dear lady."

Lacy noticed Aaron had been unusually quiet. Maybe it was because Jill had already cozied up to her boss, Timothy Mullins, and the idea of her disloyalty still lingered. Or maybe the real reason was that he knew and had seen what had clearly transpired between her and Will. She needed to see him privately before they continued on because his friendship meant everything to her and losing him would feel like losing Jay all over again. "Hey, can I talk to you for a minute, in private?"

Aaron regarded her with a small measure of contempt and then peered at Caison. "Yeah. Sure."

She started into the corridor while Aaron followed. She could feel the entire team watching them walk away, but she refused to look back. This was between her and Aaron and she had to nip it in the bud because who knew what would come to pass in the next twenty-four hours.

She waited inside the break room as he trailed a few steps behind. And on his arrival, she began, "You want to sit down?"

"Not really. There's a lot we have to do today, so maybe you should make this quick."

"Sure. Listen, Aaron, I don't really know what to say."

He grunted. "Then why am I here, Lace?" His stance was firm, his gaze, unwavering.

"I know you're upset about what you saw this morning and for that, I'm truly sorry. You weren't supposed to..."

"To what? See you and Caison, half-dressed, walking down your staircase? Clearly having slept together. That was what you didn't want me to see? Sorry to have burst your bubble."

"It was—unexpected, Aaron. I swear."

"Well, that makes me feel a whole lot better. We should be getting back." He started toward the door.

"Wait." Lacy pulled on his arm. "Please. I don't want to leave things like this. You're my best friend. I can't lose you. The kids and me..."

"The kids and you." He shook his head. "Don't you dare. Don't sit there and try to tell me how much I mean to you and Olivia and Jackson. If I meant that much to you, it wouldn't have been Caison at the foot of your stairs. It would've been me. And you knew that was what I wanted. You knew."

"I did know. And I used your feelings for my own needs sometimes. I shouldn't have. I knew how you felt and I did nothing about it, except let you continue feeling that way, leading you on. It was a mistake I'll never forgive myself for."

"You know what, Lace. Me neither. Jay would be so proud." Aaron turned on his heel and disappeared.

CHAPTER
TWENTY-NINE

DIRECTOR ELIZABETH WARD walked into the task force headquarters, where the team was set up in the communications room. "They're ready to go."

"Good. Liski should be here soon and then we can move forward." Axell turned to Mullins. "Any word on Abramov's whereabouts?"

"At last I heard, he was meeting with the Russian Ambassador. Not a good sign."

"No," Axell replied. "We need to shut this down now before the ambassador runs this up the food chain. Word gets to the president and he'll want answers, answers I don't have for him."

"What about shutting down Abramov's operation here? At least in the interim," Lacy began. "That'll keep him busy here while we do what we need to do in Ukraine. We can use Balfour for that, you know she'll talk."

Caison turned to Axell. "I can contact Mobley and brief him on the situation. He'll move on Balfour with the intel we have now. It'll be done in a matter of hours. I should lead that charge."

"Especially after the way she used you." Hunter appeared angry and it had spilled over onto Caison.

"Right. I'll take care of that now while we wait for Liski's arrival." Caison regarded Lacy before making his way to the front exit.

Axell studied Lacy for a moment. "Are we good here?"

"We're good."

"Okay." He turned back to the monitors. "Mullins has us set up in several locations inside the building."

"It looks to be vacant," Aaron said.

"It's down to a skeleton crew," Mullins began. "They've still ceased operations until they get the all-clear from Koslov, which now seems highly unlikely to happen."

"So how are we to shut down this operation?"

"We just need to get inside, get their files, and the deed will be done. They'll be out of commission permanently once the rest of the board discovers what's happened. They'll lose all their bidders."

"We don't stand a chance of locating any of them, do we?" Lacy asked.

"Not at the moment. That's a discussion for another time, perhaps," Mullins replied.

Daria Liski was escorted inside by a member of Ward's team. "She's here." Ward approached the officer. "Thank you for bringing her down."

The man nodded before quickly departing.

Daria peered with frightened eyes at the people in the room. She recognized none of them. "Which one of you is Graybear?"

"That would be me, miss." Mullins offered his hand. "It's a great pleasure to finally meet you in person. I am a massive admirer of your work."

"Thank you for clearing your schedule, Director." Caison entered Mobley's office. "As you know, the timing here is critical."

"Yes, I'm aware. Axell briefed me on the situation, and first, let me say how sorry I am. I don't know how Balfour was able to do what she did without being discovered."

"Must've learned it from her parents."

Mobley returned to his desk. "Yes, I suppose so. What do you need from me to bring her in? We have to assume she's heard about the incident. Meaning..."

"Meaning she could be readying herself to go into hiding."

"That, or she has turned to Abramov for help. The two of them together will cause a great many problems for all concerned."

"We need to cut that loose end before it unravels on us," Caison replied.

"Agreed."

"That said, I'd like to call on an old friend, one who I know we can trust," Caison added.

"Fraser."

"Yes, sir."

"You'll need more than the two of you. Who else are you certain you can trust?"

"Well, Delgado, but he's UC right now with CIA. I need another field agent like Fraser."

"Then you should ask him. There's bound to be someone he can place his trust in. Between the three of you, you'll have to track her down and bring her in. I'll take it from there."

"Thank you, sir. I'm sure Balfour's already MIA, so I'll see Fraser and we'll put together a plan."

"Go. Do what you need to do to bring in the traitor," Mobley replied.

Caison nodded and started back into the corridor. He made his way out of the FBI's headquarters, where he'd spent a fair amount of time before transferring out to the task force. Now he would seek help from Agent Adam Fraser, once again.

He returned to his car and started toward the WFO, making the call along the way. "Fraser, it's Caison. I'm heading your way. Can we meet?"

"Caison, hey man, it's good to hear from you. Yeah, I'll be here for a couple hours. Come on by. Don't suppose this is a social call?"

"No. I'll explain when I see you. I'm on my way." Caison ended the call.

The building was coming into view and he parked in the visitors' section. Within moments, he was inside, displaying his credentials to security. As he was waved through, he made it to the elevators and to Fraser's floor in CID.

The offices were busy, as usual, and Caison hustled to the man he needed to see.

Fraser looked away from his computer to see his friend standing in the doorway. "That was quick. Come in."

"Thanks." Caison closed the door and sat down. "Hey, you remember when I asked you to keep tabs on Anya Balfour?"

"Sure. And I put a couple guys on her yesterday, but they lost her. Don't know how, but it sure as shit raised a red flag for me. I figured that's what this was about. What happened with her?"

"She's turned."

"What?" Fraser leaned over his desk. "As in, 'turned,' like she's not working for our side anymore?"

"Bingo. She was always playing us, but we have proof now and I need your help."

"Anything. Just name it."

———

Axell pulled away from the monitors. "So that's it." He folded his arms. "Ward's team gets in, gets the goods, and gets the hell out of Dodge."

"That does appear to be the plan," Mullins said. "Thank you, Daria, for your help. I know what this has cost you, and suffice it to say, you will be well compensated."

"You know I won't be able to go back."

"I know. I won't let them send you back. Isn't that right, Mr. Axell?"

"That's right."

Ward shot a look at him, but Axell brushed it off.

"We should have boots on the ground in twenty," Ward said. "Let's get ready to roll out." She retrieved her cell phone and made a call, walking away from the team.

Axell followed and waited until she finished.

"You already know what I'm going to say, so how about we just don't say it?" Ward said to him.

"Thank you. We'll deal with that whole issue later. What we need now is a team in place."

"We have that. We're almost there, Trevor. Your people are here and they're safe."

"For now. But until Balfour's found and Abramov is brought in, I don't think any of us will get any rest."

"What about Lacy? How's she holding up after what happened to Koslov?"

"Better than I would've expected. Then again, she's been through the wringer."

"Haven't we all?" Ward replied. "Okay, we need to keep an eye on Mullins. I'm not sure he's to be trusted, even if he's doing this for us."

"He and I made a deal. I think he'll stick to it because if he doesn't he knows all bets are off. He won't make it out of this country."

"Good." Ward's phone buzzed. "It's my team leader." She held the phone to her ear. "Go ahead."

Axell turned away and headed back to the others. "We go live in ten. Everyone, get to your stations. We'll be monitoring it live and in color."

Lacy sat down at one of the tables and she was joined by Mullins.

"You seem to be handling things quite well, all things considered," he said.

"I'm no wallflower, Timothy, in case you haven't figured that out."

"Oh, I figured that out from the moment I engaged you as Graybear. What I didn't figure you for was a player."

"Excuse me?"

"Oh, please. You could cut the sexual tension with the proverbial knife in this office. Something clearly happened between you and Will Caison and it appears as though your other co-worker is not very happy about it." He held her gaze. "Pity. I thought you and I had a connection. A spark, if you will."

"I'm sorry to disappoint you, Timothy. Maybe in another life. Then again, I'm not one for getting involved with criminals. Or haven't you figured that out about me yet?"

"We're live, people!" Axell said.

The screens on the walls lit up as Ward's team on the ground entered the secured building. A voice sounded through the speakers. "We're in, ma'am."

Ward had an earpiece as she watched the screens with Axell at her side. "I got you loud and clear, Murphy. Move in."

The team started through the halls of the building. It was 1 am in Ukraine and a few staffers were on site, according to Daria Liski. And so far, it appeared she was right.

"I see movement on the second floor," Mullins said as he peered at the cameras on his own screen.

"Steer clear of the second floor," Ward said.

"Copy." The team leader continued through as they headed to the server room. "Jackpot."

"They'll need to enter the code," Daria said.

"Right. Murphy, enter code 147249."

He entered the code and the door unlocked. "It worked. We're going in to extract the hard drives."

The screens went dark.

"Shit. We just lost visual." Axell peered at Mullins. "What the hell happened?"

He appeared to scramble on his keyboard. "It's not me. My cameras are working, but I don't have anything inside the server room."

"Shit. Ward?" Axell said.

"Murphy, come in? We've lost visual." She waited.

Sounds of the men shouting inside sounded through the speakers.

"What the hell is happening, Murphy?"

Gunfire erupted.

"Shit! Shit!" Axell moved in front of the monitors as though he could somehow help them. "What's happening here? Come on, damn it." He turned again to Mullins. "Can't you do anything?"

"No. I'm sorry. It's not me."

"Hunter?" Axell pleaded.

"It's not us, Axell. It's Ward's equipment."

"Son of a bitch!" He slammed down his fist amid the sound of more weapons firing. "Get the hell out of there!"

Lacy rushed to her feet, unable to breathe, her eyes glued to the screens that were nothing but static. All they had was audio and it was muffled behind the sounds of gunshots. She walked to Aaron. "What's happening?"

"I don't know. Christ. I don't know."

The tone of his voice sent tremors down her spine. She approached the girl. "Did you do this? Is this your fault?"

"No. I swear. They have a lot of security. I told you that."

The gunfire stopped.

"Murphy, come in," Ward said. "Murphy, do you copy?"

They all stood frozen while voices still sounded through the speakers.

"Copy. We're okay," Murphy replied. "We came across hostiles and took 'em out."

"Thank God," Ward began. "Do you have the drives?"

"Almost."

"Get 'em and get the hell out of there."

"Um, you might want to tell them they've got three more security staff headed their way now," Mullins said.

"Where?"

"One floor above."

"Get them out of there, Elizabeth," Axell said. "Get them out or we'll lose them."

"Murphy, you have three more heading your way. Whatever you have now, take it and run."

"We're almost there," he replied.

"Run! Now!"

―――――

"We're tracking her down now," Fraser began. "Last she was seen was at Koslov's apartment building. We contacted the manager and he confirmed it."

"She's looking for something," Caison said. "There must be something that ties him to her in his place. Meaning she already knows." He turned again to Fraser. "Can you run airport checks? Let's make sure she doesn't skip town and head back to good ol' Mother Russia."

"On it. What about her place? Is it worth taking a trip?"

"She'd be stupid to go back there, and if there's anything I learned about her is that she's not stupid." Caison paused to consider his next move. "She'll want to meet with Abramov, who, at last check, was meeting with the Russian Ambassador."

"Great. Well, that'll be easy, then. We'll take her while she's inside the embassy."

Caison smiled sardonically. "Yeah, piece of cake. What I mean is that we can wait for her there. You have another you trust, right?"

"I do."

"Can you send him to the embassy and I'll head back to her place to see if she's packed a bag? Or left anything behind."

"You want me to go with you?" Fraser asked.

"No. I got this one. But if you have any Russian embassy contacts, now might be a good time to call and ask for a favor."

"I don't, but I know who does. I'll make the call now."

Caison started toward the door. "I'll be in touch when I get there. Thanks, man."

"You got it."

Caison started once again and headed back to his car. He knew where Balfour lived and while it would be arbitrary to expect she would be there, he hoped to find out where she might be going, or if she even returned home. Which could mean a laptop or tablet might've been left behind if she hadn't. It was best to cover all the bases.

He arrived within minutes to Balfour's place. He wasn't going to bother with the formalities of a key. As he made his way toward her apartment, Caison pulled out his weapon and fired on the door handle. The lock shattered. "That ought to get the cops here." But he wouldn't be there long enough. Get in, get out.

Caison headed straight for her bedroom, where he had seen a tablet on her bedside table on the night he slept with her. The thought of it turned his stomach. How could he have let himself get caught up in her web? And then there was Lacy. The woman he truly wanted. He would have to tell her about Anya if she didn't already know. But Lacy was smart.

He pulled out the drawers of the side table, but there was no tablet to be found. "Shit." He started back toward the living room and rummaged through every drawer or cabinet he could find and still—nothing. "Damn it! I knew you wouldn't come back here."

"Until now."

Caison spun around to see her with a gun trained on his head. "Anya. Nice to see you."

"You too, Will. Come back for more?"

He smiled. "Oh, I think I've had my fill of American traitors, but thanks."

"Traitor. Is that what you think I am? A traitor?"

"Pretty much sums it up, yeah. I saw you with Koslov."

Her brow furrowed for a split second as though this was actually news to her. "And you think, what, that I'm working for him?"

"Were."

"Right. Were. I heard what happened. Glad to see Merrick made it out okay. Sergei always did have a temper."

"You must've known him well, then," Caison said.

"Not as well as you might think. I was working him, Caison. That's my job."

"You really expect me to believe that? So, what, you were sleeping with him too?"

"Jealous?"

"Not one bit," he replied.

"I did what I had to do. I'm sorry if that hurts your feelings. Koslov was mine to get, not yours."

"You really expect me to believe that? If that was the case, why didn't Mobley come to your defense? I went to him first. I got the go-ahead to find you."

"You found me. Now what are you going to do? Shoot me?"

"You're the one with a gun to my head."

"Because I need to be sure you hear my side of the story. I'm not who you think I am, Will. And I'm going to need you to believe me on that."

"I don't believe a word you say. You're going to prison for a very long time."

She waved the gun toward the sofa. "Cops will be here soon after you fire your gun. Have a seat. Let's wait this out and see what they have to say."

"Why don't you just tell me now so we can get this over with? I got shit to do."

"Yes, which is exactly the reason I tracked you down. Sit. You're not leaving until I get through to you."

CHAPTER
THIRTY

THE TEAM WAITED FOR WORD, standing in front of the monitors as if images would again appear. Lacy looked at Aaron. He wouldn't return the gaze. She turned to Axell. Ward had gripped his hand as they all awaited word. Had the team extracted the drives? Did they have what they needed to shut down the operation?

"Murphy here, anyone copy?"

A collective sigh of relief sounded in the room.

"Ward here. We copy you, Murphy. We copy."

"We're out of the building and have secured the drives. We're heading back to base. Murphy out."

Ward pulled the earpiece from her ear and dropped into a chair. "Oh, thank God."

"There, you see? Everything turned out just as planned," Mullins said. "You're about to get what you needed and then we're square, as they say."

Lacy turned to Daria. "Thank you. I'm sure you did what you did for a good reason. And you didn't have to help us."

"I believed in him." She pointed to Mullins. "I believed in what Graybear was doing. And now it is over."

"Ward's team will bring the drives here themselves. No stops, they'll come straight here. Then we can take the intel to the president. This will be over soon." Axell turned to Aaron. "You did good, Hunter. We're shutting this thing down and you had a big part to play in making that happen."

"What about Jill?" he asked. "Does she get the same deal as Mullins?"

"Yes. Your boss has already agreed to that," Mullins interrupted. "She helped you and she's one hell of a good hacker." He turned back to Axell. "So I reckon I'll be getting those tickets home soon? I did hold up my end of the bargain. The time has come for you to hold up yours."

"Not until those drives are in my hands," Axell said. "Then the deal goes through. I'm afraid you'll have to stick it out here with us until that happens. So have a seat, it's going to be a long night."

Caison pushed through the door with Balfour in tow. "What did I miss?"

Lacy turned at his arrival. "Will. What's going on? Why is she here and not in a federal jail?"

Balfour followed him into the bullpen. "Timothy Mullins. How are you? It's been a long time."

"I'm sorry? Do we know each other?"

"Oh yes. And how is your Bulgarian friend, by the way? I hear he's going to be next in line to run the operation. Although," she turned to the others, "I feel like maybe we did miss something here."

"What the hell is going on, Caison?" Axell asked.

"Whatever deal you made with Mullins is now null and void."

Caison peered at him. "We know you were the one who was helping the Bulgarian unseat Koslov so he could run the operation. Which, from what I understand, would have meant a boon for you."

"Wait." Lacy held up her hands. "She was the one working with Koslov. Will, what happened?"

"Well, I had a nice chat with the Moscow station chief earlier."

"Excuse me?" Ward asked.

"Yeah. So apparently, he and Balfour's ASAC agreed to have her get close to Koslov, primarily because she had an in with Maxim Abramov. It was all designed to take down the mafia operation in New York. Only she started to find out more about Koslov."

"I couldn't allude to any of this because I needed Mullins to work with you. It was the only way I could confirm what I already suspected, especially when Merrick mentioned the name Graybear. I'd heard Sergei reference that name before. He also mentioned a Bulgarian. The closer I got to him, the more intel I gathered."

"From there," Will added, "she learned about Mullins and Barkov and how it appeared they were working together on something."

"That something was to unseat Koslov," Balfour said. "I want to thank you all for your hard work. Without Merrick's involvement with Graybear, I wouldn't have gotten much farther than pinning charges on the mob boss."

"Will, are you sure about this? We saw that video," Lacy said.

"That's right, you did," Balfour replied. "Because he wanted you to see it. I was playing a part. Mullins used it to convince you I was a double agent. Which, I guess, technically, I was."

"Elizabeth, why didn't we know about this?" Axell asked.

"Because undercover ops are highly compartmentalized. It's entirely possible Nichols ran this through without me knowing about it. Which would also mean Mobley wouldn't have been made aware. You should remember it's part of the deal sometimes when there's a risk of exposure to the undercover officer." She peered at Balfour. "But the only way to confirm it is to speak to Nichols directly, which I'll do right now." Ward left the room and headed to Axell's office to make the call.

"What about Jill?" Aaron asked.

"What about her? She's been working for him the entire time too, just like she said," Balfour replied.

Lacy turned to Mullins. "Who's the Bulgarian?"

"Lukas Barkov," Balfour replied. "And he should be in Nichol's custody right about now. I told him about the op you were running. The servers."

"We still have the servers," Axell said. "They're in our possession now."

"Good. We'll need them to prove Mullins was in with a member of the consortium as well as Koslov's role." Balfour turned to Lacy. "But you took care of him."

Ward returned to the bullpen. "It's confirmed. Lukas Barkov is in custody. Nichols has instructed us to take Mullins and Jill Goddard in as well."

"She is, as you Americans say, 'in the wind,'" Mullins replied. "But I'm happy to go with you." He turned to Lacy. "It was such a pleasure getting to know you, Lacy Merrick. I'm sure our paths will cross again."

"Doesn't sound like it, Timothy. Not from where I stand."

He smiled. "As I mentioned earlier, the consortium's tentacles reach far into many governments. Maybe even here, in the United States. So even if I am to be extradited, an almost certainty, by the Ukrainian government, don't think I'll be in their hands for long." He approached Lacy. "I do regret not getting to know you better. It wasn't a lie that I am very much attracted to you. But I have a feeling we will meet again. I do know where you live."

———

Lacy stood outside on her front lawn. "Thank you for this." She smiled at the woman.

"I'm excited to get this house sold for you, Mrs. Merrick. After what you've done for this country, the president should give you a house."

She laughed. "I don't think so, but thank you." Lacy turned away. "You'll send me those listings so we can schedule a time to take a look at a few new houses?"

"I'll get on that tonight. Goodbye, Lacy."

Lacy returned inside. "Well, that's settled. The house is officially on the market."

"Mom, I'm glad we get to move. I think it will help," Olivia said.

"I think it will too, baby. Now go on upstairs and play with your brother while I talk to Uncle Aaron for a little bit."

"Okay." She rushed up the steps.

Lacy walked into the living room, where Aaron sat on the couch. "You want something to drink?"

"No. I'm fine. Glad you got everything worked out on the house."

"Me too. I think it's time for a fresh start. I've been putting it off for too long."

"Do you know where you want to move to yet?" he asked.

"Not yet. I'll see what's out there. I just know I can't stay here. For a great many reasons." She studied him. "Are we okay, Aaron? I know we haven't talked much since they took Mullins in. And I can't stand that."

"Lace, I want you to be happy. And I understand that it's not with me. It hurts—a little. I won't lie."

She reached for his hand. "I need you, Aaron. You're my best friend. I know what happened with Will and he and I have talked and it won't get in the way of our jobs. It just happened and we both recognize it for what it was, which was nothing."

"If you say so." Aaron stood. "So, back to work tomorrow. No rest for the weary." He started toward the door.

"Nope. Not for us."

"Any idea what Axell's got going on?"

"Not yet. I'm sure it'll be another Koslov or Janz or Shen Yang. There seems to be no shortage of people who pose a threat to us. We just have to keep doing what we're doing because it's what's best for the country." She opened the door.

"Have a good night, Lace."

"You too, Aaron." Lacy closed the door behind him and returned to the living room. She reached for her phone and noticed a text.

"Has he left yet?"

She typed her reply. *"Yes."*

"Everything go okay?"

Again, she replied. *"It's okay. We'll be okay."*

"Good. When can I see you?"

"Tonight. After the kids go to bed. You know the drill. Kids can't see you. No one can know."

"I know. See you tonight," he replied.

Lacy returned her phone to the side table and turned on the television. She didn't know what, if anything, would come of this situation with Will. Whether it would last or whether the team could accept it. Right now, she didn't take much stock in the future.

At the end of it all, she knew she was no hero, no role model. She was just a woman who sought retribution for the life that had been stolen from her. And what was left was a woman who was a little harder, a little colder, who no longer wore her heart on her sleeve. What was left was a woman who would follow Trevor Axell to the ends of the earth if it meant they could prevent one more attack.

If what Timothy Mullins said was correct, the team would be in the cross-hairs of a powerful society with political influence, criminal organization ties, and a lot of money. He warned her, offering thinly veiled threats, and believed himself to be above the law. He was who she would hunt down next.

THE END

ABOUT THE AUTHOR

Bestselling author Robin Mahle lives in Virginia with her husband and two children. Her Kate Reid mysteries have drawn praise for grabbing hold of the reader and refusing to let go. And the intense, fast-paced style of storytelling led her to create another series, the Lacy Merrick thrillers, which readers have called "believable, and ripped from today's headlines." With powerful leading ladies and action-packed thrill rides, Robin hopes to continue taking readers on roller-coaster adventures that will leave them breathless.

If you enjoyed Ms. Mahle's work, please share your experience by leaving a review on your ebook retailer website.

ALSO BY ROBIN MAHLE

State of Denial - A Lacy Merrick Thriller (Book 1)

Shadow Rising – A Lacy Merrick Thriller (Book 2)

First Target – A Lacy Merrick Thriller (Book 3)

The Kate Reid FBI Thrillers (17 books)

The Det. Rebecca Ellis Thrillers (5 books)

The Remy Fontaine Fugitive Hunter Thrillers (5 books)

The Allison Hart PI Thrillers (5 books)

The Chef (stand-alone psych thriller)

The Man in My Attich (stand-alone psych thriller)

The Compound (stand-alone psych thriller)

**Sign up to receive Robin's Newsletter so you can stay up to date on her new releases, events, contests, and even exclusive new material!

uct-compliance